Married to the Shooter

Married to the Shooter

Ms. Michel Moore

www.urbanbooks.net

Urban Books, LLC
300 Farmingdale Road, NY-Route 109
Farmingdale, NY 11735

Married to the Shooter
Copyright © 2020 Ms. Michel Moore

All rights reserved. No part of this book may be reproduced in any form or by any means without prior consent of the Publisher, except brief quotes used in reviews.

ISBN 13: 978-1-64556-069-2
ISBN 10: 1-64556-069-4

First Trade Paperback Printing August 2020
Printed in the United States of America

10 9 8 7 6 5 4 3 2 1

This is a work of fiction. Any references or similarities to actual events, real people, living or dead, or to real locales are intended to give the novel a sense of reality. Any similarity in other names, characters, places, and incidents is entirely coincidental.

Distributed by Kensington Publishing Corp.
Submit Orders to:
Customer Service
400 Hahn Road
Westminster, MD 21157-4627
Phone: 1-800-733-3000
Fax: 1-800-659-2436

Married to the Shooter

Ms. Michel Moore

Dedication

MW–MW
12/28/15
Long live love—What was still is
Big as the world is round

Acknowledgments

As I have crafted numerous novels throughout the years, the list of people that support me has continued to grow. I'm so very thankful. And beyond all, I'm often humbled. Sometimes, it all seems like a wonderful dream being blessed to do what you love. I started this incredible journey back in 2005, and when my first release titled *Say U Promise* made the Essence Magazine Bestseller List, I thought it could get no better. But it did. I now have over fifty various projects to smile about and am still counting.

To my husband, best friend, and rock, Author *Marlon PS White*. You've been holding me down behind the scenes since 1999. Now, you have stepped out of the shadows and are doing ya own thing in this book industry. (*Young and Hungry, I Can Touch the Bottom, Goodfellas, Around the Way Girls 10, Caged Passion, The Other Part of the Game, Detroit Black Bottom Gangster, On Parole,* and *The Penitentiary Raised Me*) I love you big as the world is round and support your endeavors just as you've done mine. What was still is.

My mother, *Ella Fletcher,* has had my back in each and every way a parent should. She has stood by me and supported my dreams. She believed in me even when I didn't believe in myself. I know I don't say it enough, but I love you.

My daughter, Essence Bestseller, Author *T. C. Littles* is a writing machine in her own right. She has been here to see my visions and assist me in making them a reality. We have spent numerous hours on the phone plotting and scheming how we can take over the world. One day, we just might make it happen (smile). Thanks for my grandkids, *Jayden* and *Lil Ella*.

My brother *Dwayne Fletcher* and cousin *Othello Lewis,* it's always love. *Rita Fletcher,* continue to RIP. I miss you still. At Aretha Franklin's funeral, Jesse Jackson was posted beginning to end and never left her or the family's side. I remarked, "I wish I had a friend like that." Truth be told, I do. My best friend, Dorothea Lewis, is and has been my road dawg for decades. I love ya, sis! Even when you clown, I will pull out my red nose and clown with you (smile). My homeboy for life, Thomas Walker, aka Bone Capone. Man, we have been through the trenches for years. We are always gonna be family. One Love!

Several folks in this industry have made my journey more than interesting, and each I hold in high regard. K'wan Foye was the first author that I considered my friend. Also, the first author to sign his novels at my bookstore. Nikki Turner prayed for me when times were hard. Carl Weber blessed me with a deal and constant advice. Karen Mitchell and George Denard are like true family. Jeff Dumpson and Jewels, Chelle, and Jada's cousin (smile). When the chips were down, Faye Wilkes, K'wan Foye, Danielle Green, and Blacc Topp stepped all the way up. I will never forget the love you showed me and mines. We appreciate you—nothing but respect and gratitude. People talk shit all day long, but these four backed it up. If you want to know the definition of loyalty, look no further.

To Monique S. Hall, Racquel Williams, Spud Johnson, Ty Marshal, Danielle Bigsby, Avery Goode, Joe Awsum, and, of course, my li'l hometown soul sista for life, India-Johnson Williams . . . Collectively, y'all have had my back, shown love, and been nothing short of one hundred from day one. In this industry, that's rare.

A special thank-you to Tonya Woodfolk, Johnnay Johnson, Stacy Jabo, Papaya, Jenise Brown, and Ne-c Virgo for always traveling to my events. And to Qiana Drennen, you created something great. DRMRAB was legendary. That book club and all its chapters impacted the paperback world in ways unimaginable. I salute you for that. To the other Detroit-based book clubs that rock with me, The Plot Seekers and EyeCu, thanks for the continued support.

Lastly, to the Hood Book Ambassadors, Trina Crenshaw, Yolanda McCormick, Nia Smith, Krystal Robinson, Jay Knox, Desiree Bailey, La Kiesha Wright, Renita Walker, Chanelle Patton, Eurydice Lofton, Martha Falconer, Tina Brown, Vickie Juncaj, Passion Beauford, Margaret Waleed, T. C. Littles, you are the greatest book club and moral support a girl could ever have. I salute you all. We stay rocking that blue and orange at the Detroit Hustle & Grind Book Fair. Ain't nothing betta than my HBA family!

God bless you reading this. Make sure you check out the following titles:

Coldhearted & Crazy
Ruthless and Rotten
No Home Training
Tick Tick Boom
A Product of the System
The System Has Failed
Homeless
Testify
I Can Touch the Bottom
Young and Hungry
Say U Promise Saga
Full Figured 9
Around the Way Girls 10
Get It How Ya Live
Girls from da Hood 13
Married to the Shooter
A Big Girl's Revenge
Kingpins Detroit
Hustle Bag
When You Cross a Crazy Bitch
Stage Hustle

and many more . . .

Prologue

The Game Makes the World Go Round

Pimping ain't easy. And it shouldn't be. Selling drugs is even harder. That's a fact. And finding any true honor among thieves is worse than both of them combined. It had to be. That was the way it was set up to be a long time ago. The game was, is, and would always be what it was in Detroit . . . the motherfucking game. Harsh as they may be at times, some street rules and specific regulations couldn't be broken or taken advantage of. That part was always consistent if you were selling pussy, heroin, crack, or bottled water on the corner in the hood.

Today, in the basement of a stash house, was another part of playing that game that was consistent as well—retribution for your sins. Thick tension filled the air, as it should have. Somebody had fucked around and broken a rule and had to pay. Lines had been clearly drawn. Unfortunately, now those lines had been blatantly crossed. Sometimes, "sorry" or "my bad" didn't work out in the real world when dealing with real-life gangsters. Like the hood saying goes, "God forgives. . . . The streets don't."

The keyword for playing the game was *consequences*. And there would always be some based upon your actions. And the sobering follow-up was if you were ready to suffer behind them. In that crucial time, some men stood tall—some folded. But in the end, there was still an ultimate price to pay for fucking up or running off on the plug. If your character was that of a snitch at that dreaded crossroads, all bets were off as well. The true colors of your manhood would start to show, no-holds-barred.

Chapter One

It never failed. No matter how much you'd try to be fair and give a person a chance, they'd fuck it up. No matter how many times they promised to make shit right, chances are, they never did. That meant if you were the boss, doing what had to be done. Nolan was known for being all of the above, but when pushed to his limits, he would snap. Not just curse you out or raise-your-voice snap, but all-the-way-out-there-and-back—full-blown snap. It didn't matter if it was gunplay or a nigga caught them hands, Nolan had time for it. There would be no turning back, and his vicious disposition couldn't be tamed. No ifs, ands, or buts. He was an animal—a *wild* one at that. This time was no different.

Joe Brezzy-Bey had fucked up. Once, twice, three times, or more. It was like the fool had a death wish or just didn't give a shit. He kept testing the water and coming up short. Now, unfortunately for Brezzy-Bey, the worker was in the middle of getting taught a life lesson he'd never forget. Nolan was heated, and "Nigga, you got me fucked up" school was in session. His bright yellow skin was fire engine red, and each moment that passed, he grew angrier.

"Nolan, come on, dawg. Hold up. Wait, I can't breathe. I can't breathe, pleeeas—"

"Shut the fuck up! You can't say nothing else to me. I warned you over and over again. I tried my best to be reasonable. But, naw, you wouldn't let that shit be."

Clenched fist, Nolan beat on his chest with his free hand. He was madder than he'd been in weeks, maybe months. "You think I'm a joke, like a clown or some shit? Like I'm soft? Is *that* what you think?"

"Naw, dawg, wait. Let me explain." The effort to explain was real but did no good. Joe Brezzy-Bey's frail frame was lightweight work for Nolan.

"Naw, guy, I'm tired of repeating myself. I said I wasn't gonna tolerate no more of that 'short money' bullshit. Now, here you go for the hundredth time, bringing me a gang of change. I told you shitting on me was gonna be bad for your health. So now, it's whatever. You asked for this, not me."

Temporarily, Nolan let go of Brezzy-Bey's throat. Removing his shirt, the winter-white wife beater Nolan had on underneath was snug fitting, showing off his prison-chiseled body. Cracking his knuckles, he was ready for round two. The pain he'd inflicted on his worker so far was only the warm-up. There would be no more leniency extended.

"I warned you I wasn't to be fucked with. But you out here shaking my goddamn bag like it's yours. Making up the damn rules as you see fit."

"I know but—"

"But *what,* guy? Besides the damn change, from what I counted so far, it's maybe four less than the ticket supposed to be." Nolan then strong-arm yoked his worker up even more. They knocked a card table over where a paper bag sat filled with pennies, nickels, and dimes. The change scattered across the basement floor. Momentarily, Nolan stared at the change on the ground. It gave him a ghastly flashback memory of his childhood. Knowing the past was what it was—the past—he quickly shook off those thoughts. But not before socking Brezzy-Bey a few good times in the stomach. Then he grinned as Brezzy-Bey slumped over in pure agony.

Nolan didn't usually wake up with murder on his mind. He had a good heart . . . buried deep within. He attempted to keep a smile plastered on his face even when he was ready to pull the trigger. That trait made a soon-to-be victim not sure what or when they'd see death. For the most part, his emotions were tame since his youth. He'd found out early on that if a person thought they could hurt you, they would, be it physically or mentally. So, after learning those things the hard way at the hands of his parents, Nolan shut down. Once he linked up with Kapri, she was the only one he confided in. And that was when he felt she could handle the hellish demons he fought that tormented his soul. The young killer tried to keep those feelings embedded, not bringing them to the surface.

After receiving a text, Nolan was reminded he had other business on the floor across town. There was no more time to waste. Hastily, he got back to the task at hand. He continued where he'd left off, beating the brakes off of his worker. His victim could only count his blessings, knowing at least he hadn't got a bat against the head like Nolan usually did to random fuckups. This form of torture was slow and deliberate, leaving Brezzy-Bey to think he might have a chance for some small bit of compassion. However, taking several quick hits to the face changed that notion as he grimaced, urinating on himself.

"Wow, I know you ain't piss on ya damn self. Stop being a little pussy. You earned this ass kicking, period." Unhinged, Nolan's fury continued. Every move the penitentiary-raised beast made was cold and calculated. His mind-set was on violence and doing great bodily harm. So he did just that. Using one hand, he roughly pressed his thumb inward on the center of the man's throat.

"But wait, please, hold up, fam." Brezzy-Bey's eyes bucked as he struggled to speak. Fumbling over his words, he felt as if his windpipe were being crushed. He tried to explain himself. He wished an aggravated Nolan would just see things from his perspective. The worker knew had it not been for his cousin's homeboy, he'd be out in the alleys collecting discarded bottles or old scrap metal. But Joe Brezzy-Bey accepted he was dead wrong as he tried his luck with his boss just the same.

"Listen up and hear me good, you piece of garbage motherfucker. I ain't ya fam. We ain't cool. We ain't hanging out nowhere or nothing like that. You understand me?" Having gone to the gym earlier in the day, this had become a second full workout for Nolan as his biceps bulged in size.

The untrustworthy worker attempted to nod, showing that he understood what was being said, but it was hard doing so. His entire body was under attack and suffering from the countless blows. It could barely tolerate any more. The basement walls seemed to be closing in on him. Brezzy-Bey wanted to try to get away but knew that was impossible. Taking the ass whipping was the only thing he could do, or risk possibly taking a bullet in the spine if he made a run for the stairs. In those moments, he regretted that he'd come over to the stash house in the first place with the remaining short-ticket money. Nolan was right. He had been warned repeatedly, but the monkey on his back had other plans that won out.

"See, boy, you's a bitch-made worker, and I'ma boss. You get headaches, I give the motherfuckers. You think 'cause ole girl cool with me from way back when ya crack-smoking life matters? You got shit twisted." Sweat was starting to soak through the rear portion of Nolan's wife beater. And the fuck boy he was beating's blood from a busted nose decorated the front. But none of that slowed him down. He was and always had been trained to go. "It's like I said, you think I'm some ho or something. And I know damn well you old enough to know better. You just like these young niggas," Nolan agitatedly snarled.

"No, but—" Defeated, he still was trying to take a cop. Yet, his sorrowful pleas fell upon deaf ears. There was no answer to his desperate prayers. He'd have to ride this wave out the best he possibly could. This was one of those dreaded consequences in the game if caught stealing.

Nolan was nearing the end of his rope. Hiring the generic, off-brand nigga was a favor for a childhood friend from the West Side. She once did a solid for him, so, in return, Nolan gave her cousin a job when he came home from doing a bid for breaking and entering. That charge alone should have been a red flag to putting Brezzy-Bey on a bag, but Nolan tried to give people a chance and let them hang themselves. But back in the day, friend loyalty or not, something had to give to ensure the ticket would be correct moving forward. The favor he'd done was quickly costing him money on the regular. And besides his wife, there was nothing the smooth street menace loved more than money.

Seeing that ole boy was gagging, about to black out, Nolan eased up some on the pressure he was applying. His muscular frame could easily do some serious damage if he allowed things to get all the way out of control. So he fell back. However, his wrath was far from over. He wanted to teach Brezzy-Bey a lesson about stealing from him, not kill the bum. A dead worker would bring no revenue at all. But sending one to a receiving hospital to prove a point would.

Wrapping both hands around Joe Brezzy-Bey's neck, Nolan lifted him off his feet. Fed up with all of his excuses, Nolan continued the punishment. Nolan then slammed him against the wall several times. Amused at his strength, Nolan watched a few pieces of peeling paint fall from the ceiling and onto the floor. The utter fear in his victim's eyes motivated Nolan in what he was about to do next. In a series of full-drawn back punches to the jaw, which caused more blood to leak from Brezzy-Bey's mouth, then a few midsection kidney blows, Nolan topped those off with punching his worker dead in the Adam's apple.

Releasing the near-death grip, he allowed his wounded prey's body to slide down the wall onto the pieces of fallen paint chips. Once he was on the ground, Nolan raised his gym shoe, smashing it down on Joe Brezzy-Bey's forehead. A huge unicorn lump immediately formed, then split wide open. Small spackles of blood adorned the toe portion of Nolan's shoes. Seeing that, his enthusiasm to draw more increased. Nolan not only wanted to, but he also *craved* to see more. He'd become totally zoned out and bloodthirsty on getting satisfaction. If you stole from Nolan White, there was a bigger price to pay in the long run. And Joe Brezzy-Bey was now finding that out firsthand.

Chapter Two

What was taking place in the basement was starting to get way out of control. Nolan had gone beyond proving his point. Thankfully, before any more harm could be inflicted, he was interrupted by his wife. Kapri was the only one besides himself who had keys to the stash house. So when he heard the side door open and close, Nolan knew it was she. He also quickly recognized Kapri's routine hearing her footsteps above. She'd no doubt put her purse and keys on the kitchen counter, then went to the rear bedroom to see if the floor safe in the back of the closet was good. Nolan knew his spouse like the back of his hand. Like him, she never played around when their money was concerned. Listening to the sounds of her heels click down the stairs, Nolan smirked. No matter the circumstances, he loved to see his reason for living coming. Kapri was his peace, even in the midst of chaos.

"Hey, bae, what you doing down there? I got some shit to tell you that your ass ain't gonna believe." Stepping foot in the basement, Kapri raised one eyebrow. Usually, she was upbeat. However, there was no smile on her face. She was perplexed, immediately noticing something was weirdly wrong and off. Her man's wife beater was drenched and bloodied. She rushed over toward him, then stopped, wondering if she should run back upstairs and grab her gun. Locking eyes with her husband, she saw the death gaze expression he proudly wore. Kapri knew that look. Her husband was on one, but what?

Then Kapri saw the obvious and went ballistic. "Ain't this some shit? How fucking ironic. Just the slithering snake I wanted to see—Brezzy-Bey's foul rotten ass. You ho-made motherfucker! You ain't shit! I should fuck you up, bitch nigga!" Kapri shouted, calling him every name in the book. With grave intentions and contempt, she viciously lunged in his direction. She didn't care that Joe Brezzy-Bey was already fucked the fuck up. She wanted nothing more than to lay hands on him herself. Knowing what she'd just discovered about him had her vexed.

Nolan was thrown off by her initial reaction to see Brezzy-Bey. He knew she despised him. The entire crew did. But right now, Kapri was being extra as hell. In one quick movement, Nolan caught his girl up by the waist, slowing her intended attack down. Although his wife didn't know the latest antics by the worker she never trusted, the fool had certainly done enough since being on the team to cause her to clown. But she was going too far with it.

"Whoa, whoa, baby. Slow ya roll, bae. I got this. Ya already know he back on that same bullshit, fucking up the bag. But you can see I'm handling it. So—"

"Naw, love, let me go. This time, he on a whole other level with it." Kapri's hatred for Brezzy-Bey grew with every passing moment she looked at him. She fought to get her husband's hands off of her. Her body twisted, then turned, then twisted some more. But Nolan's strength was too much to break free from, so she chilled.

"Say what now? What you mean 'another level'?" Shifting his full attention to his wife, Nolan took a brief break from the beating. He let her go, seeing his better half had slightly calmed down. "Okay, bae, you good now or what?"

Kapri had to take a few deep breaths to get all the way steady. Her pressure was sky-high. She started pacing in a circle, shaking her head, trying to find the words to describe how angry she truly was. She was now also annoyed that her expensive cream-colored linen suit had a mixture of blood and sweat soaked into the blazer. Today just wasn't her day, and in her view, it was one person's fault.

"Damn, I swear to God it's like this is Karma or some shit that this slimeball-ass buster is down here," she nodded toward the corner of the basement where Joe Brezzy-Bey was trying to catch his breath and regain his composure. "Oh my God, this bitch-ass nigga! Fuck! I'm pissed!"

Nolan took a few steps in his wife's direction, still keeping a watchful eye on Joe Brezzy-Bey. Kapri was acting as if someone had run over her dog on purpose or something. And that enraged disposition had him dumbfounded. "Hey, baby, what up, doe, with all this? What's good with you? Why you bugging? And what you mean, 'another level and Karma'?"

"Niggaaaaa," she dragged the word out while taking off her blazer, throwing it on the step near her purse. "You just don't under-damn-stand! I swear shit is crazy!" Kapri covered her face with both hands and screamed into her palms. It was if she were having a nervous breakdown or one of her episodes. Kapri had psychological issues like her husband, but neither was on meds. They just lived life and took it how it came.

Nolan had to find out what the problem was. He'd been dealing with Joe Brezzy-Bey and his mess and was mentally drained, and it showed on his face. "Damn, girl, slow your ass down! You got me confused as hell right about now."

Kapri stood barely just over five feet. Yet, using all her strength, she yanked her husband over to the side near an old washing machine. They were now standing face-to-face, and Nolan saw tears form in his wife's eyes.

Then a few dropped. Her lower lip started to quiver, causing Nolan to realize something else was going on with his woman besides the ticket money being short again—something more serious. Before he knew what was happening next, Kapri bolted back to the stairs only to return quickly with her purse. Opening the designer handbag, she took out an envelope. Setting her purse on the step again, she then opened the envelope. Removing some papers, she could only shake her head in disgust and roll her tear-filled eyes at Joe Brezzy-Bey.

"Boy, I don't know why you don't be listening to me when I tell you shit. I knew that throwback broad you insist on being halfway cool with was nothing but trouble. But, naw, you always gotta be with that loyal bullshit. You just as much to blame as that nothing-ass bitch and his punk ass!"

"Baby, what you talking about now? What she do? I told you it ain't nothing between her and me like that and never was. So what's all the shade for? You tripping up in here." Nolan could easily see his wife was pissed but couldn't understand why. Whenever wifey brought up ole girl, an attitude always lurked behind it. Nolan couldn't win for losing, always trying to be stand up. Like Brezzy-Bey, he too looked at the stairs wishing he could just walk the hell away.

"Shade? Tripping? For real? Oh, Negro, please. You funny as hell." Kapri grabbed a handful of her shoulder-length, blond-streaked hair, pulling it all to the back. Poking her lips out, she firmly placed her hands on her hips, bossing up on her husband. "Trust and believe, ain't no insecurities this damn way. What kinda weed ya ass done smoked, or is you getting high with that bum over there?"

"Bae, I was just saying. Damn, now, you *really* bugging." Nolan knew once his wife started going, she went hard, even on him if called for. And whatever the deal was, she was taking no prisoners.

"Look now, ain't no trick out here can go toe-to-toe with me. So, boy, bye. You can straight go on with all that set tripping." Kapri bucked her eyes. There were no more tears, only anger. She waved her hand, dismissing her husband's immediate assumptions of her being jealous.

"Well, umm . . ." Nolan folded his arms up to his chest, giving her the eye.

"Well, umm, nothing! I wish that was all it was where her dumb ass was concerned. But that thirsty whore the one that brought that snitch over there into our lives. And even when I told you he was gonna be a problem, you put the rat on a bag anyway. A damn snitch! So, yeah, like I said, check your damn self behind this uncalled for bullshit. And while you at it, take off that damn bloody-ass shirt. *You* the one bugging!"

Nolan took off the once-clean wife beater, tossing it off to the side. Bare chest, he then paused, taking in the moment. He wanted to make sure he heard correctly. Kapri was high-strung and used to going from zero to a hundred in no time flat. The devoted husband had to make sure this wasn't one of those occasions. But this was far from an ordinary once-a-month, "I'm on my cycle" type of outburst. Regardless, Nolan had her back either way, but he at least wanted to understand the reason. "Whoa, slow it down, baby girl. What you mean a rat and a snitch? What you talking about? Him? That motherfucker over there? I'm confused as hell."

Joe Brezzy-Bey was attempting to regain his composure. He was just starting to breathe normally again when he heard his boss's wife say the words "rat," followed by "snitch," pointing directly at him. Once again, he started to spaz out, this time without Nolan's hands even being wrapped around his throat. By the sound of things, Brezzy-Bey feared what may have been coming next. He thought his heart was going to jump out of his body. He started to tremble in fear, and the lump on his head began to ache even more. Now he had to deal with *two* of them, so the stairs as a means of escape, even risking that bullet in the spine, was definitely out of the equation. Joe Brezzy-Bey was trapped, and he would soon be exposed.

Kapri cut her dagger eyes back at the man held captive. Annoyed, she handed her husband the stapled, folded, three-page document she'd gotten from their lawyer. The information was supposed to be confidential. But thankfully, their attorney had inside connects that he'd pay for information if need be. This go-around, clear-cut, was money well spent. "Yeah, bae, check this out. This what that beloved lame over there really think about your yellow ass. I promise he got down on you. Truth be told, *all* our asses!"

"What's this?" Nolan took the papers from his wife. Quickly he unfolded them. He glanced over at Brezzy-Bey before he started to read what exactly had Kapri so gone. It had to be major, so he braced himself.

"Yeah, I told you when you caught his ass selling burn bags, he was gonna be a problem. But, naw, getting rid of him was a no-go for you. When his dusty ass kept snorting that shit, you still kept him down. I swear, I should've just got somebody to kill this weak link a long time ago. So now we fucked in the game 'cause you was showing favoritism to that basic bitch cousin of his." Kapri's Red Bottom heels scraped across the basement concrete floor. She marched from one side to the other mean-muggin' their injured guest. She hated him *and* his entire generation, for that matter. He needed to die for his betrayal.

"Damn, what the fuck." Nolan saw the official heading on the top of the paperwork . . . *Wayne County Prose-*

cutor's Office. He couldn't believe what he was seeing. A sudden migraine shot through his head. Immediately, it caused his temples to pulsate at a steady, rapid rate. With that bronze-colored raised letter insignia, he knew the words to follow after that would be all bad. Anything that had to do with the Prosecutor's Office had no choice but to be. *This shit is fucked up. What these sons of bitches want? I know this shit can't be about me.* The hardcore hustler tried to brace himself even more, but it was no good. After being in the game making moves since a teen, a drug dealer's most dreaded nightmare was coming into play.

What his girl was saying was true. She, his team, he, and all they had built up in the streets were in jeopardy. Now he understood why Kapri was emotionally and physically off the chain. It all made sense. His wife had every right to be in her feelings because he was now in his too. Sentence after sentence, Nolan, known around Detroit as the "Shooter," started to bleed with anger for the ultimate betrayal. For the most part, Joe Brezzy-Bey was treated like family. But now, he had broken the deadly foremost street hustle commandment: thou shall not snitch on your peoples. His fate would soon be sealed.

Chapter Three

Kapri knew the first domino had been pushed. *Well, it's really 'bout to go down now.* She left her husband on the other side of the stash house basement to come to grips with what he was about to read. But now she had her own overdue business with Brezzy-Bey to tend to. Without closing her eyes, she prayed to God to calm her down some before she had a stroke.

Damn, let me get my shit together. Heart racing like a motherfucker!

Wasting no more time, she removed her .380 Ruger out of her purse. As she put one up top, her anger level shot back up to a solid ten. Just in case he had any ideas of trying to make a run for it, she'd be ready. Aiming it at Joe Brezzy-Bey's head, he raised his arms, trying to shield himself from potential gunfire. The dime piece-educated diva wasn't a killer by any means. That trait was solely her man's department as well as her father's. Nonetheless, she'd step up to be one if it meant the difference between her going to prison for life and remaining free.

"I knew you was a piece of filth from off rip. I told Nolan you was weak as fuck. I told him you was still getting high, ole dope fiend." Kapri pressed the barrel of her pistol into Brezzy-Bey's already shattered jaw. "But, naw, he was too caught up on trying to be loyal to that low-down cousin of yours for some payback bullshit a decade old."

Kapri watched his one eye that wasn't swollen shut widen. Then a single tear dropped. It was no secret to Brezzy-Bey or the rest of the crew how she felt about him. The otherwise devoted wife never accepted him as family or being a part of her husband's team. Now, knowing what she knew, Kapri was glad she clowned on him on sight. Anytime she'd be in Brezzy-Bey's presence, there was quickly a problem or misunderstanding to be had between her better half and her.

"I swear to God I wish I could just pull this trigger right damn now. You ain't shit. Nolan been good to your ugly ass, and *this* how you do him? *This* how you do a man that's had your back no matter what? I swear you straight pussy. What all you tell them damn police?" She nudged the pistol deeper into his perspiration-drenched, bloodied skin. "And matter of fact, take off them motherfucking clothes. And hurry the fuck up, ole bitch-ass nigga!"

"Fiona—"

"Hold up. I know you ain't trying to say that busto's name to me like it means something. You done ruined everything. I swear I hope you rot in hell. And if I have my way, that walking-virus-in-a-skirt-Fiona will be right along with you! Now, like I said, strip and hurry your ass up." After spitting directly into Joe Brezzy-Bey's face, Kapri's mind started to race, wondering what Nolan's and her next move would be. The lawyer didn't say how much the cops knew about their operation or when they might act on it. He just gave his longtime clients the heads-up that the "house of hustle" they'd built was about to fall. The only thing Kapri could do was pray Nolan could make shit right. Now fully nude, she checked to make sure Joe Brezzy-Bey wasn't wearing a wire. Kapri was streetwise enough to know if the documented snitch was, she and Nolan would be locked up by now facing life.

Nolan concentrated. Holding the paperwork under the light, he read over everything twice, carefully, then once more. His mind was speeding. He had to make sure he was getting the full picture of what the documents said. Joe Brezzy-Bey had given him up to the cops, that much was evident. And by some of the statements written, the worker-turned-informant had flipped on a few more guys out in the city making moves. But none of those dealers concerned Nolan. His business was his to worry about. And this unloyal move Brezzy-Bey had made was indeed on another level. The consequences were life, death, and freedom . . . or lack thereof. Nolan realized that much.

Kapri could easily tell her husband was about to bust a vein on the side of his neck. The more Nolan read, the more that vein started to bulge. His lip turned up in disgust more than once. It was apparent that what he had just read had caught him off guard. This was the last thing he was expecting to see. It was no great secret that Joe Brezzy-Bey was a royal fuckup where the ticket money was concerned. That's why Nolan was in the middle of beating his ass. But this outta-the-blue revelation right here was a whole different animal. The punishment for this was way more than just laying hands on a person. This meant death. It had to. After all, what Joe Brezzy-Bey had done would change the lives of Nolan and Kapri forever. Their hard-fought perfect dream world had just become a ghoulish nightmare—one from which they probably would never wake up. Now, the way his girl was behaving all made perfect sense.

With the gun still aimed at a panicked, nude Joe Brezzy-Bey, Kapri leaned upward. She snatched the documents out of Nolan's hands, throwing them on the floor at their feet. Having the paperwork in her possession for a little over an hour, she had time to calm down and process what the outcome of dealing with a snitch could bring. But she still nutted up when she laid eyes on the punk-ass nigga. So, now it was her husband's turn to do the same. Only thing is, Nolan had no time to think or process shit—just react. Over the years, the bond couple had been in and through some really wild, over-the-top situations. Most they sat back and now would laugh about. But none of this jumping off was humorous to any degree. Standing face-to-face, Kapri asked her man what he planned on doing next. Of course, she threw in her two cents about what she thought should occur.

"So, bae, you see what I was saying? That dirtbag Fiona done brought this good mouth-running fool into our lives. So real talk, whatever you do to him, you need to do to that wanna-be-me tramp too. I mean, seriously, we don't know how much he has told them." Using her free hand, she caressed Nolan's muscular arm. She knew whenever she would do that, nine outta ten, she'd get her way.

"Yeah, baby, you right." Nolan instantly agreed, regretting he hadn't listened to her in never giving Brezzy-Bey work from jump. "My bad, booboo, on not doing what you thought was best. You be seeing shit a nigga like me be overlooking. That's why I married your pretty ass. You always got me in good times and bad. And it looks like this some of the bad." Nolan held his wife's chin up, then kissed her on the lips. "But don't be worried. I ain't 'bout to let some judge break us up again. Fuck walking that yard. A nigga built to do that time, but fuck that. I need to be home with you, building and shit. Ya feel me?"

"No doubt, baby, I'ma stand strong no matter what. I mean, so far, the papers only name him as an informant against you and some of the fellas. But like I fucking said, who knows?" Kapri was usually hard as nails but fought back the tears as she spoke, lowering her gun. "Damn, this is so fucked up. Shit, for all we know, the hook is parked on the corner, waiting to kick the damn doors in. We probably under surveillance now by the Feds or DEA."

Those words did something to Nolan's spirit. Kapri was right. They didn't know what kind of time frame they were working with when it came to this situation. There was no telling how long they'd been under investigation. And she was also right. This was all his fault for bringing the virus into their world. He had let not only her down, but also himself as well.

Fuck! Fuck! Fuck! Let me think! Damn, this shit is fucked!

For a few minutes, the seasoned criminal paced the floor as his aggression increased. Every muscle on Nolan's chiseled frame was on swollen. The prison ink on his back was covered in beads of sweat, and his green eyes were now bloodshot. Finally, he eased up on pacing and pounding his fist into his palm. Nolan had more than enough of reflecting on what could or would be. He paused, turning to face his visibly distraught wife. "Baby, you already know what has to come next, right?"

With no love lost where Joe Brezzy-Bey was concerned, it didn't take much convincing for Kapri's confident response. She was always down with the termination of anything standing in the way of their happiness, be it family, friends, associates, workers, or in this case, a turncoat snake that deserved what he got.

"Of course. Simple, my king. This nigga gotta die." Kapri grinned at last, thinking of getting rid of Fiona's cousin once and for all. Grabbing Nolan's manhood, she slowly stroked it through his jeans, licking the remaining of the day's gloss off her lips. "And, baby, I say the sooner, the better. So, yeah, do what you gotta do. If you run outta bullets, feel free to use mine as well. I'm here for it."

In the midst of all that was going on, Nolan was still aroused by his girl's touch. He pulled her close and deep tongue kissed his constant partner in crime. "Yeah, Kapri, even if we do get knocked hard for the bullshit he done told the damn police, he won't live to see the outcome of being a snitch." Nolan turned, mean-muggin' his soon-to-be-dead worker. "Say them nighty-nighty prayers, bitch, 'cause ya time is 'bout up!" His main focus was back to Brezzy-Bey and going straight ham.

Pouncing on the traitor, Nolan pounded his face with his fist until his knuckles started to swell. He knew he should have never trusted an addict off rip, but he did. After all he'd done in the way of letting this lame slide on continuous short tickets, for Joe Brezzy-Bey to fuck him over like he had was unreal and unexpected. But Nolan had just read the bullshit in black and white. Ole boy had his own issued informant number and everything. There would be a double salute awaiting his lawyer whenever Nolan saw him. Because whoever Attorney Mims had working with him inside of the Detroit Police Department and Prosecutor's Office had gone beyond the call of duty with this paperwork. They had basically signed, sealed, and delivered Joe Brezzy-Bey's death warrant.

I swear a nigga did everything he could to live righteously. A guy like me tried his best to repay his debts and make shit right. I went against my damn wife. I stayed up some nights hearing Kapri go bat-shit nuts on me for even dealing with you. Now, I gotta hear her mouth about this. Now, I gotta hear her tell me that I was wrong and should've listened to her off rip. And as for your damn cousin, I promise on my life if I find out she got shit to do with this for real, for real, I'ma send that ass to the upper room too. You done ran your mouth and fucked shit up for Kapri, me, and all the crew who depend on shaking that bag to pay they bills.

Because you a coward and couldn't take that little bit of time you probably would've got for whatever, you went straight foul. Ooo-wee, my dude, you gonna feel every bit of this beat down before you don't feel shit no more! That's my word!

Not yet ready to be calm, Nolan wiped the multitude of sweat beads off of his forehead. Resentment for the betrayal boiled over. He declined to slow down, ready to snatch a soul. Imagining the number of crew secrets Joe Brezzy-Bey might have divulged to the law, Nolan started stumping the disloyal worker in the midsection. Deliberate in where his shoe landed, the premeditated pain would be unbearable. By the time Nolan finished, a suffering Brezzy-Bey would be begging for death to take him away. Every part of the man's nude body was being battered and bruised by Nolan's kicks and punches. At one point, he even picked up an old kitchen table and beat Brezzy-Bey across the back with it.

Kapri stood by with a smile of satisfaction on her face. Mesmerized with the heinous work her husband was putting in, she remembered what first attracted her to Nolan. He was an official beast. Watching him do what he did made Kapri want to spend the rest of her life with him even more. Her mother had long since warned Kapri that dealing with a man just like her father would bring her nothing but heartache, problems, and grief. Yet, none of that advice mattered. Nolan was her soul mate, so the risk and hazards that came with being his wife were irrelevant.

In the midst of watching the one-sided melee, she held the gun down at her side, angry enough to pull the trigger herself. The mood was nothing less than chaotic. The man that lived on point and principal was furious that, against his wife's word, he had given this idiot a chance. And now he had fucked him over. Knowing what he now knew, there was no turning back and no time to figure things out. Nolan had no choice. They couldn't allow this traitor to leave the house alive. By the expression on Joe Brezzy-Bey's beaten face, he knew his fate as well.

Nolan searched the basement. Finally, he found an old telephone cord in a cardboard box of trash. Infuriated, he tied up a physically defeated, nude Joe Brezzy-Bey, hands first, then feet. He was then propped up on the side of the washing machine. The newly discovered informant now had the muzzle of two guns pressed to the sides of his head after Nolan produced his. Each passing second, Joe Brezzy-Bey came to the harsh realization his time on the earth was rapidly growing to a close. He mustered up the energy to yell out for help before Nolan socked him in his already busted mouth. However, as much as he shouted and fought the notion of death, the clock was ticking. It was about to go down.

Chapter Four

Quick thinking was the ultimate key. The couple needed to reduce the possibility of drawing unwanted attention. As always, Kapri had a plan. "So, yeah, bae, I already know his crybaby ass gonna be making even more noise than he just was. Even though there's no neighbors on either side of the crib, fuck somebody walking by on the humble hear his ass. Shiiid, then we gonna have to cancel they asses too." For the first time since coming down into the basement, Kapri gave a sincere smile with no sinister intent. "So, I know what we gonna do." She darted upstairs, but not before taking the liberty to kick their captive in his nuts as hard as she could.

Seizing the opportunity while Kapri was gone, Joe Brezzy-Bey turned his head to the side, allowing thick clots of blood to fall out of his busted mouth. Visibly, he was in bad shape but knew his life depended on trying to fight through the excruciating pain he felt. Frantic, he thought he could at least try to get Nolan to chill and give him a break. Regretting that he'd even been working with the police, he didn't try to deny nor confirm his affiliation at first. After urinating on himself even more, he gave in to telling the truth. Desperate, he attempted to explain what led him in that foul direction. Off rip, he claimed the narcos had beaten him up after catching him with some drugs that they said they would use to lock him up for years if he didn't cooperate. But Nolan didn't want to believe it was that simple. He hoped Brezzy-Bey wasn't that much of a pussy.

"Oh shit, what the fuck! I know this ain't the cops about to pull me over." Joe Brezzy-Bey looked up in the rearview mirror of his used Ford Taurus. Knowing he was slightly under the influence of a pint of Seagram's and a few lines of powder, he prayed the unmarked cop car would just turn off. Because he was twisted and blew through a stop sign, he'd got caught slipping. Nolan had long warned him to get his taillights fixed before riding around dirty, especially at night. But Brezzy-Bey had failed to listen, needing every spare dollar to get high and still keep the ticket correct. This could be the reason the boys were on him, not because of the drug-infested block he'd just left.

Everyone around the way had been made aware that some plainclothes narcotics officers had been lurking trying to find a reason to harass everyone in that general neighborhood. It didn't matter to the overly eager cops one bit if you were young or old. Everyone African American was a suspect to the white law. After them following close behind his vehicle for almost two blocks, his luck had run out. He was being flicked. Bright blue and red flashing lights accompanied by that siren . . . a driver's worst nightmare. Before pulling over to the side of the road, Brezzy-Bey's mind raced. He was still on parole and didn't want to risk going back behind the wall. The three years he'd just spent locked up, not being able to snort quality dope whenever he wanted, were more than enough. Just the thought of it made the once-proud Moabite sick to his stomach.

Besides being under the influence, he had a small brown paper bag with some product in it and a portion of the ticket money due to Nolan. Whereas his first mind told him to jump out and run, he knew their dirty ass might shoot him in the back. He then thought about attempting to take them on a high-speed chase, but unfortunately, his gas tank was on E. He wouldn't make it over two miles. Out of options, Brezzy-Bey reached over on the passenger side, grabbing the bag. Knowing he would be asked to step out of the car, he stuffed it down the front of his pants, hoping they wouldn't dick frisk him. Then maybe he could talk his way out of the rest.

"Turn the engine off and toss the keys out the window," a stern voice rang out over the speaker. "Then place your hands on the steering wheel. Do it now!"

Doing as told, he nervously watched through the side mirror as three policemen approached his car, weapons drawn. Soon, he was surrounded. A gun pointed at his head from the passenger side. Another pointed at his head from the driver's side. And the third officer posted up by the hood of the vehicle, which was a guaranteed straight-through-the-heart shot. It was evident by the expressions on their faces that this was going to be no average traffic stop. Under the influence or not, it was at that point Joe Brezzy-Bey knew he wasn't going home anytime soon.

Within seconds, he was snatched out of the Taurus and body slammed to the pavement. He'd not once tried to resist but was still roughed up. Back in the day, Brezzy-Bey used to be able to take a beating from the boys, but those days had long since disappeared.

Handcuffed, sitting on the curb, the trio of narcos had already discovered the paper bag containing two bundles of raw and cash stuffed under his nut sack. That led them to believe more could be found inside the filthy interior of the vehicle. With malice, they pulled down wires from here and there, yanked the headrests away from the seats, and snatched the entire dashboard damn near off. In the midst of all of that, one officer held up one of the beige-colored extra small envelopes with a black cat stamp. He grinned as if he'd won the lottery. It was their job to find out what drug dealer was doing what and what product came out of what camp. And that black cat package had been making more noise in the streets of Detroit than the other products for months on end. Although it was two baker's dozen bundles, the cop made it clear that they knew Brezzy-Bey's drugged out ass wasn't actually the man, but he could point them in the right direction.

The risk of being violated and sent back to Jackson shook him. The fear of getting his ass handed to him day after day in the penitentiary had Joe Brezzy-Bey ready to tell on his own mother. So getting him to flip over would be effortless. They didn't have to lay hands on him anymore. The inebriated coward was giving up Nolan White and his entire crew before even reaching the precinct. The plainclothes officers knew they'd struck hood solid gold with this random traffic stop.

Nolan couldn't wrap his mind around anyone being so weak that they were that scared of doing a few months to a year, maybe, for a parole violation. Especially a man who'd already done time. It made no sense. There had to be more to the reason Brezzy-Bey turned on the team. After being backhanded slapped a few good times, Brezzy-Bey switched it up some. He claimed his homeboy Trenton had convinced him to work with the cops and turn on Nolan so they could take over the entire narcotics operation. Nolan gave him the side eye about that, knowing Trenton's shaky drug-using pedigree. And besides, it wasn't like they had access to a solid plug.

Lastly, in desperation to get Nolan to ease up on the physical assault he was enduring, Brezzy-Bey mumbled something about Fiona just wanted him to get Kapri locked up so she could finally be with Nolan and be his girl.

This was becoming too much to take. Nolan didn't want to hear any of it if he wasn't telling him what he'd actually told the police. Especially the part about Fiona's off-the-wall, stalker-inspired motives. Nolan could only shake his head. If Kapri heard that bullshit, she'd fly off the deep end and kill Fiona with her bare hands. She was already sensitive when it came to even hear that trick's name mentioned in passing. If that statement Joe Brezzy-Bey claimed ever proved to be indeed factual, Nolan would deal with Fiona later in his own way. But no matter what, in his opinion, there was no good reason for a guy that ran the streets or who even dabbled in the game to tell on the next man. Even if Nolan wanted to give the slimeball a chance to make things right, he couldn't turn back the hands of time. The ride-or-die couple knew they couldn't erase what was presently known by the cops, but at least, maybe, they could do some sort of damage control.

Kapri returned with the black noisemaker and set it under the window closest to where their victim lay. She explained they would plug the small boom box in to drown out any sounds Joe Brezzy-Bey might make. After plugging it in, she pushed the button to a station known for playing back-to-back, nonstop music. She made sure it was loud enough so that even when the commercials did play, they too would be a distraction for any cry for help.

"Okay, bae, this should be good. That way, if his dumb ass tries to scream for help, nobody will hear him. And even if they do hear something walking by, they gonna just think it's the music playing loud the way black people like it." Kapri grinned somewhat now, believing there was a way outta what Brezzy-Bey had done. Deep down inside, she knew there wasn't, but for the time being, she outwardly kept the faith. Her energy level for cutting up was low.

"You right, 'cause you already know his punk ass would yell all night long if he could. This nigga straight pussy." Nolan watched his wife reach for her purse along with her stained blazer. "Boo, where you about to go? You good?"

"Yeah, I'm good. I just had some things to take care of before Attorney Mims called to meet up with me and fuck my day up."

"Who you telling, wifey? This shit was supposed to be a regular beat down for fucking up the money. Now, it's about to be murder."

"As well as it should be, all things considered. So, yeah, handle ya business," Kapri nonchalantly advised. "Then, when I get back, you can tell me the game plan." She kissed her warrior on the cheek before making her exit. Having previous important matters to attend to, Kapri left her man to deal with the exposed hood whistle-blower. She trusted and knew that Nolan could and would do what he had to do to ensure both of their lives remained Gucci.

The next move where Nolan was concerned was plain and simple. From what little information he had read in the official paperwork, Joe Brezzy-Bey had to die—and soon. The part to figure out now was when. Nolan was anxious to pull the trigger and had no problem whatsoever doing so. But he had to ensure that Kapri was out of danger of getting knocked with him if he got caught.

And also that all the drugs and firearms they had stashed inside the house were relocated. Money wasn't an issue since Kapri had long since had them putting that up in a different location.

The telephone cord would not be enough. Using a few rolls of duct tape, Nolan took his time ensuring that his ex-worker-turned-informant was totally securely out of play. Now, Joe Brezzy-Bey could not move, see, or speak. The only thing he could do was breathe out of his nose.

Taking the rubber hose off the rear of the washing machine, Nolan used it to smack Joe Brezzy-Bey in the mouth as hard as he could, certainly breaking his teeth, until his cell rang, interrupting the beating. If the now swollen, loose-lipped snake ended up dying before he returned, then all the better! It would save Nolan a bullet later on down the line when the time came. Any way it went, the lesson learned would be that working with the police was bad for a guy's health. But for now, like his wife, it was time Nolan bent a few corners. He had to go check up on some traps he'd set deep east and hope there were no more plots of deception brewing amongst the ranks.

Chapter Five

Kapri

Things moved quickly. We had no choice. Most times, my husband thought I moved too fast without thinking out things. But I always got the job done. He could count on me like I could count on him. People from around the way often agreed with him, claiming I had a firecracker, short-fused temper and would pop off at a moment's notice. Maybe I was nuts like my father and needed to be locked up to calm me down. I don't know and damn sure didn't want to find out. But I did know what my family seemed to hate about me the most, they loved about me even more. I was loyal without a fault and always down to clown. Far from ordinary, I was a sure bet when it came to pulling up.

Thankfully, we had cash on hand. If you were in the game, you had to anticipate the need for it immediately. My husband was a thinker. He put us in the position to save for a rainy day and made sure that we always planned for trouble. And that made everything I had to accomplish much easier to do.

At this point, there was no real way of knowing when the other shoe was going to drop. If the Detroit police, the Feds, the DEA, or ATF did make an appearance, we wanted to have as few reasons as possible for them to add even more charges. It took less than twenty-four hours for us to relocate everything illegal. Nolan's aunt didn't know it yet, but he had chosen to hide most of the guns in the rafters of her basement. We had the keys to her house, so when she was at her job at the nursing home on Meyers off Seven Mile, we did what had to be done. Each weapon, no matter big or small, was wrapped up securely in bedsheets. Knowing his aunt would never go in the cobweb-covered room located off the side of the furnace area, it was perfect. Even if other family members were to visit, they'd be none the wiser.

As for the drugs, they definitely could not be in the same location as the firearms. That was a no-no. Besides, we needed around-the-clock access to them at all times, day and night. And we certainly didn't need Nolan's aunt to question why we might have been going in and out of her house so frequently. Even though she was older, she was far from being a fool. She knew what line of work her nephew was in. And even though she readily didn't condone it, she didn't condemn him for it, either.

We took the majority of the product and paraphernalia over to a new apartment I'd gotten for us under an assumed name. The management was somewhat shady, as most were within the city limits. There was no needed credit check required or proper ID . . . just first month's rent and a security deposit. Of course, we had money on deck, so that part was easy peasy. I knew Nolan's mind was preoccupied with murder, so I had to think for both of us.

I purchased some secondhand furniture from the local Salvation Army to move to our new apartment. I made sure I dressed down and wore no makeup. I had to play the part. Showing up my normal flawless self was not advisable. We didn't want the neighbors to think we had any more than most of them did. If they saw we were struggling like they were, the desire for them to break in would be far less. After stashing some of the drugs in the side of a filthy mattress I'd gotten out of one of our spots, I felt content. I'd done well. The remaining drugs, Nolan put out in the street, running a two-for-one special. The game plan was to press a hard run on the bag until everything was gone.

Our first mind was to pack some clothes and whatever we couldn't bear to part with. Then Nolan would gather all the money we had out in the streets owed to us. Next thing would be simple . . . get out of Dodge. We could drive down to Kentucky and get our whip crushed at a junkyard. We had a clean title, and at the end of the day, money made the world go around. So, if Nolan wanted our brand-new Lincoln Navigator with the top-of-the-line package and custom-embroidered his-and-her seats compacted into no more than a compressed lump of steel, then so be it. He'd pay the yard worker top dollar to do as he was told, no questions asked.

Once that was done, I'd get my homegirl to purchase us another vehicle, then drive that down to Miami. After chilling for a minute or two on the beach, we could leave the country. I would get in touch with my mother somewhere down the line. Nolan's people meant nothing to him, so he'd just be ghost. However, my husband knew that if we didn't at least get rid of Brezzy-Bey, he would be a direct link to the cops staying on our black asses. So, for a while, we chilled and prayed the hook would not come knocking anytime soon.

With all of the drugs, firearms, and the temporary stash house set and in place, I shot to the Dollar Store. I grabbed a bucket, a few mops, several sponges, and a couple of those thin, papery masks painters wear. I had more than enough towels I'd purchased from Walmart when I slid by to get five huge bottles of Clorox Bleach. I needed the smell to be something serious, and the weak chemical ones from the Dollar Store wouldn't cut it. I was all set to move forward.

As Joe Brezzy-Bey still lay bound and gagged in the basement, I thoroughly cleaned the rest of the house from top to bottom. The strong smell of the Clorox caused my eyes to water and my nose to run. That was good because I knew that I was doing a proper job of removing any traces of any human who had been here the previous weeks. The only time I stopped was when my mother called to tell me my father was back in jail, which came as no huge surprise. That was his life since I was a small child. After ending our brief conversation, I returned to the task at hand. I'd bagged up some personal items belonging to Nolan and me, placing them in my car.

My husband had removed the closet safe and dumped it in the Detroit River. He made a trip to Home Depot to purchase three additional security locks. Whereas we already had one on the front, rear, and side doors, he reinforced them by installing an extra one on all of the points of entry. He was good with the tools and whatnot, so no one else had to be involved. Thinking ahead, he pulled all of the shades around the lower level of the house and taped the sides to the frames so no one could see inside even if they tried. The taxes were all paid up, and any mail that would come would be hidden behind the gates. There would be no reason for anyone to come snooping around for months. Wisely, Nolan decided we would stay away from this hot-box house until we made the move out of town for good.

It had been well over forty-one hours and counting since we had our guest held captive for his disloyal actions. Constantly forced to urinate and defecate on himself, the bastard had the basement lit up. I didn't even bother to go and check if he was dead or alive. My man told me to leave all of that "Brezzy-Bey bullshit" up to him, so I did what he requested and stayed away from that part of the basement. Thankfully, the bleach was extremely overpowering, and I only had to splatter some on top of the old washing machine. Checking my cell, I saw that it was almost time for my next step.

Snatching up the bucket, bleach, and rubber gloves, I tossed them inside of a garbage bag, then put them in the trunk of my car. I took the damp mops and threw them over the back fence in the already garbage-filled alley.

It was time for me to break out. I was already packed and had a late flight to catch to Atlanta. After a quick walk around the perimeter of the house, I was ready to put phase three of Nolan's plan into action. Slowly, I pulled out of the driveway. I turned the radio on and got off in my zone. There was nothing but slow songs playing, which was fine by me. I thought about my husband killing Brezzy-Bey to protect us and our freedom. No doubt that put a smile on my face. The thought of a bullet in that dude's skull for being a snitch warmed my heart. I felt absolutely no remorse for Brezzy-Bey or his stanking-ass cousin, for that matter. The only thing that would make my night better is if I were guaranteed that she and her cousin would be buried side by side in a double grave. My hubby always asked me what I wanted for my birthday or Christmas. Well, this year, that would be my first choice. Fiona's ass dead before my flight landed.

Dodging a few potholes, I hit the freeway. Randomly, I pulled over and discarded the garbage bag out my trunk somewhere along the way on I-94 W while heading toward the airport. It was right after I passed the huge landmark tire, so I knew that was far enough from the house. Nolan felt it was best for me to get out of town. My beloved wanted to ensure I'd have an airtight alibi when he did what had to be done. And what was better than being screened through airport security, then spotted shopping at a few ATL malls? We agreed I would check into one of the best hotels. The plan was even to order room service. Then I would go down to the front desk to complain about it. I would make a big deal out of it so that everyone that I came in contact with would remember me. The next morning, I would hit up the mall.

I most definitely hated that my husband had to make wild moves solo like he was about to make, but I loved the fact that he protected his queen in every way possible. My king's frame of mind was that there was no good reason for both of us to fall if he got knocked. In our team of two, one of us had to be able to remain free and hold us down when and if the time came. I was his ace.

Nolan arrived at the stash house dressed to handle business. He backed up in the driveway and called his wife, but there was no answer. After waiting ten minutes, he tried again. "Damn. Hey, love, what up, doe? You good with it?"

"Yeah, bae. I was going through the security checkpoint when you called. As soon as I got through to the other side, I left my ID in the tray on purpose."

"Oh, yeah?"

"Yeah, bae. Then I went back to ask one of the TSA agents if it was in one of them. They checked, and, of course, there it was in the bottom just as I had left it. I know they will remember that because they had to go through like eighty trays."

"See, that's why I married your ass. Always on top of ya game." Nolan sat back in the stolen pickup truck and smirked. "Other than that, how did shit go inside? I'm in the driveway now about to go in."

"That shit was quiet as hell when I left. I went down there briefly to clean off prints from the washing machine, but like you said, I never went over toward that door."

"Okay, love, good looking. Go ahead and have a safe flight. I'm 'bout to do what needs to be done, ya feel me?"

"Be safe, and I'll text you when I touch down and get straight. I love you. And, oh yeah, shoot that rat bitch in the ass one time for me!"

Nolan couldn't help but laugh, knowing his girl was as serious as they come. "All right, girl. I gotcha. I love you too, baby, big as the world is round. What was still is."

Nolan put out the blunt he was smoking and left it on the windowsill. It was time to put in work. He was known to handle situations out in the street most men couldn't. If you were a true boss like he was, you ran to responsibility, not from it. Gun in hand, the seasoned shooter made his way down the basement stairs. The small radio was still playing just as they had left it days ago. A faint smell of bleach came from over where the washing machine stood but not enough to make a huge difference.

Overwhelmed by the pungent smell of a mixture of piss and shit, Nolan used his free hand to pull his shirt up over his mouth and nose. It was a far cry from the lemon-scented bleach aroma that filled the upper level of the house.

As he neared the corner of the basement, Nolan stared at the doorknob of one of the small rooms. Just in case Joe Brezzy-Bey had the strength to break free of all that had held him almost motionless for days, Nolan yelled over the sounds of the radio. "Okay, I promise on God, if you try any dumb shit, I'ma light that ass up without question!" With pistol ready to ring, the door was swung open. The awful smell was ten times worse and hit Nolan in the face, almost causing him to throw up. This stench was worse than the one of death. "Damn, you foul as fuck! What the hell. Damn!"

Nolan took a few steps back to see what was what. There were no immediate signs of any movement, which was good. Maybe the naked, shitty-ass rat had indeed expired like he and his wife both hoped. He had possession of Brezzy-Bey's cell phone. Ironically, not one person had called to check on they people. Not even his supposed homeboy with the bright takeover idea and not that backstabbing Fiona, who, after all these years, was still trying to get the dick. And not the police who he was working with. Nolan had searched through his call log and read all of his text messages. Nothing out of the ordinary noticeably stuck out. He even tapped the Facebook icon and scanned through that inbox as well. Once again, nothing. It seemed as if nobody gave two damns about the nigga. So, offing Joe Brezzy-Bey would not bring heat right off the rip. If lucky, time would pass for things to cool off and the corpse to be identified. With any luck, Joe Brezzy-Bey would lie in the Wayne County Morgue unclaimed as a John Doe. Nolan didn't know his arrangement with the hook on how often he had to check in, so he hoped that they would just think their informant was lying low or just plain skipped town.

With gardening gloves on top of the two rubber ones, Nolan grabbed Joe Brezzy-Bey's duct taped feet. With ease, he snatched him out into the open. That's when he realized the creep was still alive. . . . Well, at least, barely. He kicked his head over to the side. Using a box cutter, Nolan sliced the tape on the side of Brezzy-Bey's battered and bruised face, cutting deep into his skin. Blood started to trickle down into his ear slowly. Callously, he then ripped the gray tape, snatching off both eyelashes as well as his wounded victim's eyebrows instantly. Basically nonresponsive, the police informant was numb to any more pain. He didn't move or flinch at what had to be excruciating pain.

On point and principal, Nolan wanted to see his face. The man who came from nothing and clawed his way up the ladder of Detroit's drug underworld wanted the unfit street soldier to see—not just feel—what happens to assholes that recklessly turn on they own peoples. With his index fingers, he forced Brezzy-Bey's swollen eyes open. Nolan was annoyed that he was too weak to keep them open, but he was fed up with trying. After what this snake had done, Nolan wanted to take his sweet time in sending this motherfucker on his way, but there was no time. The unknown raids and potential arrests were looming, so Nolan got on with it.

Tired of all of the preparation to commit murder, he turned up the radio's volume a little bit more. The house was on a block with many vacant lots and bandos, so there were not many neighbors to be nosy. And the ones that were still living there were probably accustomed to the sounds of what may be gunshots. After all, most of Detroit was. There was no more hesitation in what would come next.

Nonchalantly, Nolan rolled him over on his stomach. Totally defeated, Brezzy-Bey didn't even moan or protest being on the verge of death. He'd suffered terribly since the first blow he'd endured in the basement of horrors even before being exposed. No more words were needed anyhow. The time for excuses, procrastination, and pardons was a done deal.

When Nolan pressed an old couch cushion down on the rear of Fiona's kin's head, letting off a single round, Brezzy-Bey's naked body jerked once. Then it went limp. Finally, the deadly deed was done. Nolan showed no emotion as he removed the sweaty gloves. Why would he? That was what all who betrayed the street code deserved, both young or old, black or white.

Reaching in his back pocket, he took out another pair of gardening gloves. He slipped those on top of the two pairs of rubber gloves he was already wearing. He'd cuffed an entire box from where his aunt worked, which he used for hooking up dope. Now they had another use. With the aid of an old oriental area rug Nolan had found in an alley a good mile or so away, he proceeded to roll the corpse on top of it. Bending down, he tucked the ends of the rug. Thinking about all the things he had to do later, Nolan sped up his mission. After all, time was money. Using the duct tape, he then folded the ends of the rug up like a burrito.

The next part would be a little harder to accomplish since he was alone. But Nolan and Kapri had decided that at this point, they didn't know who they could trust, so it was best to act solo.

Your ass heavy as a mug, Nolan thought as he yanked and pulled on the rug. Almost at the top of the wooden stairs, he paused to catch his breath. *I should've just chopped that ass up in pieces and threw you into the sewer. But a nigga ain't got time for all that.*

Two more good times of pulling and Nolan had gotten the job done. Opening both security gates, he stepped outside to make sure the block was deserted as it always was. He also wanted to see if the sound of the single gunshot had alarmed anyone. But in true Detroit style and fashion, it had not. The block was quiet.

After pushing the metal brackets to hold both doors wide open, Nolan dragged the body outside. Luckily, he was in good health. Otherwise, he would be even more exhausted after all he'd just done to get Joe Brezzy-Bey this far.

Lifting the rug, he struggled to shove it into the rear of the stolen Dodge Dakota pickup. From the shape it was in and the filthy condition inside, it was apparent it was a work truck. Nolan had taken it out of a service garage parking lot, so it being missing probably would not be discovered until the next morning.

Knowing that he had no time to waste, Nolan checked his cell once more. It was near midnight. Kapri should have been well off into making sure she was seen at the Atlanta terminal and in the hotel ordering that room service. She would text him when she was about to go down to the front desk. That was his signal. That would be when Nolan would finish up the rest of the plan. Locking up the house, he went to the backyard. Sitting by the side of the shed, he picked up a bottle of lighter fluid. There would be no more cookouts for him and his wife at this house, so the flammable chemical would come in better use later on.

After walking to the front yard, he posted on the front porch and waited for the text. Damn near two in the morning, his notification alert went off. Glancing at the screen of his cell, he saw a bunch of hearts. There it was, his signal. It was go time. He hit the weed once more. Tossing the rest of the blunt he'd left on the windowsill out onto the sidewalk, Nolan went around to the driveway. He pushed the flathead screwdriver down into the side of the busted ignition, and the truck started.

Pulling out of the driveway, he made his way onto East Warren. Making sure he obeyed the speed limit, Nolan stopped at every light. He couldn't run the risk of getting pulled over. What he was doing was risky enough, especially driving a stolen vehicle. But the fact that he had a dead body in the rear flatbed was another issue altogether, an issue that could get him natural life if caught.

Yeah, cool. I'm here. This right here is good. Having driven clear across town, Nolan made sure he went by the Southwest Detroit spot he'd left his low-key hoopty parked.

Going at least seven blocks past that spot, he pulled over. He checked his surroundings as always before shooting a move. *Damn, hell yeah, this what I'm talking 'bout. It's deserted as fuck!* It was easy to see that no one was outside stirring around. The smooth assassin took out a surgical mask and covered his face. Then hurriedly, he once again put on gardening gloves over the two pairs of plastic ones he was already wearing. Ready to finish the job, Nolan killed the engine.

He stepped outside of the truck and looked around to see if he'd left anything behind by accident. Seeing that he was good in that aspect, it was go time. *All right, let's get it, get it!* He placed the screwdriver in his back pocket. Making sure the mask was tight, he retrieved lighter fluid out the side of the flatbed. Embracing his demented mind-set, Nolan drenched the rug containing Joe Brezzy-Bey's corpse. *Yeah, no open casket for your disloyal ass. Unless ya people wanna sit in front of a piece of charcoal, that is.*

Making sure the rug was thoroughly soaked, he squirted the remainder of the fluid on the body of the truck itself. There were several old grocery store sales papers on the floor of the passenger side. He gathered all of them. Lighting three at a time, they became like a torch. Not wanting to waste any of the flames, he tossed them into the flatbed. Instantly, the rug started to blaze up a little, then seconds later, it'd become a mini inferno.

Burn in hellfire, Joe Brezzy-Bey, with your diseased-rat ass! You earned every bit of this hot shit! Never bite the hand that feeds you. But you act just like them new breed of young pillheads who don't get that part of the game! Y'all just wanna be out here in these streets getting high on lean like shit's a game!

Stuffing the last rubber banded paper down into the gas tank, Nolan lit that as well. This time, there was no delay. It was about to blow. There was no more time to lose. He had to get out of Dodge. The brightness of the flames would surely bring attention even to the otherwise deserted block. But hopefully not before Brezzy-Bey's skin was damn near melted off the bone. With the gloves still on, Nolan took off hitting the vacant lots. Content with his actions, he grinned as the sounds of the stolen, fully engulfed vehicle crackled in the background.

Nolan came back to his hoopty and damn near crossed Woodward Avenue before the fire trucks could even get the call. After bending a few more corners, he jumped down on the freeway. Foot to the pedal, he headed deep east. He had to put in work one more time before he called it a night.

Driving past the Van Dyke exit, he reached under his seat and retrieved a throwaway cell phone. Powering it on, he placed a call to his wife. It was nearing four in the morning, but he had to hear her voice. He had to assure her that the deed was done, and things had gone as planned.

"Bae, what you doing, what you got on?" he softly whispered as if someone else were inside of the car trying to ear hustle. "Talk dirty to a nigga that done took a life!"

"Don't bae-what-the-hell-you-doing-and-got-on me, crazy fool. What's the deal?" Kapri demanded to know right off rip. She'd been up all evening playing the role for the hotel staff and was wired. "You know I'm over here bugging. So, what's up? How did shit go with your take-a-life ass?"

"Well, don't trip. We good this way. I got you. You know how I do what I do when I do it," he gleefully boasted as he drove.

"Baby, are you *sure* we good?" she questioned, finally feeling as if she could set her troubled mind to ease. "'Cause like I said, a bitch been on edge here."

"Girl, don't you ever doubt my skills. You already know I'ma handle my business. Especially on some bullshit like this. Now, like I said off jump, bae, what you got on?"

Kapri lightened up her mood, knowing that devious mole to their team was no more. Since boarding the plane, she'd been on edge. Loyal beyond words, she wanted to be there to see the rat bastard take his final breath, but she followed her husband's instructions instead. Kicking off her shoes, she finally fell back on the bed to relax. "Look, I'm just glad that part is over. But we still need to get with the lawyer and find out what else he knows. Just because ole boy outta the picture don't mean we good."

Nolan agreed. He promised he'd hit him up first thing in the morning. In the meantime, he told his wife to get some sleep and buy him some fly shit from the mall when she went shopping to be seen around ATL some more. "Now, tell me you love me."

"You know I do, Nolan. Now, do you love me?"

"Of course, I do."

"How much?" she smiled, knowing what his answer was going to be.

"Big as the world is round. Now, bye. Get some rest. I'm about to do the same."

"Oh yeah, Nolan, before you hang up, your damn no-good father called me from some strange number tryin'a get in touch with you. He claims it's important."

"Bae, fuck that begging nigga. I don't know why he keep trying. His shady, backstabbing ass gonna stay blocked—period! Now, get some rest."

Chapter Six

Now that one problem was out of the way, Nolan had to focus on the next. Even though he claimed he was going to take it in for the night, he lied. What he was about to do next, he didn't need his wife to worry about. She had enough on her plate. Besides, an airtight alibi for one murder was just as good as two or three, if need be. Nevertheless, Nolan would deal with it alone. Thinking back on one of the excuses Joe Brezzy-Bey gave for giving the team up to the law was his homeboy put him on to the idea. Well, whether he did was far beyond the case now. With all that had taken place over the previous day, he had to go as well, even if on the humble.

Nolan never ran with the likes of Trenton Franks. He was no more than an old, washed up ex-semipro basketball player. The longtime East Side resident never made it to the pros here in the United States but played one season overseas before a tragic, career-ending occurrence. Damage done to his kneecap and a severe ligament injury made him dependent on pain meds for relief. Trenton, like most, graduated to needing much more to get off the edge. His new drug of choice was heroin, aka raw, and sometimes crack. And the package Nolan and his crew, including Joe Brezzy-Bey, was handling was the strongest, most consistent thing running for almost four months straight, which was unheard of. At some point, the dope a dealer would cop would be weak and not be able to take a major cut. But what Nolan was working with could be stepped on many times with lactose, dormin, quinine, and it would still be very potent, strong, and desirable, and still stand strong in the streets. Even addicts trying to get the monkey off their backs and take methadone couldn't shake that craving. Mr. White's name was definitely ringing bells in certain circles and considered a target for jealous dealers and the police alike.

When Joe Brezzy-Bey muttered Trenton's slimeball name, it wasn't very hard to believe he had a hand in the turncoat bullshit. Those two had been best friends since eighth or ninth grade. They always looked out for each other, come hell or high water. So it would be a sure benefit for his manz to come up in the game, even though they were both getting high. Nolan had an idea where his soon-to-be victim laid his head. When you ran the streets, it was easy to find out just about anything, especially for a price. And even though heroin was the bag he was pushing to the middle age and younger set, the new popping drug crack was running wild. People were selling their souls and the souls of a newborn to get a rock. One suck on that glass dick, and a person was gone if their mind was weak.

Armed with a few rocks, Nolan had been pointed in the right direction the night he'd first tied up Brezzy-Bey after discovering he was a snitch. And now that he was burned and gone, Trenton's fate awaited him. On a mission, Nolan drove by his destination to see if any cars were parked in front, if there were any lights on inside the house, and lastly, if there was any form of movement on the dimly lit block. Besides a stray cat, no signs of life occurred. He parked the next block over near the opposite corner. As he crept through the trash-filled alley, he saw the boys ride by with their lights off. They were either trying to sneak a nigga too or just too plain lazy to risk a resident in need flagging them down. Whatever the case, Detroit's Finest was not a deterrent for what had to be done.

Like a ninja, Nolan moved accordingly. Once in the back area of the dilapidated shack Trenton called home, Nolan got ready. It was go time. Removing a full-face wool mask out of his rear pocket, he checked around his surroundings once more. Everything was clear. He pulled the mask down, covering all but his eyes and a small portion of his lips. The Black Bottom-trained killer placed a pair of rubber gloves on as he always did before doing unforgivable mischief.

Nolan eased his way up toward the rear of the dwelling as the dry, dead grass smashed beneath his feet. The backyard was littered with discarded debris and an old refrigerator missing the doors. Each wooden stair seemed to creak louder than the last, step by step. Hopefully, the disturbance in silence would not alert Trenton and any other of the house's occupants. But if it did, the way Nolan was feeling, the play could go down out there in the moonlight.

Strap in hand, Nolan reached the top stair. He took in a deep breath of the night air. Cautiously, he opened the raggedy screen door on the enclosed porch. Only two yards away and a swift kick, he'd be inside ready to settle the score. Whether Trenton truly had something to do with it, at this point, it didn't matter. Shit was in full motion. If he didn't, he could thank his best friend Joe Brezzy-Bey when he got to hell. They could both snort dope down there for eternity for all Nolan cared. His conscience would be clear.

The little female crackhead Nolan blessed with a few rocks swore Trenton lived alone in the bungalow-style house. . . . That was, if she wasn't there keeping him company. So this would be an easy kill for Nolan . . . in and out. Or so he was anticipating.

Nolan was seeking retribution, and his movements were extremely guarded. From this point on, the habitual criminal had to be in both defensive and offensive mode. Those traits were required if he wished to come out victorious in what was sure to be a one-sided battle.

As he lifted his foot, prepared to slam it against the door, he paused. Tugging slightly downward on his mask, he noticed something strange. The door was ajar. At this time of night, especially on the East Side of Detroit, that was abnormal. However, with the door being as it was, that meant Nolan did not need to kick it in and make noise, alerting Trenton that death was coming.

On the other hand, it could also be a sign of two looming options. One being that someone from the inside had peeped a masked intruder coming and was lying in wait, ready to pull an ambush move. Or the other being that God had blessed this soon-to-be exterminator of life and left the door open. The latter of the two would be favorable for most, but Nolan White was a Black Bottom-born warrior who showed no real fear since birth. If, indeed, it was a potential ambush in the making, that would make the bloodthirsty game of murder even more enjoyable to Kapri's wild-minded husband.

Ready to die on point and principal, Nolan had zero insecurities or reservations of what was about to take place. Inhaling a small bit of the night air, he exhaled. With murderous intent and no more delays, he burst through the door. Aiming his weapon in every direction as if he were SWAT executing a raid, the revenge mission advanced. Although the room was dark, Nolan aimed the pistol over to the right, then strategically to the left. With his finger eager to pull the trigger, the hood-trained assassin then made sure no one was hiding behind the flimsy door. No visible movement took place.

It took no time to realize the first room he'd entered was empty. Nolan continued his gamble with death as he thankfully discovered the second and third rooms were clear as well. Not surprisingly, from the shabby looks of the exterior of the house, none of the rooms had furniture. Not even the kitchen had a refrigerator. It was likely the one out back. A white stove stood there that, even in the dark, Nolan could tell was not fit to cook on. Many dishes, pots, and pans were stacked in the sink. Trying not to breathe in the awful household stench through the mask, Nolan wondered who would want to eat here, let alone sleep in the filth.

Not allowing his mind to be distracted, Nolan maintained his gun at a defensive level. With each passing step, the vindictive felon was met with darkness and uncertainty. *What the fuck! Does anybody even live in this raggedy, stankin' son of a bitch? I mean . . . damn.*

Firearm drawn, eager to shoot, cautiously, he turned the corner. Without hesitation, the same steps he'd made when he first entered the dwelling that Trenton supposedly resided at were reenacted. He aimed his gun in every conceivable direction in anticipation of trouble. Yet, once more, nothing was lurking. That didn't sit well with Nolan. Something wasn't right. Motionless, he stood in the hallway of what appeared to be a deserted dwelling. There was no movement or sign of life in the house, other than his own, which Nolan found strange.

He hoped for the young crackhead's sake that she had not lied to him about the address just to get the rocks. He'd hate to have to find and deal with her for sending him on a dummy mission. He knew her name, Roberta Tanner.

Just as the lone gunman started to question her information as being false, he saw a small bit of light illuminating from under one of the closed doors. *Oh shit, okay, damn, maybe that bitch was telling the truth after all. Trenton's ho ass must be in there. So good, then there where he's gonna die.*

Time was ticking, and enough of it had been wasted on the creep. Now, action had to be put in play. On the stalk, Nolan now headed toward the light. The other bedrooms he passed were dark, so he didn't even bother to check them. The street assassin just kept his eye focused on the prize. Nearing the shut door, he leaned inward. Faintly, he heard the sounds of snoring, mixed with a rerun of *The Golden Girls. Yeah, this it. It's go time in this motherfucker.*

Thinking of Joe Brezzy-Bey's rat ass and what that paperwork said, Nolan went into full killing mode. Gripping up on the handle of the pistol, he used his free hand to reach down and turn the knob. Slowly, the Black Bottom-gangster twisted it until he knew it had clicked. Once he flung the door open, he bum-rushed in, ready to let off a few rounds, if need be. The smell trapped inside of that room hit him in the face like a brick. It was ten times worse than that of the entire house, causing Nolan's throat to grow increasingly dry. But there was no time to deal with hygiene issues in that house. He had other, more pressing matters to handle.

With malicious intent, Nolan headed over to a mattress and box spring that lay on the floor. From the light from the small television sitting on top of a milk crate, it was easy to see that more than one person lay in the bed, knocked out. *Damn, there's two motherfuckers in this stankin' son of a bitch they call a house. Oh well, fuck it. I got enough bullets for both they asses!*

It was easy to make out his mark. Trenton's extralong legs and feet extended far beyond the length of the mattress and box spring. Whoever was lying next to him was petite in the frame. Although Nolan could have just as well easily shot them both in their drugged out, zombie slumber, he wanted to look Trenton in his eyes. Nolan wanted it to be known that just like his homeboy had ratted him out to the law to save his own ass, Joe Brezzy-Bey had done the same to him as well. Nolan wanted the junkie to see his certain death coming straight on for aiding and abetting an informant. Assisting a rat was just as bad as being one yourself. So, for that, the infamous Mr. White needed a face-to-face before pulling the trigger. For some strange reason, Nolan got off on that type of shit, even making it his "thing" before sending someone on their way.

He nudged them both with his pistol. The female was the first to squirm a bit, then, somewhat, wake up. Finally, she turned over, and Nolan saw a portion of her face. The light from the television was not too good, but it was fairly easy to see, she was no stranger. He recognized her as his apparently reliable source of information from the other day. Sadly, the girl had no way of knowing that she had basically signed her own death certificate giving up Trenton's whereabouts. But she did, so that was about to be that. Nolan felt no guilt or shame killing the opposite sex, if need be.

Seconds later, more movement occurred. Trenton was now semiawake as well. Both their reactions were the same. . . utter confusion thinking that the heroin they'd snorted and crack pipe they'd hit had them hallucinating. Their minds and eyes had to be playing tricks on them. Within seconds of making sure they weren't having a nightmare of sorts, it became alarmingly clear to both drug addicts what was happening was indeed a horrible reality. A man towered over them in a black, full-face mask. And the gun he was holding was pointed directly at them, poised to fire. While the girl was not capable of forming words, Trenton was the first to find the ability to respond verbally.

"What the fuck! What in the hell is this? What's happening? Who is you?" Instinctively, he attempted to get up, but he held up, realizing the masked gunman meant business.

"Shut up, nigga. You'll find all that out soon enough." Nolan felt negative energy rush through his body. He was more than ready to settle the score.

"Yo, why you here like this? I ain't got no money or nothing." Confused, the once basketball star rattled off question after question while cowardly attempting to use the female as a human shield.

"Look, my nigga, didn't I tell you to shut the fuck up? Now, if you say one more thing, I'ma put one in your head just because," he growled, ready to make good on his word.

"Dawg, it ain't no more of that shit." He pointed toward the drug residue plate on the floor. "We used it last night. I swear to God. And you can check. And I ain't got no money."

"I see you think I'm bullshitting with you about that fucking mouth." Nolan quickly put the gun over the girl's shoulder, shoving the barrel into Trenton's forehead. "And I don't give a shit about no drugs or little cash you might have. This ain't that."

"Please, oh my God, please. I didn't do anything." Finding her voice, the distraught girl professed to be faultless in whatever was going down. While doing so, she sobbed as she tried to get away from her "get high partner's" strong-arm hold.

With an advantage, Nolan looked down at Trenton with disgust. Here, this oversized man had the nerve to hold a female much too young for him from jump, closely, as if bullets don't go through flesh. He was a real waste of skin, and the world would surely be a better place without him occupying space. Obviously, being scared was no reason for a real man to turn straight bitch as he was. Trenton apparently didn't care that the filthy bedsheet was now on the floor, and his girl's flat-chested breasts were exposed. He was out for self, and she would have to deal with her own pride later. That was . . . if the couple made it to see daybreak.

Panicked, Trenton would not shut up as ordered. Nolan was weary of his theatrics and laid his cards on the table before pulling the trigger. The strong smell would not allow him to stay confined in the room much longer without getting sick to his stomach. He'd had enough nose hair burning stenches filling his nostrils earlier from Joe Brezzy-Bey's rotten rat ass. "Look here, faggot, fuck you, this bony bitch, and that shit y'all be talking. This right here ain't even about all of that. I'm here on some other type level shit."

"Okay, man. What, what is this about?" Trenton begged for his life, ready and willing to say just about anything to get out of that house and dire situation.

"Dawg, look, I know what the fuck you tried doing, with ya ho ass. But it ain't work. It ain't work out for him, and damn showl ain't gonna work out for you. Both you lames gonna fall."

Having a gun shoved in his face and the promise of great bodily harm being done to him, Trenton totally shook off his narcotic high. He was now wide awake and somewhat in his right mind. He was listening to his masked captor but was lost in what he meant. Terrified but having a desire to live, Trenton's voice raised, almost demanding an explanation. "Listen, dude, I don't know what you talking about. You got to have the wrong person. I ain't did jack shit to nobody. Why you doing this? If this is about this bitch and some fucked-up bullshit she did—here—take her." He roughly pushed his companion onto the floor. "She yours. I don't want no trouble. You can take her ass and go."

Taking a few steps back, Nolan now had the sobbing female at his feet begging for mercy. This entire scene was beginning to be too much to deal with. Ready to reveal his motives for murder, Nolan used his free hand to pull up the mask uncovering his face. Even though the light from the television was dim, it was still easy for Trenton and the girl to see Nolan's face.

"Naw, my nigga, this ain't about her. This about your lame ass trying to boss up and mix and mingle in my business affairs."

"Wait, hold up. Is that . . ." Trenton said, puzzled, wide-eyed, and almost in tears.

"Yeah, you slimeball motherfucker, it's me."

"But I don't understand." Trenton went on with trying to play with Nolan's intelligence, and doing that didn't sit well with him.

"Look, pussy, enough with the games. I know what you and that punk-ass snake Brezzy-Bey was up to."

"Huh?" Trenton's facial expression told the tale.

"Yeah, nigga, he gave you up right before he took one to the back of the head."

"What in the hell? Damn, Nolan, hold up." Trenton tried to stand to his feet again but was forced to remain on the far side of the filthy mattress, sensing a bullet coming his way.

"Yeah? For what? Fool, like I said, I know what you put ole boy up to."

"Hey, big dawg, it's me, Trenton. Come on, now. You know who I am. Remember me from around the way? Why you here like this, man? I mean, what's going on?" He continued to stumble over each word that came out of his mouth, further proving his guilt.

"Oh my God! I know you," the young, once drug-free girl blurted out still on her knees in search of clemency from whatever was about to go down. "You gave me—"

Frustrated with the mere sound of her voice, Nolan cut her off midsentence. There was no great need to expose that her ratchet crackhead ass was a rat too. "Whatever, girl. You might just need to shut the fuck up and let grown men talk. And maybe you might make it up out this bitch alive. Ya feel me? Now, be your ass quiet."

"Okay, okay, I will. I promise." Instantly, the petrified female did as she was told, wanting nothing more than to live. Trembling in fear, she wanted nothing more than to go back to the days before she smoked her first rock. But now, it was too late for all of that. Her life seemed doomed.

Nolan then briefly ran down to Trenton why he knew he was not innocent in even whispering in the ear of his manz to turn on him. "Real rap, my dude, I find it amazing I done just said ya boy from back in the day Brezzy-Bey took one to the back of the head, and you ain't even blinked once behind the shit. Y'all two been like Batman and Robin, and you just like blank face he dead?"

"Dawg, I swear I was just going to ask you what—"

"Come on, guy, don't try to run none of them dope fiend games on me. You and that fool been getting high for years and heavy hitting my bag up short for the last few months or so." Nolan's voice grew more agitated as the gun he was holding was begging for him to pull the trigger. "Dig this here. Before I let this bitch sing, I just wanted you to see my face and go to hell knowing a nigga like you could never!"

Hearing the promise of impending murder, the dopesick female was once again crying loudly, this time pointing toward the door. She was panic-stricken. She was frantic. She thought about trying to jump out of the window or maybe make a run for the door. She was visibly on the verge of a nervous breakdown as the tears poured from her eyes and confusion set in. She wanted nothing more than to leave Trenton to die on his own just as he was willing for her to do. Off the chain, she would only be silent again after Nolan slapped her in the center of the face with the gun's handle. The force of the blow caused a nice-size gash and sent her crawling off into the corner like an injured animal. Horrified, she pressed the palm of her hand tightly over her mouth to keep herself quiet. Blood trickled down from the fresh head wound. She was about to black out. Nude as the day she was born, the self-degraded addicted whore who'd given Nolan the location in the first place rocked back and forth, staring at the doorway.

Rushing closer to the bed, Nolan slightly tilted his head. He was all the way in his zone. With contempt, his upper lip snarled as he gave Trenton a message for Joe Brezzy-Bey. "Tell that little faggot I said never bite the hand that feeds you."

"Dawg, wait, wait! Let me explain. Come on, Nolan. Damn, dawg, for old time's sake, just hear me out, please." Out of his mind dreading what was about to take place, Trenton made a final attempt at getting a stay of execution.

"Yo, my nigga, real rap. . . . Ain't no good come from those that snitch. I already told him once before he took his last breath, but you go to hellfire and reinforce my words."

Trenton scrambled in an attempt to get down in between the wall and the soiled mattress, but to no avail. He put his needle-tracked, scarred arms up in hopes of shielding what was coming next and started to snivel. At that moment, he reflected on why he had even put that thought into his homeboy's mind. When Brezzy-Bey came to him explaining what the police wanted him to do, he should have warned him just to man up and take the time. From the beginning of time, snitches always met a cruel fate. But the drugs had clouded his judgment. All Trenton wanted was maybe a little extra play when he went to cop if Brezzy-Bey had actually taken over. But now that greediness for a temporary come-up in the hood had Trenton cooked. He, just like his childhood friend, had overplayed his position. At one point, the ex-basketball player had traveled all over Europe, staying in some of the finest hotels. Now, Trenton Franks would die a broke drug addict on a filthy mattress, wishing he could turn back the hands of time.

Aggressive in nature, Nolan then acted. He got what he came for . . . complete utter satisfaction. He pulled the trigger. A single gunshot rang out. If nothing else, Nolan could find his target in pitch-black circumstances without a flashlight. He was a ghetto-trained marksman, to say the least. The bullet found its way dead in the middle of his victim's forehead. In slow motion, Trenton's body lost all signs of life. He slumped over, going limp. Nolan lowered his gun.

Watching the female out of the corner of his eye, he bent over to double-check, making sure Trenton was indeed deceased. Skilled in his deadly craft, "the Shooter" learned early on not to leave any witnesses alive to tell the tale. At least not if you could help it. That part of the game was universal.

The loud, ear-piercing sound of the gunshot echoed off the walls of the bedroom. It seemed to shake the frame of the dwelling. Already hysterical, the young female had urinated on herself and could keep quiet no longer. She screamed out, witnessing Trenton take his final breath. Not knowing how nosy the nearby residents were in the neighborhood, Nolan knew he had to make tracks before anyone decided to call the police to investigate. As he turned, he saw the girl still over in the corner now hyperventilating. Although Nolan was thankful she had given him the address to Trenton's whereabouts, she had been paid for her services in crack cocaine. So, to him, she'd enjoyed her payment in full for unknowingly being a rat. But it was that ratlike quality that meant she had to go as well as Trenton and Joe Brezzy-Bey. No matter how much she claimed she would not snitch, she'd seen his face and could not be trusted. He pointed his pistol in her direction. She was up next. This would be a record for Nolan . . . three bodies in less than twelve hours.

In desperation, the drug-dazed female spoke out. In the middle of all her tears and pleas of mercy, she managed to remind Nolan that he said if she would just shut the fuck up, she would be able to make it out alive. "Buuuut, you said—"

Nolan laughed some at her nerve and stupidity. How could he not? She was straight fooling. This was one for the books. He couldn't wait to tell his wife about this bullshit later on down the line. "Come on, now, girl, you can't be serious with this. Sorry for ya luck, but you what's called collateral damage."

More tears flowed as she gasped repeatedly. "Wait, please, but you said—"

There was no need to degrade her further. Nolan could only shake his head in disbelief. Out of respect, he held back his laughter as he simply explained, "Damn, little lady, it's safe to assume if I'm a murderer, I'm a liar too!" No more words had a chance to come out of her mouth as Nolan let off another round. It found its mark in her lower throat area. Her head jerked back twice. Like most people terrified during their final moments alive, she died with her eyes wide open. It was as if she'd just smoked a rock and was on the search for another blast. Nolan looked at her, not with regret or remorse, but with a smile. *Girl, you was funny as hell. You should've been a comedian instead of a crackhead. Wait until I tell Kapri what you said.*

It was time to be out. Nolan looked at both deceased bodies, then headed down the hallway to make his escape. Overall, he'd had a productive, although busy, day. Content with himself, suddenly, he heard a sound from one of the dark bedrooms he'd initially assumed were empty. Weapon raised again, Nolan was ready to put in more work, if need be. One more on his body count would be nothing to do. He had enough bullets, so it was what it was.

He stepped back some into the shadow, his finger slowly caressed the trigger. The sound was getting closer. Nolan aimed at the open doorway, ready to react to whatever the looming potential threat was. *Oh hell, fucking naw! Ain't this about some shit,* he thought, looking downward. To Nolan's surprise, a sniffling baby no more than nine, maybe ten months, crawled off of a pile of dirty clothes that were serving as a crib of sorts. The loud, alarming sound of the gunshot must have awakened the sleeping child.

Once in the hallway, the diaper-clad infant and Nolan locked eyes. The baby whined, wanting comfort. He wanted to be picked up, but that was definitely *not* going to happen. Taking a few steps out of the way, Nolan allowed the fussy baby to crawl into the other bedroom. He realized once inside of that room, the innocent baby would discover its deceased mother slumped over on the floor, and Trenton in the same condition not too far away. Nolan was an inhuman, ruthless brute when need be. And the vicious shooter stood by his rule of never leaving a witness who could testify, but the type of heartless shit of being labeled a "baby killer" wasn't in him. That was going too far, even for him. Savage, yes—animal, never.

In the midst of all the bodies Kapri's husband had accumulated over the past twelve or so hours, this was his one good deed for the day. The tiny child would be blessed with remaining in the land of the living, knowing it couldn't identify Nolan White as the shooter. With a clear conscience, he pulled his mask back down, covering his face. Content in his actions, he left the same way he'd entered, heading toward his car, knowing he had settled the score on betrayal.

The following day, Nolan knew he would have to gather the crew. His new mission would be trying to low-key peep out if there were any more weak links like Joe Brezzy-Bey that needed to be dealt with. And if there were any, a bullet to their head would be their fate as well.

Everything was everything, picture-perfect. No compromise and no negotiations. The caper had gone just as Nolan and Kapri mapped out for the untimely demise of Joe Brezzy-Bey. And now, Nolan had two more bodies for the night he'd have to explain to Kapri and God one day. He reasoned that leaving the baby alive would bring him a blessing somewhere down the road, so he was good, Karma-wise. For now, as it stood, the couple had just gotten away with triple murders. However, things like cold-blooded, premeditated murder could never be as simple as the assailant would want.

Unfortunately, there was always a hiccup in every supposed perfect plan, along with a price to pay. And someone getting caught up on the humble was always a big risk and strong possibility. As time passed, Nolan and Kapri White found themselves not exempt from that destiny. Their roosters would certainly come home to roost.

Chapter Seven

Kapri

It damn straight ain't easy being me, but I'ma make that shit look that way fo'sho, fo'sho. I ain't never gonna let 'em see me sweat. They can all move around! Me and my husband been way past motherfuckers judging us and how we do what we do when we do it. We been showing out since day one and ain't shit gonna change that, not even the penitentiary. If my man rocking, I'm rolling. I'm built for this life.

I exhaled, glancing up in the rearview mirror. Cautiously, I checked my surroundings. My eyes slowly darted from side to side of the packed parking lot. Reaching over on the passenger seat, I smirked, then grabbed for my best friend. Tucking the pretty pearl-plated gun underneath the seat, I then opened the glove compartment. There was a single shot warm bottle of Moscato. Yeah, it was before nine in the morning, but a girl needed something to steady her nerves.

Twisting off the cap, I leaned my head back and took it straight to the head. I closed my eyes and prayed to God to give me patience and extreme tolerance. I prayed that I didn't have to chin check a nigga or ho this morning. For the past few days, I'd been put to the test. I was exhausted but still representing strong for my husband.

After placing my sunglasses just so, I removed the keys from the ignition. I checked the mirror once more, this time to make sure my hair was on point. As always, my hairdresser had my 'do laid. With confidence, I stepped one Red Bottom stiletto out of the truck. The other followed, touching the pavement, and in a few brief seconds, the drama jumped off. The numerous attention-seeking vultures were once again ready to attack. I was prepared for whatever, so I was beyond good.

As if I had not one care in the world, I tossed my hair over my shoulder and held my hand upward toward my face, shielding direct facial contact. If that was not enough to bring the hate temperature up a few degrees, my oversized 4-caret flawless diamond wedding ring was a showstopper. So yeah, I flossed on they ass. Of course, that in itself brought swift attitude from the female gawkers as my huge center stone glistened in the morning sunlight.

Eye level, I slowly took notice of each and every perfectly manicured design waiting for traffic to clear so I could cross the street. I'd paid my nail tech more than usual for the full VIP treatment. The black-and-white tips matched my suit and were worth every single penny. This week was a special occasion. This week and probably a few more days to follow would have me on full blast display. Every hater, naysayer, and even the parking lot attendant would look for signs of weakness from me. But I continuously shined. There would be none. Despite my current situation, I was still living my best life. Well, at least, outwardly.

"How can you deal with a twisted-mind monster like that?"

I rolled my eyes as I slow strolled past, face flawlessly beat. I was glad I chose the Viva Glam color lipstick shade. I was camera-ready knowing my courtroom entrances always made the evening news.

"Bitch, he killed my only son!"

I remained unbothered, nose in the air as if she were not speaking to me. And on any other regular day, a thang dressed as she was could never—the nerve.

"Look at her stank ass, acting like she better than everybody!"

I swung my authentic Gucci purse on my arm with my head held high, presidential style. I was the shit and knew it. And the best part was, the haters knew it as well.

"Let's see how you feel when his punk ass gets triple life."

I never eased my arrogant stride. I was poised with each step seeing the long line entrance was near. *Damn, is that even a sentence?* That man was definitely doing too much trying to make his point.

"I hope he rot in double-hot hellfire."

Damn, that was harsh. Not double-hot hellfire, I amusingly thought when an elderly lady yelled it out. I made a mental note that I'd have to use that saying one day when I was talking shit. It sounded over the top.

"One day, you gonna be behind bars with your man. You need to be right alongside him. You ain't shit either. Joe's blood is on your hands too!"

And there we have it. At least that unpolished tramp Fiona was finally showing her true feelings. I'd get with that whore later. But that part right there she blurted out about me being in jail made me slightly pause and break character. Knowing all eyes were on me, especially hers, I then gave the judgmental crowd the biggest smug, "Hey, Kool-Aid smile" I could. Imagine me, Kapri James White, locked up. Never that! I was married to the Shooter, and that was as close as a jail cell I was going to see. Nolan always made sure of that, and this time was no different. Entertained at the sheer notion, I winked at the many news reporters assigned to the high-profile case hubby was fighting.

Repeating "No comment," while still flashing my ring, I pulled open one of the double doors. Short-staffed, the Wayne County Sheriffs had their hands full trying to keep order as well as me out of harm's way. It was a crazed madhouse to gain entry into the building, seeing as my husband's murder trial wasn't the only one taking place that week. Yet, make no mistake . . . It was definitely the most popular. I had been there every day, beginning to end. So my face had become familiar to the male sheriffs who often flirted, knowing my husband would probably be locked up for years to come. I was always fake cordial and smiled. I was an opportunist and got in where I fitted in. They rushed me through the courthouse metal detectors and barely watched the scan monitor when my purse went by. I could tell they were over the circus I brought with me every time I came in or left. And truthfully, so the hell was I.

I exhaled deeply before heading toward the elevators. It was easy to see that all eyes were still on me. Day after day, it was the same thing. Monday, Tuesday, Wednesday, and now, here it was, Thursday. The insults, accusations, and threats of retaliation violence never let up. They never changed. It was as if these people had nothing else better to do but to try to make my life a living hell.

Although I didn't give a fuck about their particular plight, yeah, I get it. I truly do. Their son, brother, daddy, cousin, and uncle was dead by way of a hollow point nine slug lodged in the left rear portion of his skull and then set on fire. The near mob mentality family reunion being held in the courtroom was livid. They feel my better half is at fault for their grief.

So, okay, yeah, they bitter. However, calling me all the rotten bitches and whores in the book ain't gonna bring they ole, good-snitching-ass-family-member Joe Brezzy-Bey back from the grave. He gone and good the fuck riddance, I say. You would think the extra money they raised from the Go Fund Me and the chicken dinners they sold to bury that burnt rat would be enough to keep them on the hush. But just like the deceased, trying to bald-faced lie his way out of being killed, they wanted to be heard. They lived to be seen, hence, all the extra.

Dressed in a modest-looking, but extremely expensive skirt suit and blouse, I played my role perfectly. My paternal DNA-inherited bloodline dictated that I did. As much as I wanted to break down in tears, I wouldn't. Matter of fact, I couldn't. I could not give them the satisfaction. And more than that, I could not let my husband see me in that state. I was his backbone, his ride or die as the young kids say, and his soldier. In reality, I was his only soldier and link to the outside world. His so-called family had long since abandoned their post as far as he was concerned with his first bid. So when they came around with their hands stuck out or wanting to be a part of our shine, rightfully so, we ignored their existence. They weren't there for him as a kid, so we would not be there for them now that he was grown. My baby was straight renegade where his bloodline was concerned, which was all right by me. I had no problem embracing the black sheep.

Besides the high-priced lawyer with all the connections we kept on retainer, I was the only one that knew the truth about my husband and how he moved. With that knowledge, naturally, the Prosecutor's Office tried every trick in the book to get me to turn on my better half, even threatening to bring separate charges against me for petty bullshit like "Accessory to Murder" and whatnot. This was crazy, because I was way down in Atlanta during their supposed time frame of the murder, just as we planned. So my alibi was airtight.

Thankfully, our lawyer shut those allegations down every time they surfaced. But like I said earlier, my paternal DNA foundation was solid. My birth father had done a twenty-piece straight with no interruptions, never once considering snitching, dry or otherwise. And I was built the same way as my sperm donor, Ram Tough. I wasn't scared of sitting down if I had to. Fuck any penalty before I'd be disloyal.

Over the years, Nolan and I had stashed money for a rainy day, and now, we had severe heavy storms to weather. What was the sense of playing the game if you didn't have an exit plan when the time came? Cash was always king.

Planted in the front row behind the defense table, I leaned upward. With certainty, I assured Attorney Mims he'd indeed be paid another huge chunk of his promised bonus before we parted ways. Suited and booted, he was always casket clean. And most importantly, the man was well known around town as a miracle worker for beating hard-to-beat cases. Our lawyer made the impossible . . . possible. Thus far, our paid mouthpiece had definitely earned every bit of his extravagant fee, beginning with those confidential documents.

With various motions filed and getting supposed witnesses dismissed citing creditability issues, things were going better than expected on our behalf. We were fighting the uphill battle difference between numbers and letters, but so was the prosecution. Sure, my husband had no bond, but even God couldn't convince the judge to offer that luxury considering the extremely violent nature of what crime Nolan had "allegedly" committed and his record. And as for the other multiple murders they tried to tie him to unsuccessfully, Trenton Franks and Roberta Tanner, they were a no-go. My husband was clear where those two untimely killings were concerned. Thank God. Yet, the name Nolan White was still burning on the lips of the judicial system.

Chapter Eight

Kapri

It was nearing a little past nine when the inmate entrance door cracked. My heart raced with anticipation. It felt as if it were going to jump out of my blouse. I kept my eyes focused on the door. One armed Wayne County Sheriff appeared, followed by two more, all looking stern-faced. This entire trial, they were obviously in cahoots with the prosecutors trying to portray to the jury Nolan was out of control even in their guarded custody. Watching them put on a show for the twelve didn't shake my faith. God had the last say-so—period.

In a matter of seconds, I soon saw the absolute love of my life once again led out in shackles. Even though he was badly in need of a haircut and a shave, he was still as handsome as hell. Those green eyes . . . that body. My bae, the Shooter, was allowed to wear the black dress pants and cream-colored button-up I'd left for him. Yet, despite an objection from our lawyer, the judge shot us down. The metal restraints stayed as if he were Public Enemy Number One. Nolan was far from the ruthless wild animal the media outlets were portraying him to be, but at this point, it was what it was. We had to roll with the punches.

In the midst of some of the people making snide remarks loud enough for the judge and jury to hear, I tuned them out. They weren't my main focus. My husband was.

It didn't take long before our eyes locked. I had the same lump in my throat that I did the day we first met. My love and loyalty ran deep. I mouthed the words, "I got you," which was the same thing I said to him when he'd gotten arrested months ago. My king never cracked a smile but nodded, letting me know that he appreciated me sticking by him. The few times he was able to call from the county jail, it was made perfectly clear to me that as a team, we would not allow others to see us bend, buckle, or break. The lawyer had also reinforced my husband's wishes, where emotions were concerned. We were all three a united front. I loved my man more than life itself and had his back in good times and the bad ones as well. I continued to hold it together when several more of the victims' family members had to be restrained and were forcefully removed from the courtroom.

"You sorry-ass motherfucker. You think you a tough guy? Bitch, do me like you did my peoples. I'll kill your ass for real. I ain't like all them other lames you done put in the ground."

"Get your hands off me so I can show pussy what's really good. That was my fucking cousin he did like that. He put a bullet in the back of his head and left him to die—bleed out like he was a dog in the streets. That shit was uncalled for—burning a nigga up." One man tried his best to break free from the sheriff's strong-arm grip.

"Let me get that uppity bitch of his sitting over there like her shit don't stank! Ole tramp ass sucking a murderer's dick." That sleazeball Fiona was back at it. She tried her luck at climbing over the small wooden wall but was stopped dead in her tracks as well—which was good for her because I would have head-mopped the floor with her just as I always dreamed about.

Collectively, they all lunged at both Nolan and me, but like the Gs that we are, neither of us flinched. I merely crossed my ankles and stared straight-ahead. And as for Nolan, he had on his "I wish a fucker would" face. I guess that was that Black Bottom gangster in him and that calm NFL (Niggas From Linwood) in me . . . definitely a powerful combination. He had no family members of his own showing support or loyalty, and neither did I. We were all each other had in the world, which was more than all right with me.

The team of prosecutors, headed by Ms. Sylvia Campbell, the youngest on their team, found utter satisfaction that the victims' family had clowned in front of the jury. Their outburst gave them a chance for things to be heard that were previously ruled out by the judge. But our lawyer was far from shaken. Like Nolan and me, he was unbothered. Finally, things calmed down in the courtroom, and the judge restored order. The trial then proceeded. Like the previous days, more testimony and more finger-pointing of guilt came from the other side. The prosecutors' team was having their final stab at swaying the jury.

At one point, it took everything in my power not to leap from my seat and slap the fire out of the only black woman on their team. She, ironically, had the worst mouth. Ms. Campbell seemed especially motivated to get a conviction. Maybe it was because she was so young and wanted to prove herself. I didn't know what it was, but I shook my head every time she spoke, thinking she was probably no more than a bitter soon-to-be spinster mad at the world for not blessing her with children, let alone a husband of her own. So here she was, trying to take mine away from me the only way she knew how.

"So, yes, jury, the man you see sitting over there was seen leaving the scene where the victim's body was discovered set ablaze. There were at least two eyewitnesses. Also, a green light camera at a nearby business caught images of what appears to be Mr. White fleeing in a dark-colored Range Rover. That is the type of vehicle that is registered to the suspect's 'play' aunt. It is the same truck Mr. White has been often seen in driving around the city. To reinforce the facts, even more, Mr. White was pulled over by a traffic cop in the Tenth Precinct and issued several tickets."

"Okay, Your Honor, first, I'd like to state again for the record these entire proceedings have been nothing more than some far-fetched fabricated hoax, evidence-wise. It's circumstantial, at best. And even then, it's question-able. I'm shocked this has gone this far based on street gossip and innuendos. The Prosecution preying on the fears of a crime-ridden city doesn't equate guilt. Like now, Ms. Campbell is suggesting that there is only one dark-colored Range Rover in all of Metro Detroit. And besides, as the jury and this court already know, the truck that the Prosecution is speaking about Mr. White driving was in the service shop during that time. That proof has been verified from countless sources, including the dealership owner himself. So, why is she insisting on making that a part of this loosely strung together case?"

"Yes, go ahead." The judge nodded to the prosecution team's annoyance.

"Yes, Your Honor, and as far as those eyewitnesses are concerned, the court decided before we went to trial neither of those witnesses were credible," our lawyer firmly interjected. "They are drug addicts that admitted they were coaxed into pointing out my client's picture in exchange for cash—which is against the law in the first place and definitely cause for a mistrial. So, why is she constantly bringing up misinformation and distorting the truth? It's like she's beating a dead horse."

"But, no, wait," Ms. Campbell tried to interject but was swiftly shut down by the judge's stern glare.

Attorney Mims took a moment to observe some of the jurors' reactions to what he'd just stated and went back in on the facts despite his opponents' sneers. "And as we all know, I already introduced the video showing that at least seven trucks were fitting that description during that twelve-hour time. And countless more if we extend that net by two hours before what the prosecutors claim to be their frame of guilt. But as I just stated, his truck was in the shop. Soooo, I mean, I'm confused about what's going on here." He made sure to walk over in front of the prosecutors' table and make eye contact with each of the team.

"I mean, it's like they have built a case on falsehoods because, apparently, the deceased was a paid police informant that they lost track of. It's not my client's fault that his death occurred. Unless the government, whether it be local, state, or federal, is willing to disclose the entire true scope of any and all investigations or cases the deceased was involved in, how did they come to point the finger at Mr. White with blatant manufactured evidence? It's a modern-day witch hunt."

"If you please, Your Honor, I was only trying to link the suspect by way of vehicle association. But I will move on to more solid facts." Ms. Campbell childishly rolled her eyes at our lawyer as if she were some schoolgirl with a major attitude. She knew she was out of line but didn't care.

"I think that would be the best form of action, Ms. Campbell," the judge wisely advised knowing she was on the verge of being in contempt of his courtroom orders previously explained and agreed upon by both parties.

"Well, we all know Nolan White is infamous. Not only with our department, which is quite aware of his activities, but also with the entire Detroit Police Department as a whole. You, the jury, have heard various officers testify that Mr. White has not only been part of several ongoing investigations involving drugs, one that the deceased was assisting us with, but also a special appointed task force specifically formed to apprehend Mr. White put in overtime for weeks tracking his whereabouts. He was, and is, labeled as extremely dangerous. Nolan White is rumored to be a sharpshooter and not afraid or hesitant to pull the trigger. That much can be easily seen from the crime scene photos presented in earlier evidence that can only be described as overkill." She was right back on a roll and feeling herself.

"Ms. Campbell, I'm growing weary. You are walking a fine line with me. Consider this your last warning. Any further statements that are against guidelines will put you in hot water with me and this court as a whole."

"Okay, Judge, I just wanted them to remember, even though we can't prove it, in a horrendous act of brutality, he murdered that young girl in that house, leaving her innocent infant there playing in her deceased mother's blood," Ms. Campbell blurted out so the jury could see her visibly shaken over her last statement.

"What in the entire hell does she think she's doing?" Attorney Mims leaped from his seat, not caring if he was in contempt. "Has she lost her mind? What she said is not only unfounded speculation, but it's also totally out of line and uncalled for. Is Ms. Campbell this desperate to get a conviction that she makes wild remarks and accusations as if there were no laws in place? She is *beyond* out of order. These tactics are despicable!"

The judge sided with the defense and was livid. He'd been on the bench for years, probably before the young woman had finished grade school. From time to time, he'd seen lawyers pull stunt after stunt trying to sway the jury to their side. But Ms. Campbell had gone too far. In fact, what she had done was set the defense up to file a motion for a mistrial. The judge could not put the genie back in the bottle but warned Ms. Campbell to wrap up her closing statement swiftly, and then he'd like to meet with her in chambers after his other morning sessions. He strongly suggested she may want to place a call to her family and let them know she may not be returning home tonight.

Ms. Campbell knew she'd crossed the line, but she felt she had the jury on the edge of their seats. As much as she wanted to throw caution to the wind and keep going hard, even if it meant being held in contempt, the young woman took heed. She took a brief pause and a small sip of water before continuing to try to win the case, hands down. It was apparent she solely wanted to be the one on her team accredited to putting the final nail in my husband's coffin.

"Some people are born to help and aid society, and we have others, like Mr. White, who seem to be born to run wild and destroy the very fiber that holds us together as a decent community. The defendant needs to be off of the streets for good, ending his reign of terror against the residents of Metro Detroit. He needs to pay not only for the gruesome crime of the bullet he put in the rear of his victim's skull, shattering it and ending his life, but also to shield us all from his future actions."

The judge seemed to be just as annoyed with the woman's long-winded statements and continuous stretches of the truth as everyone else, including a few of the jurors. She was going over and over what appeared to be the same loose end facts trying to secure a conviction. With some of the worst acting I'd seen in years, she pointed at Nolan, raising her voice when she said certain words. And then that woman had the nerve to look in my general direction like she wanted to call me a few choice names for having the nerve to be married to my husband. I promise you on a stack of three church-blessed Bibles, homegirl was doing way too much for my liking. However, I had to sit there and let her do her thing. I had to tolerate it. I had to endure. I had to push through, hearing Nolan was a monster. Nolan shot him. Nolan burned him up. Nolan left him for dead. Nolan made him beg. Nolan needs to be removed from society. Nolan is a menace and a nuisance. Nolan has a history of mental illness and needs to be on some sort of medication to control his documented fits. Blah blah blah.

I swear this poor-taste-in-clothes prosecutor bitch was testing me, especially the part about my love being crazy. I mean, damn, you break one teacher's nose back in the day and spit on another, and the masses label you nuts. I took a few deep breaths praying for God to keep me seated and not jump up and do the same to her. I was off my meds too, so *anything* was possible.

It'd been days that seemed like months. Even though I was dreading hearing the words, "We rest our case," I finally did. That ugly skank finally took her foot off my husband's neck. The judge, like us all, appeared to be elated. We would not have to hear that annoying lady's voice any longer. The judge wasted no time in giving strict deliberation instructions to the multicultural jury comprised of eight men and four women. When it was crystal clear what he demanded of them as far as when they went home for the evening, he dismissed the jury. Then he allowed everyone left who was seemingly the victim's family who had controlled themselves to vacate the courtroom next.

The bailiffs surrounding Nolan, legal counsel for both sides, and I remained. Apparently impressed with how we both remained calm and respectful of his courtroom during the outbursts, the judge allowed me a few minutes to speak with my better half while his clerk was preparing paperwork that required his signature.

"Hey, Nolan," I spoke his name almost in a whisper as my heart started to shatter even more. My legs felt weak. This was the longest we'd been apart from each other since getting married.

"I see you looking good, killing these bitches as always. And them heels you got on is making daddy's shit jump." Nolan tried to keep his manhood in check. No matter the circumstances, he always made sure to let Kapri know she was looking hot. That was his mission in life . . . to make his queen happy, even from behind bars.

I blushed just at the thought of what he'd said. "You bugging, bae. I love you. You know that, right?"

"I love you too. Bigger than the world is round. So, how you holding it down, baby girl? You good out in them streets or what? What's the deal? Do I need to make some calls?"

I wanted to wrap my arms around him and beg him to come home. I wanted like hell to tell him the truth. I wanted to let him know that I was lonely and missing him like crazy. I wanted to tell him that I was on the verge of having a nervous breakdown behind all this bullshit. But I didn't. I was the soldier he'd come to depend on.

I bit the corner of my lip while fighting back the tears. I knew my outside misery was the last thing he needed or wanted to hear on the inside. I couldn't be so damn selfish. Time and time again, he'd put his life and freedom on the line so we could eat good, drive right, and live like hood royalty. So, without question, I owed it to my man to stand tall. So stand tall, I did.

"Naw, I'm good. You know me, bae. I'm gonna adapt and make do when need be. The bills paid up and them crazy dogs of yours still acting a fool on the mailman. All is well." I tried to muster a smile and bring one to his face.

"Okay, dig that." Nolan tried to reposition the upper shackles constraining his wrist but couldn't. "Good. I hope they both out there holding you down. And, yeah, fuck that mailman. I ain't like how he be looking nohow."

"Boy, you crazy."

Nolan gazed into his wife's eyes. "You and me, we done came a long way from that day in the office."

"Yeah, bae, we have. And we gonna make plenty more memories when you come home."

"For real, though, 'cause ole boy is killing that big-mouthed lying bitch with them facts. We might just come up out of this better than we think. Just keep the faith, brown eyes."

Seeing the bailiff take one step closer to us, we both knew our special big-mouthed moment was drawing to a close. "You know I got you, baby, no matter what, now and forever. What was still is and always will be. Just know I'm out here doing what needs to be done. I know our time to shine again is right around the corner."

"Yeah, I know you got my back. A guy ain't never worried where your heart is where I'm concerned. Repeatedly, you done proved that shit, no matter what. And this time ain't no different than the rest." Nolan slightly sneered as we were now surrounded, and time was up. "Be good, baby girl, and I'll hit you up as soon as a nigga can. But until then, go home and live life for both of us. Go shine bright on they ass!"

Watching my husband being led out of the courtroom yet again hurt my inner soul. It never got easier and never would. I knew the next time I would come face-to-face with him, we would know his fate as far as the verdict phase goes. And no matter what punishment they came up with, my life would never be the same.

Redirecting my attention to the lawyer, I motioned for him to slide over to the far side of the table he was sitting at. I hoped he was working on the appeal papers in anticipation of the verdict. Like I said, we were prepared for a guilty verdict. That part was nearly inevitable unless a miracle occurred. But we wanted the numbers, not letters. If Nolan got numbers, then my king was coming home sooner or later. Numbers meant hope. Numbers, if low enough, meant he would one day be free, back in my arms. But letters, they signified death behind bars. There was no coming home from that—no successful appeals, and zero hope. Straight over-the-bridge-shipped-up-north-Level-5.

Not saying a word, I placed a sealed envelope into the lawyer's open briefcase. Without much fanfare, Attorney Mims casually tossed a few papers over it in hopes of concealing our personal business from prying eyes. I, in turn, made my way to the exit, but not before making sure the mouthy, unsophisticated prosecution team hater, Ms. Campbell, had a chance to marvel at my wedding ring.

Chapter Nine

Kapri

Once out in the hall, I hoped the crowds that filled all the various courtrooms on that floor had thinned out. Well, at least the ones that had me in their crosshairs. I was offered protection to my vehicle but turned down the offer. Thankfully with ease and no conflict, I slipped into the bathroom. I exhaled, finding it was empty. Without haste, I dipped into one of the stalls. I didn't have to pee. But after hours of being front and center on display, I needed a moment of privacy to adjust my crown. It was awful seeing Nolan in those shackles. And it was growing even harder to go home without him by my side night after night. My husband wanted me to go home and live life for both of us, but how could I? *He* was my life. I was his strength, and he was my peace. I was devastated and a mess. I closed my eyes, asking God to give me the mental management to go on . . . well, at least what was needed to make it back to my truck without all the fanfare.

As I stood there gathering my thoughts, I felt a vibration. Seconds later, I felt it once more. Unzipping my purse, I soon saw the source. I shockingly discovered that the sheriffs had messed around in their hurriedness to get me through security and allowed my cell phone inside the building. *What the hell. Shit, I'm glad they didn't see this motherfucker, 'cause the way the female sheriff watching the monitor be hating on my ass, she would've tried to claim I was smuggling shit in to pass off to my husband.*

I removed my phone from my purse with intentions to just power it off until I got outside of the courthouse building. Before I did so, out of habit, automatically, my manicured nails tapped that blue and white addictive icon. I checked my Facebook page to see if any pictures of me entering earlier had hit the local crime-reporting groups. Most times, they were faster than the mainstream media updating hood news.

Damn, there goes my peace.

Suddenly, I heard the bathroom door swing open. That was followed by the sounds of cheap heels dragging across the faux marble floor. Motionless, I couldn't believe my luck. This was something out of a Lifetime movie. My expression turned from sugar to shit. As I stood in the stall with the closed door, I overheard that annoying voice. That hard-to-stomach voice belonged to the woman I had been forced to listen to smear my husband's name.

Oh, hell naw, not this mud duck chick. I swear this day can't get any worse. Ms. Campbell was on her cell, talking away. Dumbly, the cocky-mouthed whore didn't bother to see or even care if anyone else was inside of the bathroom. Absorbed in what she thought was a private conversation between the other person and her, the bad-weave vulture had mines and my names dripping off her fiery tongue. *Listen to this ho talking this garbage. She outta her shit. I swear hoes be fake as hell with it.* There was no point or a great rush to make myself known. I had nowhere to go but back home to an empty house that this bitch was trying to make a permanent situation. Quietly with my cell in hand, I leaned back and let Ms. Campbell's talkative self go to town on hers.

"Yeah, sis, like I said, we just finished up for the after-noon. I thought this day was going to go on forever. . . . Yeah, I'm on the same case, that damn Nolan White. . . . Girl, yes, of course, that uppity bitch of his was there as always. . . . Yeah, trying to look all cute like her shit don't stank. . . . Some tight-ass skirt suit with some of them Red Bottoms shoes on, probably fake. You know how them dope girls be pretending they have class."

No, this young nothing-ass bitch didn't! I wanted to check the dog shit outta her for running off at the mouth. But with a twisted face, I fought to stay quiet as she went into the very next stall. The nasty female didn't even bother to wipe the seat off before plopping her fat ass down on the toilet.

"Sis, who you telling? I know, right? . . . Yeah . . . Yeah . . . Yup . . . Hell yeah, girl, you seen his picture all over the news and on social media. That man is fine as hell, shooter or not. . . . Yeah, even in them shack-les, I made the judge keep on his wet-dream-making self. . . . Yeah, I know that was extra with the shack-les, but so what? Yup, too bad he gotta go to jail 'cause if he wasn't, I'd be all over that. . . . Yeah, girl, I bet his dick is long and thick. . . . Yeah, he married to her, but so what? You know how them dope boys roll. . . . Heck yeah, just like that other dude I ended up sexing before he got sent away. If him and me had not been fucking on the sly while he was out on bail, I would've slammed him hard too. . . . But that tongue of his was too good to keep locked away forever. . . . Yeah, sis, you can call me crazy all you want, but it is what it is. . . .

"Naw, seriously, though, on this Nolan White case, you know I doubled down on the facts with him. You know we have to stretch the truth sometimes. Hell, even lie to prevent taking an L, especially where that generational monster is involved. He got this time of lockup coming for what he did. Besides, you know how the conviction game goes. These jury members are mostly uneducated, slow, and need a little coaxing."

I couldn't resist any longer. I'd heard just about enough. For days on end, this woman had been more than disrespectful when depicting my man, me, and our entire existence. And here she was on the other side of this partition showing her true feelings, wishing she could low-key give my hubby that musty pussy of hers. And worse, she'd talked about how she'd lied and even falsified evidence to get defendants locked up. Sadly, my man was not the first and probably wouldn't be the last if she had her way. Well, now, it was time for me to show her *my* true feelings. Now, I would show her what was really good in the hood and expose that corrupt ass.

Patiently, I waited for the supposedly "educated" monster to finish her call. After listening to her pee, then flush the toilet, I timed my next move perfectly. With a huge smile plastered on my face, I opened the stall door the same time she opened hers. She and I both stepped out in unison, then paused. Me in my black tailored suit, perfect hair, flawless makeup, and, of course, those expensive, black patent leather Red Bottoms pumps that had Ms. Thang so bothered. And her, looking like a tired-face baby elephant with a synthetic, poorly styled wig on and a dress off a Family Dollar rack. We stood side by side, facing a huge, lighted mirror. However, as you can just about imagine, only one of us was smiling. And *boom!* Just like that, there it was. There was my payback for the weeklong disrespect of me and mines. Every false accusation geared toward my husband, every condescending gaze in my direction, and apparently, every time she wished she was getting the dick that belonged to me . . . The expression on her face was priceless.

"Heyyyy, homegirl, long time no damn see," I sarcastically grinned while quickly admiring how white my teeth looked in the mirror.

"Oh my God—you!" Her eyes widened, ready to pop out of her head. She looked as if someone had just punched her dead in the stomach, and she was gasping for air. I guess that flip talk mouth she'd had all this week was now dry as her jaw dropped open. The wanna-be superstar prosecutor's abrupt silence didn't bother me one bit. Besides, after all she'd said, it was now *my* time to be heard.

"Yeah, it's me. Imagine that? But now that we're here, well, damn, Ms. Campbell, where do I begin with you? I mean, so, yeah, you real funny with your ole peculiar-built ass," I started as I opened my purse, removing my lipstick and dropping my cell inside. "I'm not mad at you or even surprised that you think I'm a bitch. Most women that look like you do feel that way. So, yeah, I'm good with that title." I made sure the glossy color was perfect as well as my eyeliner.

Still very much shocked that she and I were even standing side by side, she struggled to speak. "Excuse me, but—"

I cut her off. Like I said, her time to shine was over. "Girl, don't even attempt to try me. I ain't deaf, and I know you just didn't forget that quick what you said." I chuckled at her expense. "Trust me, I already knew you thought my husband was fine as shit. We laughed about you wanting him. Matter of fact, he, our lawyer, and I all joked about the bullshit. But, girl, bye. That's old news to me. Plenty of females shoot they shot at my man. But him and me, we solid. See, I'm good with another title you will probably never have, and that's *wife*." Finally, I turned to face her as I proudly waved my ring finger. *Damn this ho ugly this close up.*

"But I—" Once more, she tried interrupting me while adjusting her cheap floral print dress. But I was having no part of that. As she stood there insecure about her appearance, she was going to hear me speak my piece.

"Please shut the fuck up, your ass is in *my* courtroom now, and you's straight outta order," I eagerly mocked the shell-shocked female.

Dumbfounded, the usually talk-a-mile-a-minute woman stood mute as she was now in the hot seat. "And, oh my God, since you was wondering, yes, girl. My husband's dick *is* extralong and *very* thick. And all that shit you was saying to whoever was on the phone, you probably can't ride it like you just said because my bae is *wild* with it. You don't seem like you can take all that shit he got dangling between his legs. All of that bullshit you was just talking is just that—talk."

I was going in hard on the youngest prosecutor in the city's history, but she definitely had it coming. And I was far from finished. I dropped my lipstick back in my purse and continued. "You got so much foul bullshit to say about my pretty ass, but the one thing you not gonna go around saying is that my motherfucking shoes is fake!" I paused my speech once more, reading her holier-than-thou ass. Like I was a shoe model, I floss profiled my heels. "'Cause see these right here? Like everything a bitch like me wears, is official and top of the line."

Giving me the ultimate stank face, I gladly returned the favor. I wished Ms. Campbell made me come out even more of my character, but she knew better. I don't know if it were that the woman was scared that I would take her head off her body or if it was that she knew she was in the wrong. Whatever the case was, I continued to make it apparent today was that day, and I had time for it. I stuck my hand damn near up in her face, touching her nose with the center stone of my ring.

"And this right here . . . that killer's dick you wanna have a taste of so badly got a whole damn wife, booboo. One that gives zero fucks about going to jail. So, please, in the future, wanna-be home wrecker, show some respect. And if you think *that* was a threat, let's be clear, baby girl, it *was!*"

Finally, Ms. Campbell swallowed the lump in her throat and found the words to speak. Putting on, she tried to act as if I had misheard what she said or her true intentions. The guilt and shame were apparent as she stumbled over every word. That confident, long-winded-speech woman was suddenly reduced to broken sentences and short statements. The paid coon for the white man's justice couldn't look me in the eye. I found that part amusing, especially since she'd been mean-muggin' me since the trial had started. But, whatever. Yeah, I could have ended my rant then, but, nope, that would be too much like right. I wanted the slut to explain what she'd said about fucking guys she was prosecuting, making up false evidence, and how she could manipulate the jury. I waited a few seconds for her response to all of those things she'd recklessly bragged about. However, she couldn't and didn't. How could anyone clean up all of that?

I was done. I'd proven my point that just because I was "Married to the Shooter" didn't mean she could treat me like shit. And just so she'd never forget our impromptu meeting, before leaving the bathroom, to her astonishment, I took my cell back out of my purse. She didn't have the nerve to inquire how I'd gotten my phone inside of the courthouse in the first place. And at this point, it didn't matter to her, but momentarily, it definitely would. With a smirk of satisfaction, I tapped the video icon. Eagerly, I then pushed *play,* hoping my Android had done its job. The recorded sounds of portions of the once-thought-private conversation clearly bounced off the walls. She knew her voice was distinctive and easily recognizable. Her expression was invaluable.

She placed one hand on the sink for support as the whore's knees seemed to buckle, knowing she was about to take a major L. No matter how qualified she thought she was in the courtroom, I was *levels* above her in this revenge bullshit. Over the years, it'd become my thang, so to speak. But this? This right here was the icing on the cake. After being forced to hold my tongue for days, I was taking every opportunity before someone came into the bathroom to interrupt us to clear the air and have my say. I was going ham with it.

"So, yeah, homegirl, you might wanna figure out how to help my falsely accused man out some. I think it'd be in both our best interests. Don't you? And for real, for real, I don't know why you going so damn hard anyway." I openly puzzled what her angle could be. "You getting paid an extra bonus or something? But whatever you trying to prove, do it with the next case and the next Negro, 'cause mine has just become special, and the clock is ticking on this real-ass Rolex."

"Say what, huh? What do you mean, Kapri?" Ms. Campbell awkwardly asked, her eyes wide open, looking as if she were about to break out in tears.

"*Kapri?* Are you fucking *serious* right now? Don't call me that. We ain't friends. It's *Mrs.* White to you." Kapri gave her the stank face and the "Bitch, who in the fuck do you think you are?" expression all rolled into one. "And second, you think they got me and mines on blast in the news every night? Wait till they get wind of you and *your* bullshit."

"Look, hold up." She was ready to try once again to take a cop.

"Naw, Ms. Campbell, *you* hold up. See, the bottom line is the next time we meet, either my man goes free, or you can be prepared to be locked up right alongside him. The choice is yours."

Throughout the trial, Prosecutor Campbell seemed pretty clever. So I know she could figure out what was on the line. She'd fucked up royally. And now, she'd have to face some of those hard-line consequences she was so hell-bent on my husband dealing with. Smugly, I never gave her another chance to respond to what I was suggesting, or should I say, *demanding*. And I never looked back when I strutted out of the bathroom door. I'd let her live with all of what just had happened, at least for the time being. The job she loved so much, as well as her freedom, was now in jeopardy if I blasted her in the media. She'd be disbarred and possibly arrested. This woman made a living embarrassing and humiliating suspects and their families for making mistakes. Now, it was *her* time to take the walk of shame and at least wonder who might find out her dirty little secrets.

Although my husband may have been guilty in the eyes of the law, they had no idea whatsoever where he came from and the type of shit he endured growing up. My man was mentally damaged, but the team of prosecutors, the judge, and no one else truly cared the way I did. All they wanted was a conviction. But now, there was a chance for us to be soon reunited because this big-mouthed bitch was cooked.

Chapter Ten

Oh my God! Oh my fucking God! Shit, shit, oh my fucking God! How could I be so damn stupid and careless? Damn! Why didn't I look on the floor to see if anyone else was in here? Damn, that sneaky little bitch didn't say a word!

Prosecutor Campbell paced around in a circle. While her mind was racing with thoughts of what to do next, her heart was racing as well. She overplayed every single thing she'd said talking on the phone to her sister. It was bad, all bad, and incriminating as hell. She felt light-headed over what had just taken place. *Damn, I really messed up. I can't believe this! What am I gonna do?*

The ordinarily calm individual took several deep breaths, exhaling slowly. Her daily condescending attitude toward life and how she moved was now collapsing. Panicked and feeling dizzy, she turned on the water in the sink. Using one hand, she splashed some up in her face a few times in hopes of thinking what had just happened was all a bad dream.

It didn't work.

What Prosecutor Sylvia Campbell had slipped up and done was no bad dream or nightmare. Her current reality was still just that . . . real. The poor woman was hyperventilating on the verge of passing out. Leaning back against the wall, she could hear the echo of Kapri's cell recording of her voice loudly in her brain.

*This is the worst thing that could ever fucking happen!
Now what? Now, what do I do? I gotta think quickly
because if that bullshit gets out, I'm ruined.* Once more,
she started to walk from one side of the bathroom to the
other. With tears in her eyes, she got her phone. Hands
nervously shaking, she pressed her sister's number,
calling her back. Hearing her younger sibling pick up,
the traditionally strong personality female started to
bawl uncontrollably. She sobbed as if someone had a
gun shoved in her face, threatening to pull the trigger.
And truth be told, Kapri James was doing just that with
the newly heard information she'd just overheard and
thrown in her lap to deal with.

"Sylvia, sis, hey, girl. Can you hear me? What's wrong?
Sylvia!"

The hard-line prosecutor heard her sister talking, yet
couldn't seem to stop crying. She wanted to answer her,
but in truth, what could she say? Would she just come
out and say that her entire career she'd worked so hard
to achieve despite harsh odds was now over? How could
she tell her little sister? She had always looked up to her
to fix things since their youth . . . tell her that she was
a careless fuckup? Fighting back the urge to just jump
out of the window and end all of her potential problems,
Prosecutor Sylvia Campbell got herself together. Finally,
she answered her now confused and worried sibling.
"Hey, girl. Hey, I messed up. I messed up big time."

"Huh, what are you talking about, sis?"

"Well, you know when I just before had called you?"
The tears had slowed down, but the usually great speaker
still struggled to get her words out.

"You talking about when you just left the courtroom?"

"Yeah, girl, that's when I made the biggest mistake of
my damn life. Sis, I done fucked up all the way. I'ma get
fired off jump or maybe even get locked up."

Prosecutor Campbell pushed the trash can in front of the door to avoid anyone coming inside. And even if they ignored the trash can, she'd still be made aware of their presence. Things were bad enough. Totally distraught, the last thing she needed or wanted was for one more person to overhear her dirty little secrets. Wiping her face with the sleeve of her clothes, she went into a stall and sat down on the toilet. Still in shock, Sylvia Campbell started to explain what had just jumped off moments before.

Her sister was, of course, dismayed. "This shit is so fucked up. Damn. Why ain't you check before you started running off at the mouth? That ho-ass nigga gotta pay!"

"I know, I know he got it coming. But I didn't check. And now that bitch of his is going to do everything she can so her husband can walk free. Or at least get a mistrial." Full of regret, she pressed her free hand against her chest, starting to hyperventilate once more.

There was dead silence on the line as the blood-line-linked pair both contemplated what was or could take place next if Kapri let the cat out of the bag. Knowing what she had to do, Prosecutor Campbell ended the conversation asking her sister to pray for her. The judge had already ordered her to his chambers this afternoon, hinting that she would be held in contempt of court for her earlier inappropriate comments. Taking into consideration what she would soon need to find the courage to confess, being held in contempt would merely be a light tap on the hand. Maybe she could get in touch with Kapri and work something out. But she was no fool. The tough young officer of the court knew anything short of Nolan White walking out the doors a free man would be unacceptable. Looking at her watch, Sylvia Campbell knew she had less than thirty minutes to figure out her next move.

Chapter Eleven

Kapri

I can't lie or even attempt to. When I initially walked out of that courtroom, I was miserable. It was hard to hold my head high. I felt a strong sense of hopelessness take hold of my spirit and beat it down. However, after that impromptu bathroom incident, I now had a new lease on my self-confidence. That little blessing in the bathroom had given me full-blown life. I had all the renewed energy generated I needed to navigate through the crime-prevention protesters, infuriated family members, and media. I felt empowered. My sunglasses were adjusted, and my game face was on.

Within seconds of me leaving the front doors of the courthouse, the drama was coming from every direction. It didn't matter that it was damn near eighty-four degrees in the shade, they were still on a hundred with it. Clenched fists were thrown in the air, and handwritten signs condemned not only my husband but also every other would-be criminal within the city limits. And then there were the microphones of the news reporters hoping for an exclusive. They were shoved in my face, forcing me to knock them away.

Despite the multiple human roadblocks and constant name-calling, I kept my composure. Just as proud as I was to be Mrs. Nolan White when I arrived this morning, I had the same energy now. Especially thanks to my little bathroom encounter. That right there would be my man's golden ticket. If I played my cards right, he could end up trading that ticket in for a get outta jail free card. Ole girl was gonna make something shake, or she was gonna be in a cell in the women's prison right down the street from my man. I'd make sure of that. In the meantime, I dipped, ducked, and dodged every step of the way toward the parking lot. Some of the more persistent, scorned people in the crowd, like that tramp Fiona, were begging to get their face smacked.

Fiona, instead of keeping her distance, closely followed behind me. I slowed my pace down long enough to whisper for her to watch her back before she ended burned the fuck up like her cousin. She saw the expression on my face and must've known I was fed up and done playing games for the day. She stopped dead in her tracks, obviously rethinking her next move.

Just as I was about to step off the curb, a hand reached out, grabbing my forearm. Ready to battle, I snatched it away. It was one thing to talk smack, but it was crossing the line touching me. Fist balled the best I could, considering my nails, I stopped in midswing, seeing an ally.

"Damn, boy, why you ain't say nothing?" I figured it must've been Fiona, and it was go time, but it wasn't. "I was about to bug all the way out on whoever the fuck was yanking on me. You was about to catch these hands!"

O. P. smiled at me, nodding his head with pride. The next second, he turned back to eye fuck the menacing crowd. His facial expression and demeanor must have given them more than enough clues that it would be in their best interest to fall back and just leave me be.

O. P. was far from average. He stood a little shy of six feet and weighed two-something. But that description of him wasn't the part that caused the majority of people he came in contact with to be alarmed. Simply put, it was his face. Or at least the half that seemed to had been sewn back together.

O. P. took a hit in the jaw a few years back. The force and caliber of the bullet ripped a fist-sized crater on the entire left portion. The emergency room doctor on duty that fateful night was obviously inexperienced as the end result of O. P.'s stitches made him look like he had three permanent zippers holding his skin in place. It still looked horrendous, and I had seen it countless times.

"Girl, you was moving so damn fast I could hardly keep up. You know I still got that damn bullet in my leg and shit." Yet another hood souvenir he carried daily like most black men born in the struggle. It was like being shot, in jail, or growing up without a father was a rite of passage for most black men. And O. P. had earned all three of his stripes.

O. P. stood for "On Point." And just like right now, he was definitely that. He and Nolan went way back. Way back to peanut butter and jelly sandwiches after school and King of the Mountain. Throughout the years, when either of them would get locked up, the other stepped up and made sure their families ate. By the time I'd come along and met Nolan, he and O. P. had been in and out of handcuffs numerous times between them. But sadly, for my man, this go-around was going to end up being much different than all of the others combined. Although Nolan was on the verge of getting ready to get banged extra hard on this case, I had to be thankful he dodged the bullet for the other murders I know for a fact he committed.

It wasn't like my husband just went around town collecting bodies for the hell of it, but youngins is mad disrespectful in this day and age. These new modern-day dope fiend teenagers, popping pills and drinking lean feel like they're untouchable. They feel like the rules don't apply to them, or they bigger than the game. So every so once in a while, a real certified gangster gotta step up, intervene, and put in work. Most times, their parents or even the police can't restore order. Yet, when they homeboy takes a dirt nap in front of they eyes, they get wise and sober up or risk suffering the same consequences. Or in Trenton and that crackhead's case, you'd catch something hot on the humble. Either way, that was the evolution of life in the hood we grew up in.

We were back at my truck, and all was well. O. P. explained once again that he didn't want to go to the trial and draw attention to himself. Everyone in the city knew my husband and O. P. ran together, and he was right. He would have been a distraction and not welcome—first, his face. And then, of course, Brezzy-Bey's people may have mustered up the courage to try O. P. If that happened, it'd really be on. They would need more than the bailiff to restore order. The Gang Squad and the state police would make the evening news rushing into the courtroom. He then informed me that he'd spoken to Nolan and what their plan was moving forward.

"Damn. Okay, O. P. He didn't tell me. So, what's the deal, so I'll know what to do?"

O. P. reached in his rear pocket. After looking around, he handed me a nice-sized manila-colored envelope. "Here, Kapri, take this. It's yours."

With it now in my hands, there was no mistake. I could easily tell the envelope was stuffed with cash. What the amount was, I couldn't tell off rip, but I knew it was a nice amount unless it was all singles.

"Damn, guy, what's this all about? What you need me to do with this? You need me to hold it for you or what?"

"Naw, baby girl. It's Nolan's cut of some business we had put together awhile back before he got knocked. Plus, some extra he wants you to pass on to them fucked-up-ass supposed baby mommas a little bit at a time. You know how that goes."

Tucking it in the side compartment of my purse, I was happy that it was there to replace the one from earlier I'd given to the lawyer. *Look at my husband, still taking care of me from behind bars. Who don't love a nigga like that?* I was already good and sitting pretty. But who didn't need or want money? This I put away. I would save it for a rainy day and possibly attempt to make sure them two envious females he had kids with would be able to buy back-to-school clothes for his seeds. Those "outta jurisdiction situations," as he often referred to them, were way before Nolan and I got serious, when he was out of state running wild. So I had no real problem with them. But the "baby mommas" collectively had issues with me running things where *their* money was concerned. The reason being was because no matter what Nolan did since the day we first met, I was always around in his life in some sort of fashion. Like I stated before, he was my strength, and I was his peace. But right about now, all of the past animosity they possessed for me didn't much matter.

My husband, they baby daddy, although there was never any blood test involved, was locked up. And what that meant was *I* was the one fully controlling that money flow. I was his wife and bottom bitch. So just like it had always been since he and I linked up for real, for real, they could get right or get on—their choice. "See you later, bye" was my motto. It was obvious. I was levels above them. What they hated about me was what was missing in them. Any way it went, I had no time for entertaining their silly project-ho bullshit. If either mammy wanted to hold their kids hostage from being in their father's life, it meant nothing to me but more on-hand revenue to spend for my lavish lifestyle to continue. I needed to upgrade my truck anyway.

I hugged O. P. Sincerely, I thanked him not only for escorting me to my truck but also for being one of the only real friends Nolan had. The rest of the dudes he and O. P. ran with were no more than workers or lames trying to get put on. But O. P. was solid; matter of fact, more like family. We parted ways with my promise to get at him if I had any problems or needed help with crowd control the day the verdict would be read. I dreaded the thought of that day, but it was a reality—unless my newly discovered "friend," Prosecutor Campbell, could work some black girl magic. For now, I would keep our little secret. But if things didn't go my way, she'd be cooked.

Now safely inside of my truck, out of instinct, I reached for my gun. With it resting back on the passenger seat, I was almost ready to pull off. Unlike my husband, I was not a felon, so I could and did legally carry a pistol twenty-four/seven. In most cases and places I went, if my gun was not welcome, neither was I. We were like known Siamese twins. People in my old neighborhood had long since spread the word I wasn't afraid to pull the motherfucker, let alone let that bitch sing. I was just lucky enough not to have caught a body or a case.

Grabbing my cell out of my purse, I powered it back on. Waiting for it to reboot, I laughed at the look on the bitch's face when she came out of the stall. The shit was priceless. Times like this made me wish I had a homegirl or BFF to kick it with, but that wasn't my nature to be "cool" with other females besides my cousin. For the most part, they were messy, and that messiness I couldn't tolerate. Once my cell was back on, I listened to the bathroom audio once more. *Damn, I bet that girl will check under the doors next time.* I was amused and would later decide how her corrupt revelations and controversial statements could benefit me and mines. But for now, as I pulled out of the parking lot, my mind was racing.

I replayed almost every minute of the trial since day one. Then I angrily relived the moments leading up to hearing the front door of our condo being kicked in. I got chills thinking about the police with guns drawn and pointed at our heads, resulting in Nolan being dragged outside wearing only his boxers. I hated the police—period—and that would never change.

I'd been through a lot over the past few months. Hell, seemed like my whole life. But nothing could prepare me for being separated from my other half. Nolan White was my soul mate. But he was also the Shooter. And since I was married to the Shooter, this was the life I chose. But, damn . . . I gripped the steering wheel and allowed the tears to fall. I felt dizzy. I felt overwhelmed, and more importantly, I felt lost and confused.

How in the fuck did we get here? How did shit go so haywire after my bae killed that diseased rat that had it coming? Him facing natural life and me left to pick up the pieces . . . How in the entire fuck? It seems like only yesterday we were teenagers.

Chapter Twelve

Kapri

It was the beginning of the tenth grade, and the devil was on my shoulder, ready to ride. Having gone to Catholic schools for years, I was far from accustomed to what I saw here at Central. I had cursed out one too many nuns at my old school, so they asked me not to return the following semester. My mother was disappointed but never talked down on me, although she did mention that being in contact with my pops was hyping me up to take on his off-the-chain characteristics, which probably did have some truth to it. Mom knew I had mild, inherited mental issues. But, in truth, that was her fault for choosing my daddy's deranged ass to lie down with in the first place. Nevertheless, now, here I was in the middle of what I could only describe as total chaos. Kids were running through the halls with no teachers around. Fights were going on, and no security interceding. It was pandemonium. And no matter how badass I was at my former schools, this was an entirely different element altogether.

The fact that the students were not wearing uniforms, as I was accustomed to doing, made matters worse. It was like a sea of colors bouncing off the walls. Everywhere I looked, some sort of a ghetto fashion show was taking place. It was easy to see which kids' families probably sold drugs and which ones did not. Top Tens, Levi's, thumb-size gold ropes, and Max Julians . . . It was the early eighties, and crack had replaced heroin as a quick high in Detroit. Yearning to get a job in one of the factories was now replaced with getting a sack. That was the thing to do if you were a teenager and wanted to be or feel important . . . secure that bag.

I was raised in a single-parent household, but we were considered upper-middle class just the same. Or at least that's what the judgmental neighbors renting the homes surrounding us felt. We owned the house we lived in, and my mother drove a new car almost every other year. Wearing new gym shoes or new jeans was second nature to me as was going on real vacations out of state, not just hanging out at the local park at the first of the month. I never understood struggle or the harsh life of poverty, thank God. My mother had a steady job since before I was born. She was an assistant supervisor for the Department of Social Services. Her checks were constant, and she and I were quick to catch a flight whenever she felt the need to leave. There was not one time that I can remember doing without or our lights being shut off or going to bed hungry. Even though she and I bumped heads often, I had to respect the job she had. She always held us down. In my book, she was the real MVP. On days when we were so-called bonding, I would let her know how I truly felt.

My father and mother were as different as night and day. He had long since been out of the picture. For lack of better words, my mother used to say he was not of the world we lived in, and getting with him was a major mistake, although my conception wasn't. He wasn't born in Detroit, like my mom. My grandparents moved the family up North from New Orleans when my father was a young child. It had long been rumored my grandmother had cast some swap black-magic spell on a well-to-do white man in their small rural town. And the result of that was she and the entire family fled to Detroit to avoid getting lynched.

Once here, my granny continued her uncanny palm and tarot card readings. She would often cover my face with her left hand and tell others that her supreme powers had skipped a generation, and I had been blessed with the same gift as she. My mother thought "my inherited gift" was all total bullshit. Needless to say, she kept me away from my black-magic granny and that side of the family as much as possible.

My father wanted to be in the streets, ripping and running. So, of course, eventually, life caught up with him. He murdered a man in cold blood, yet claimed it was self-defense. But that twenty years he was doing said something else. Me being me, I'd gone down to the main library and pulled any news article they had available with regards to my father's case. To be extra sure of what had taken place that ultimately separated him from his family, I got copies of the court transcripts. After studying the documents page after page, word for word, it was easy to see why he got twenty years. His actions earned every bit of that time. My mother was correct. My father was not of our world. But I loved him just the same. I would write to him at least once a month, although I was never allowed to visit. He was in jail locked up, not me. That was the reason my mother gave whenever the subject of visits came up in conversation. So, after a few years, I gave up on seeing my dad until he touched back down. Secretly, I held that against Mom, but it was what it was.

The only connection I kinda sorta had on his side of my family tree was Diane. She and I were first cousins and only ten months apart in age. The few times I was able to go over to my paternal grandmother's house, she'd be there, making the visit more eventful. Not superclose, no matter what I was going through, we stayed linked, and she'd pull up if need be. I guess in her case, blood was thicker than water.

"Look, Kapri, when you get to this school, just keep your head down and do your work. There's no need to make friends with those old hoes in training. And definitely, no exchanging numbers with them boys. Most of them come from bad families and probably sell drugs or worse."

"You mean worse like your baby daddy?" I knew I was pushing my mother's buttons with that snide remark, but I was already angry I even had to go to Central High School in the first place.

"Girl, like I said, stay your ass out of the way."

The first week of public school, I stuck out like a sore thumb. Sure, I had all the latest fashions at my fingertips, but just because you look the part doesn't mean fitting in was automatic. I kept my circle small, which consisted of only me. Years of going to school with white people had rubbed off on me. Well, at least, that's what the other students remarked when I would speak. So, after a while, I just decided to shut up altogether. It was better than getting ridiculed and potentially having to snap. The students there thought I was an easy target to bully because I was a loner. But bullying me? Those types of problems they truly *didn't* want. The failed to realize *I* was the actual threat. As for my studies, I didn't have to worry about my abrupt silence affecting my grades. I was miles ahead of the others in all of my classes without effort. After a few months of being enrolled at Central, I became bored. And that boredom was the spark to ignite the small fire, which resulted in the blaze that later shaped my life.

"I swear to God, you guys need to stop talking to me. Why don't y'all grow up?" I was fed up. I had just about enough and was not willing to take anymore. I missed my old friends and my old school. They may have mostly been white, and maybe some were racist, but at least they kept their hatred for me under wraps. These females here were far from being subtle when it came to them disliking me. It was not my fault that my eyes were light chestnut brown, and I was cute. It was my natural hair that reached down beyond my shoulders that I had to brush, not theirs. And as for my complexion, once more, not my own choosing. They could blame God for making me light-skinned. But all of these physical attributes about me, these hoodrat bitches ridiculed and mocked.

I continued to hold my head up because I knew they were just jealous. And in reality, I guess I would be too if some new girl came from out of nowhere catching their boyfriends' eyes and turning heads. But that still didn't give them the right to put their hands on me. Talking shit was one thing. I could handle that because I was good with my words. But now they were starting to cross the line, so I was going to have to prove to them *I* was also good with these hands.

"Why you running around here acting like you white? Like you better than the rest of us? Don't nobody give a fuck you think you pretty, 'cause you not." One sternly questioned me as if I were her child that needed repri-manding.

"Yeah, you stuck-up stank bitch. You ain't that pretty no matter how long your hair is. You think all these guys around here wanna wife your ass? Bitch, they just want the pussy." The next girl, wearing an emerald-green Michigan State hoodie, backed up her friend trying to tear me down, but I wasn't going out like that. Although I was far from arrogant, my self-esteem had always been on high even in my darkest times.

"Look, I done told y'all to stop messing with me. I'm not with all the games and certainly not in the mood for this. Go find something else to do and somebody else to do it with, 'cause I'm *not* the one." I was at the end of my rope, trying to ignore their daily rounds of tag team dogging me. I promised my mother and myself that I was going to change. I was going to do better and just finish this semester without incident. But I was nearing the point of no return if these girls kept it up. I was done playing nice. Something had to give, and it was about to.

"And okay, Kapri, what if we don't stop? What you gonna do? Go get some of your white friends to jump us? Or do you think you a beast? Is *that* what it is?" Dumbly, she had both hands tucked in the pouch of her hoodie and had the nerve to want all the smoke.

I was tired of this school, and especially these same two girls bullying me. Why wouldn't they just go somewhere and do them? I'd made it clear numerous times that I wasn't interested in them or their little ugly, broke boyfriends. They could all kick rocks. "Listen, I'm warning you both," I promised, showing no fear, ready to show them the *real* Kapri James, the one that was banned from every Catholic school in Metro Detroit. The one that could not be stopped once started.

I was on the verge. I knew what I was capable of. The mocking continued. The threats got more violent, and their need to impress the other students increased. I knew it was about to pop off soon. They had me cornered and grew more aggressive. All I wanted to do was sharpen my pencils and finish my social studies paper. But they had other plans, and I guess that was too much like right.

These girls were out of control. They were coming at me like I had actually done something to them, but I hadn't. No matter what they'd said or done since me arriving at this school, I never lashed back out. My only crime I could figure out was being me. Their voices started to get louder, and the situation grew intense. I was no fool—far from it. I knew what was about to happen next, so I readied myself and stood my ground.

Before I could look to see where the teacher was, I felt the harsh sting of a hand slap across my face from one female. The girl in the hoodie then kicked my lower leg. I didn't buckle or fold. I took each of the blows like a bona fide trooper. Then something inside of me clicked all the way on. That small amount of pain was all the motivation I needed to feel an inner wrath brewing strongly. It was like I was a prizefighter, and the bell just rang. All I saw was red. All I wanted to do was shut them down and shut up the hot-box talk they were doing. I'd had enough. I was done being their victim.

Without thinking, I raised my right hand back a little past my shoulder. My hand did not tremble one time. And I did not hesitate when I brought it forward. Strangely, I smiled when I dug the pencils I was holding deep into the first female's shoulder. I knew for sure I had done damage when she stumbled backward into the chalkboard, screaming for someone to help her.

The second girl didn't want to go out like her friend did, so she tried her best to go head up with me. Hands and fists started to fly. I gave as good as I got, but she was overweight and quickly running out of steam. I was solid, however. In a short period of time, a bitch like me was just getting warmed up. I couldn't grab her hair, because she had so little. Instead, I used my palm and smashed her head into the side of a desk twice, maybe three good times. Fist tightly clenched, I socked her dead in the mouth before grabbing a globe off the shelf and bringing it crashing down on her face.

With all the other students yelling and urging us on, I didn't hear the teacher reenter the room. The teacher was screaming for the other students to help break it up, but they knew better. The middle-aged woman tried her best to get me off of the girl who I had knocked to the ground, but I was in full-blown beast mode. I had the bitch by the hood, fast-track dragging her near the window with thoughts of throwing her out of the motherfucker. At that moment, I had already manifested it into taking place and me fighting a murder case.

Nearing the end of the clash, the girl was leaking badly from her nose and mouth, and a tooth was missing. Her eye was starting to swell, and she was in tears. As for me, I had a tiny gash on my right cheekbone, but that didn't slow me down any. In reality, I had tasted my own blood, and it made me go insane. The more the teacher and now security attempted to drag me away, I would break loose and attack once more.

"I warned you bitches to stop playing with me like I'm some sort of a game. But, naw, y'all kept thinking I was weak because I wasn't saying nothing back. And now y'all both done caught these hands. Trick hoes got the nerve to be crying, pointing the finger of blame at me. Well, fuck y'all, and matter of fact, fuck this school. Yeah, I beat the shit outta both you bitches, and I'm still pretty!" I wiped a small bit of blood off my cheekbone, swearing shit wasn't over, and I'd see both of them in the streets one day or another.

By the time I had decided to settle down, both females, the entire classroom, school, and staff knew I wasn't to be fucked with. I'd made that clear. I'd come to Central High School, minding my own business wanting to do right. But them hoes wouldn't let me be great. They put me to the test, and needless to say, I passed. Today, they learned to never judge a book by its cover. Pretty bitches can buck too.

Not being able to get me back in a civil state of mind, the dean of students looked up my records file and called my mother. I knew when that woman placed the call, she didn't know what consequences she was about to endure, especially when she tried to slip in the fact that I had been injured. You can only imagine that conversation ended abruptly after *that* revelation. We lived only a few blocks from the school, and as fate would have it, my mother was on vacation. So, yeah, my mother arrived quickly.

When she stormed into the office, she searched the room with her eyes. She saw me sitting off in the far corner with a damp paper towel pressed to my face. I could tell she was about to be on the warpath. Normally, I'd be ready to give her some lame, made-up excuse for my behavior, but this time I was innocent. I'd done no wrong but defended myself. They struck first, so there it was.

"Hello, Ms. James, I'm the dean of students that called you." She extended her hand as if my mother were in the mood for pleasantries. She didn't know my parent. My mother looked at her with sheer resentment as if the dean of students were the devil himself offering to buy her soul.

"Please don't be condescending to me, whoever you are—not now, not ever." She took a few steps back, giving the dean the once-over.

Despite other staff members trying to explain the details of what went on, my mother irritably breezed past them all. As I sat there, my adrenalin was still at an all-time high, and I was still on go status. Despite our differences and clashes throughout the years, my mother knew her child and could sense that emotion in me. Not saying a word, she pulled my wrist down so she could see the damage. Needless to say, her eyes bucked at the sight of her child's face. She was livid. I'd never seen my mother so angry. I'd done a lot of wild things throughout the years, and she never reacted as she was now. All along, I believed that my firecracker temper and mental deficiencies came from my father. Now, seeing my mother act as she did, I wasn't so sure. I just prayed she didn't have her gun in her purse. Because the way she was carrying on in the middle of the office, pulling that thing out and letting it sing revenge seemed like it was coming next.

"What in the entire hell have you let happen to my daughter? What kind of wild kingdom zoo is this? I should have all you sons of bitches arrested." My mother was adamant that someone was going to pay for my injury.

"Ms. James, please. If you just wait and calm down, I can explain." The dean put her hands up in hopes of changing the hostile climate and the huge problem she was now facing.

"Look, lady, just get on with it and tell me what the fuck happened to my damn child in this place," she raged, flinging her arms with her purse hanging off her shoulder. "*Somebody* better tell me something—and quick! I swear to God, somebody better start talking!"

"Ms. James, please calm down. Please, please, and let me explain."

"First of all, it is *Mrs.* James, thank you very damn much, and second, explain what? All I know is I sent my child to school this morning and in your care, and she ends up looking like this." In one furious motion, I was yanked up out of the chair as my mother grabbed my chin, showcasing my face. "This right here is criminal. I'm calling the damn police and pressing charges on whoever did this to my daughter." She swiftly scanned the office but saw no other child. "Matter of fact, where is the little animal bastard? I want to see their parents too. I'm pressing charges on them too!"

Then my mother was told that not only had I probably fractured one girl's jaw, but I also punctured a girl's upper shoulder area with some pencils, and they had currently both been rushed to the hospital. You would think the fact that I was victorious in whooping not one, but *two* supposedly bad bitches would have calmed my mother down. But it did the complete opposite. The teacher stood idle while two girls jumped on her baby? Naw! *That* part was not sitting well with her.

My mother grilled the principal until it was further disclosed that there had been no adult supervision when the altercation occurred. That was all my mother needed to hear. I knew her and how she moved. She didn't like all of the stunts I was known to pull, but she never stopped backing me up, especially if I were in the right. She swore that everyone involved with my injury was going to fall. My mother assured them that it would now be her job to make sure someone else lost theirs.

As the staff started pointing fingers, not wanting to take the fall, we stormed out of the building. Once in the car, she tossed her purse in the backseat. Her gun didn't fall out, but a hammer with a wooden handle that we always kept in the junk drawer and a butcher knife did.

I just turned around and faced the front, knowing my mother was still heated. I kept a wet paper towel pressed to my upper jaw area. The car was silent as we headed straight to Sinai Grace Hospital to see if I would need stitches. Sadly, I did and was informed it would forever leave a small scar. I tried not to cry as I looked in a mirror but reasoned with myself that I was still fly. The doctor gave me some antibiotic ointment, a script for a few pain meds, and discharged me. I wanted to beat those bum bitches' asses all over again. And someday I would.

"Kapri, you have to do better. I know this time it was not your fault, but your temper and that mouth are gonna cause you trouble. And one day, I'm not going to be able to save you. One day, you might have to pay the price. Just like that no-good father of yours."

"Ma, like I said, I was minding my own business. They came to me starting it, so I finished it. And as for this," I looked in the mirror at my stitches as my mother drove us home, "I guess I'ma just be a cute girl with a scar 'cause I'm still gonna be serving them hoes."

"Girl, didn't I just tell you about that mouth. Now I gotta deal with all they asses up at that damn school." My mother shook her head as she turned onto Lodge Service Drive.

"Dang, okay, my bad. Sorry, Ma, I meant serving them bitches," I joked, trying to lighten the mood as she drove. "And FYI, you was in that office going on they asses. You was on the heads, for real, for real."

My mother looked at me and could only laugh because she knew I was telling the truth. She had bossed all the way up on them. Thankfully, she didn't have to swing that hammer or skin gut a bitch. I'm not sure what she thought she was going to be going against when she got up to that school, but one thing for sure . . . My mother was prepared to go hard in the paint on my behalf.

After that incident, I left Central High for good, which was okay with me. I had grown weary of any type of authority figure by then, except for maybe my mother. I felt I had bottomed out and had learned all I needed to know to survive. Usually, my mother was on my side, and I was spoiled. She'd just proven that again by following through with her threat to sue the school district along with the parents of the two females who had attacked me. The lawyer advised my mother her best bet for a financial settlement would be though DPS because the girls' parents were drug addicts on that pipe.

After searching for another district schooling that would allow me to enroll midsemester, we discovered I was blackballed because of the pending lawsuit. Without so much as blinking an eye, my mother sued them too for discrimination. In the time being, before I would start homeschooling, I was enrolled in a charter alternative school specifically opened for at-risk youth. And that is where I would first lay eyes on who would be my future husband.

Chapter Thirteen

Nolan

As far back as I can remember, things ain't been right. I used to think I was tripping, and my life was what it was supposed to be. But how could it be? How could any kid deserve to see what I'd seen, been a part of the bullshit antics my mother had going on? It was like I was born into some weird Twilight Zone-like type of existence. Some days I used to sit back on my grandmother's porch and wonder . . . Why the hell me? Why other motherfuckers had so much, and I didn't? Why they had family that was family for real? The only time mine seemed to come together was if it were a fight or one of my cousins was throwing a card party. And those usually resulted in a fight too. Damn, as I really look back now, I came out of the womb to struggle with immoral behavior that most religious people called ungodly. I was a bastard. But that was normal in the hood, back in the day and now. The ungodly part had to do with my parents. Like I said, I was considered a bastard, but I knew who my pops was, although, to this day, I wish I didn't. He was everything I aspired *not* to be as a man.

He claimed he kinda cared for my old girl when he first got with her, but that quickly changed. No sooner than he knocked her up with me, he was on to the next female he could con out of the pussy and money. I was told he tried denying me for a good ten months or so, but my grandmother forced her son to step up to the plate. I don't know how he thought he could get away with saying my mother had cheated on him when she got pregnant because I had the exact same birthmark as he did . . . a dime-sized mole on my wrist. But my grandmother making him "claim me" didn't make him a real father. He was just a sperm donor and proved that trait time after time.

It was the middle of summer back in eighty-four or -five. Because of my mother's unstable circumstances, I'll get to her and her bullshit later, I was made to go live with Pops. I knew when the idea was first brought to me, it wouldn't work out. He had ruined my life years before with treating me like I was garbage as far as I was concerned. Yet, I had nowhere else to go, so that was that. The decision was made, and it was time for me to leave the East Side.

I was eagerly given just enough for bus fare and a transfer from my mother. I received not a goodbye. Not an "I'm sorry to see you go," or even, "I love you." It was as if I were no more than a mere stranger or a nuisance to her partying. My entire existence seemed irrelevant to her. I fought to remain silent as I begrudgingly gathered up my things. The little belongings I did have were dirty, torn, or just plain outdated. At school, I was often ridiculed, and sadly, that degrading humiliation had become the norm. Nevertheless, they were mine and all I had. With a lump in my throat, I stuffed them in two plastic grocery bags and a small duffle bag I had stolen out of Kingsway Department Store.

I wanted to ask my grandmother why she had agreed to my parents' new agreement with my living arrangements but didn't bother. At the end of the day, if she weren't okay with it, it wouldn't be going down. It was what it was. I would just have to make the best of it. There was no sense in continuing to try to reason with my mother.

It was pouring down rain on my way to the Far West Side of Detroit. I was confused about what exact stop to get off at and was far too proud to ask the driver. Unfortunately for me, I had gone three stops too many and had to walk back in the downpour.

By the time I reached my father's girlfriend's house, I was drenched as well as my bags of clothes. Standing on the porch, I remember looking at not one, but *two* vehicles in the driveway. *Look at this bullshit here!* Used to reacting with violence, I had to calm down. I counted to ten like the school psychiatrist had me to do each time I was beside myself. It took everything in my power not to sock my old man straight off in the jaw when he finally opened the front door, asking me what took me so long. I didn't say a word. I just looked at him as if he were crazy. His voice grew more agitated, insisting he had places to go, and I was holding him up.

"Boy, what the hell is wrong with you? You must think the world revolves around you. And if that deranged mother of yours got you thinking that, then y'all both wrong. Shit like that don't fly around here." He made sure that any neighbors in ear range could hear his declaration of authority.

"Yo, what you mean? It was the bus, plus, it's raining. You don't see that or me?" I smartly pointed out toward the wet streets, then my clothes. I tried to reason with him, knowing that feat would be nearly impossible. I just closed my mouth once more, wishing I could hit him.

Ironically, my father's expression seemed as if he wanted to sock me in my jaw too. The hatred he'd always felt for me was apparent. After taking a few steps backward, I thought he'd found the courage to do so, but he came to his senses. Even though his unkind words made him feel like a big man, he was far from that. Though just a teenager, I stood half a foot taller than he did. I had not been around him on the regular for well over a year, so he didn't know what I was capable of if pushed too far, especially physically. So, for now, the coward didn't force his hand. He stuck to the verbal assaults, which sometimes hurt more than getting kicked in the back of the head.

"Excuse me? Nolan, just who in the hell you think you talking to like that? You don't think I see the damn rain? I done had enough of that mouth of yours already. I told my mother this shit was a fucked-up idea. But, naw, she thought it'd be good for you. But you over here showing your ass already and ain't even stepped a foot in the door."

Even though I knew my father's sentiments for me were barely lukewarm, at best, it was second nature for him to be cold, even brutal, when it came to someone else's feelings. I was exhausted and soaked down to my underwear. I continued to be mute and let him get off. I just let him callously dog me out like he always did. The quicker he talked down on me, the sooner it would be over.

When I finally stepped inside of where my sperm donor was laying his head, it was like I was in a whole different world than what I was accustomed to. He had living room furniture that matched, a floor-model television, and the inviting aroma of food floated from the kitchen. His girlfriend welcomed me with a warm smile, handing me a fluffy burgundy towel to dry off. She told me to make myself at home, asking me if I was hungry. That was the first time I felt like someone was genuine and nice to me since a teacher back in third grade.

"Woman, don't be telling no other man to make they self at home. What the fuck is wrong with you? And, naw, he ain't hungry. His ass should've had his good-for-nothing mammy feed him before he came this way. And if he didn't, too bad."

The louder he got, the more I could see he had low self-esteem. That "make myself at home" statement almost caused an all-out war. My father jumped up once more, cursing me out for no good reason. He made it clear that I was only staying there temporarily, and he was waiting for the time to come when he could send me back to my mother. He then shifted his mean-spirited words on his girlfriend. She, in turn, reminded him that this was *her* house, *not* his. And she was grown, not to be spoken to like he sadly talked to his children. Once again, I remained silent even though I was cheering inside. Back in the day, I used to be devastated when he'd treat me like filth, but now, I was numb to those actions. Even if anyone would bring the mistreatment to the forefront, he would still believe himself to be faultless.

Instead of staying in one of the spare, comfortable bedrooms upstairs, my father maliciously escorted me down to the basement. Once down there, I shook my head. I was low-key pissed. It wasn't like it was finished and kinda plush. Yeah, it was nicer than some of the places my mother had us recently living at, but still . . . It was a basement with a twin-size raggedy mattress and box spring on the floor when I could have just as easily been upstairs. I dropped my wet bags on the floor and watched him disappear back up the stairs. In true disrespectful fashion, he slammed the door behind him.

Why that ho-ass nigga gotta be so damn extra all the fucking time? One day, he gonna try me, and I'ma test his jaw. I looked up toward the small bit of light shining from underneath the door. Seconds later, his girlfriend opened it, handing me a plate and a few more towels. For that, I was thankful. As I ate, my hatred for my father grew even more. It was like he was jealous of me or something. I had long since learned how to stay out of his way or just plain be invisible whenever he came around to berate my mother. Those actions had become second nature when dealing with my father and his evil existence. To this day, I still don't get his resentment. The only difference is, now, I don't give a fuck. He doing him, and I'm out in these streets doing me. If and when he died, I probably wouldn't even go to his funeral. On second thought, I might, only to make sure he was dead and gone on his way straight to hell.

The summer living under that roof seemed to fly by. I had made plenty of friends in the new neighborhood I'd now referred to as "home." But oddly, I'd also made just as many enemies. For some reason, the hate was real from some of the dudes. The strange thing is most come from two-parent, middle-class households. Every new pair of jeans or gym shoes that came out they had. They didn't have to hustle to buy gold chains or impress a female with lavish gifts. Their parents blessed them with an allowance. But me, I was on my own. By this time, not only was my father fed up with my bad-boy antics, but also so was his girlfriend. No matter how hard I tried to do the right thing, bad shit just kept pulling me in. So I couldn't blame her wanting me to leave either. She had other kids of her own to consider. And me, I was a bad influence on the verge to corrupt them all.

"Here comes that pretty-boy, nothing-ass bum with them green eyes from the East Side. Walking like he a beast or some shit." That was all most guys had when wanting to go up against me, the fact that I was light-skinned and had green eyes. And the next was, of course, my clothes . . . or lack thereof.

"Where that Salvation Army-dressing fool at?" the second boy joked while looking around. "I'm tired of him thinking he pulling all the females."

The third in the crew pointed in my direction, calling me bitches. I heard them talking fly way from across the vacant lot I was at. I saw them keep gesturing while a few random girls from around the way stood off to the side, giggling. The trio was death-stare mugging me as if they were daring me to get any nearer. I knew what was about to come next if I did, but I didn't care. I was feeling reckless and invincible. I was fed up with these soft momma boys thinking they could ho me. I was truly about that life and didn't mind proving it. An average person would have turned around and gone the other way, maybe even run. But not me. Imagine that . . . Nolan White, running from a fight. I had made up my mind a long time back that I'd rather get my ass handed to me than go out like a pussy, especially in front of some females. So, that in mind, I didn't slow my pace. I picked it up.

In no time flat, I was at the playground ready for whatever. I had no more patience for their verbal games and them trying to make me look bad in front of they girls. Standing toe-to-toe, I locked eyes with one of them. Before any words could pass, I swung. Then I kept swinging, never losing focus of what I'd come to do, which was at least prove I was far from a bitch. Thank God I had been held up in the basement using some old weights that I'd found in the furnace room. My arms were cut up and ready to help on my mission. I knew for a fact I had shattered one of their top dog dreams because I heard one of the females scream that it looked like ole boy's shit was leaking bad. That gave me an extra boost of energy and incentive to keep swinging. I was left-handed, a southpaw. So I knew my blows from that side held more power. So that's what I led with while keeping a steady pace with my right.

With no end in sight, the three of them eventually got the best of me. I was on the ground getting stumped, but still was talking shit as I struggled to get back on my feet. The end result was them dotting my eye and leaving my back bruised black and blue. But I knew for a fact that I'd done some damage too. It didn't take long to notice that one was indeed leaking like a waterfall from his mouth. Although it hurt like hell, I stood tall. Still having my pride intact, I walked away with only a slight limp. I was bleeding from the corner of my lip as well. The other guy was trying to catch his breath, while the third one threatened to slap one of the females for pointing out that it took three of them to win against me. It was true. However, it wasn't no thang. I temporarily took my L like a man. But I'd be back, and much sooner than they all thought.

These busters think this shit is over. But it ain't no way they gonna have me out here looking like this. Like some sucker! I'ma show them what's really good in the hood.

Nolan was still pissed, showing no signs of calming down. Like a soldier returning from the war, the rebellious teen proudly stood in the mirror. With his torn shirt now off, thrown onto the floor, he swallowed hard. His head was pounding, having taken a shoe to his temple. Dizzy, he turned on the cold water in the sink, hoping to shake it off. Cupping his hands underneath the faucet, he splashed the water upward. Unfortunately, all the wetness in the world couldn't alter Nolan's swelling face or his intense pain. It was easy to see that by morning, his right eye was going to be all the way closed. It was already changing colors, just as his back was. Moving his shoulder over as far as he could, he saw one of the guy's shoe print stamp across the lower area.

Got my shit saying Nike! I swear, I'ma kill one of them faggots for this bullshit. Fuck all they gump asses. They think shit is all sweet, but it ain't. They gonna pay. I swear to God they is!

Nolan went through the small duffle bag he still kept his clothes in. He threw on a clean T-shirt, mad the other was ruined. Scorned, without saying a single word to anyone else in the house, he slipped out of the side door as quietly as he entered. The only difference now was that he was armed with a bat. This was not just a normal bat, but one he'd modified weeks before when he was bored. It had industrial-sized staples duct taped around the top portion. The metal staples were sharp, and there were plenty of them to do some real significant harm. Nolan had been using the makeshift weapon up until now to hit small garden snakes with it in the backyard. But today, his bat would make its mainstream debut as evidence in three attempted murder cases.

It didn't take long for Nolan to hunt his prey. Cocky, two of the three lames were at the same spot he'd left them. Obviously believing that there would be no retaliation, Nolan could hear them talking about how they had done this and that to him. On the prowl, he lay back behind a vacant house, now watching them act out what had just taken place. The females were still there, giggling, feeding their egos. Apparently, the one dude with the busted mouth had done the same as he had—went about his way to treat his wounds—only Nolan was now back seeking retribution.

Malicious intent flowed through Nolan's veins. It quickly fueled his need for revenge. With each passing moment, his palms grew sweaty. The East Side hood warrior briefly tightened the grip on the wooden handle of the bat. Then he loosened it as his hand trembled. He repeated this until he felt the time to pounce was right. Each one of his attackers had their backs turned, as did the females. They were focused on a pack of Jeeps riding past with their speakers working overtime. It was at that moment he bossed up making his move.

Bat in hand, Nolan bolted in their direction. Only a few yards from being upon them, one of the females turned around. She and Nolan locked eyes. She stood motionless as well as silent. Not opening her mouth to warn the two guys, Nolan assumed she must've been the female that had spoken out in his defense. He didn't have time to thank her, but would maybe get around to it later—if he wasn't in jail for murder.

Without delay, he settled his need for payback. The element of surprise was now in full play. The first dude took the brute force of Nolan's initial swing. Although he wanted to crack his skull wide open off rip, he strategically decided to go at his legs. He knew if the first guy was brought down to his knees, he could easily go to work on the second without interruption.

Just as planned, the first guy instantly fell to the ground. As he yelled out in agony, the other dude, including the females, all turned around. Stunned, once more, the girls watched in disbelief. First, they had witnessed the attack on Nolan. Now they would have a firsthand account of another fight.

Amid the girls' screams, Nolan then proceeded to break both of the second guy's arms as he put them up to shield himself. He proclaimed he was sorry, but Nolan showed no mercy to either guy. The devil had stepped up and was riding shotgun. Frustrated with his terrible home life, instead, the stressed man-child increased his swings of the now-bloody bat. The streets never gave a fuck about him, so now, Nolan was returning the favor. With his own eye rapidly closing, Nolan continued to wreak havoc. He was relentless in the blows he was dishing out to both guys who were on the ground in almost the same spot they'd had him at earlier. There was no way in hell he was going to be the only one out of the previous melee nursing wounds resulting over what had taken place.

"Yeah, so you punk-faking gangsters think y'all was just gonna jump me, and it was gonna be all good? Naw, pussies, never that. I ain't cut like no bitch. Putting ya hands or feet on a nigga like me gonna get ya ass dead, real quick." There was no turning back. The stage for bloodshed was once more set. Nolan had to satisfy his thirst for payback.

"Oh my fucking God," one shocked female screamed out, cringing at the rapid motion of the bat about to hit its mark.

"Yeah, so you momma boys over here playing like y'all about that life, when a playa like me living it on a daily basis. I does this shit for real, for real, ya feel me?" Nolan was full of pride as he put in work.

"Hold up, hold up!" one managed to get out before feeling the bat strike his wrist, cracking a bone, then his forearm. The sound of his wrist breaking along with the sound it made was heart wrenching for the squeamish females to watch and hear. The boy's pain was excruciating as he cried out for help.

"Aaaaw, fuck, shit. Nigga, is you crazy? Chill with all that!" the other begged, getting the same brutal bat treatment as his homeboy was enduring. He was now regretting jumping Nolan in the first place. If he could take it back, he would. But it was too late for all of that. The only thing he could do now was pray Nolan got tired and give him a chance to get away.

The cocky teens' pleas fell upon deaf ears. Nolan was hyped as the hits kept coming across any part of their body that wasn't shielded. Begging, crying, their appeals for him to stop only made the enraged teen go extra hard. No longer was the East Side bad boy just swinging the bat—now he was taking his turn to stump on heads and backs. "Yeah, how that shit feel? Do it feel good? Do it? Y'all out here fronting for these rat-mouthed hoes I wouldn't let suck my dick." The females took offense by rolling their eyes, simultaneously sucking their teeth. Nolan slowed down and laughed at their response. Licking his lips, he pointed the bat at the one girl who hadn't warned the rest of her crew. He then winked his eye that wasn't swollen half shut. "Yeah, well, not her. She the only one halfway pretty enough to suck my motherfucking dick. I'ma get your number later."

Instead of being offended over what he'd just announced, the girl separated herself from her friends as if she had just leveled up. "All right, then, cool," she smiled, not caring what her friends thought. Fiona had been checking Nolan out since he moved into the neighborhood, but up until now, he never noticed her.

When Nolan felt he'd gotten enough reimbursement for them rushing him at the same time, he told them to make sure they informed their homeboy he'd be getting with him as well. Before he could dip off, Fiona stepped up, handing him a piece of paper with her number scribbled on it. He stuffed it into his pocket, pledging to call. Fiona exhaled in awe, thinking Nolan was courageous. And in the bloody aftermath, the truth was the youth was crazy as hell and didn't give a fuck about living or dying. Possessed with a menacing expression, Nolan slow strolled off victorious, bat in tow. Prideful, his chest stuck out. He was certain he'd gotten his point across that he wasn't to be fucked with—now or never.

Chapter Fourteen

Nolan

The small bungalow home was quiet for the most part. Nolan crept on the side of the house. At first, being forced to live in the basement was a curse, but Nolan had come to embrace the freedom of being able to sneak in and out at will. His father was a hard sleeper, so the side door opening was never noticeable. Today was Saturday, and he was glad that his father was not at home. He'd been fishing since the break of dawn. He would ask one of his many other friends' sons to go, but never his own, Nolan. But that was fine. Nolan hated the sight of him as well. Anytime the old man was there, an argument would break out between him and his girlfriend or anyone else under the roof he chose to be his target.

Extremely sore from both altercations, the injured teen limped toward the door using the wall of the house to steady his pace. Once inside, he fell back across his bed. The mattress and box spring were still on the floor, but Nolan had made it be his private home away from home. In deep thought about how he would handle the three guys and any of their people seeking revenge, he fell asleep. His dream was consumed about why his mother had even sent him on this side of town to live with his father from jump. . . .

***

"Ma, what did I do so bad that you don't want me around no more? I'm confused." Wanting some understanding of her out-of-the-blue decision, Nolan begged his mother for an answer and some understanding.

"Look, boy, just pack your damn stuff and get ready to leave. I just can't deal with you anymore," she slurred, turning up the small bottle of cheap wine. "All the fights. All the disobeying me. All the skipping school, and all the times you running around here looking at my black ass like you crazy or something. Acting like I owe you some money. *I'm* your parent, *not* the other way around."

Nolan frowned his brow. He couldn't conceive why she was saying these things. Over the years, his mother had been known to make rash decisions, especially when twisted. But this time, Nolan didn't see this coming. Usually, he was his mother's go-to on everything she refused to deal with. Now, this. "Ma, are you serious right now? You can't be."

"As a damn heart attack, boy. So like I said, get your little bullshit and go on now. Get the fuck on." Rubbing her fingers through her homemade brown hairstyle, she swiftly motioned toward the door as if her son were a stranger, not her firstborn.

Nolan was close to speechless. He had a lump in his throat, and once more, as many previous times, his mother had broken his heart. Once a homecoming queen, she had the face of an angel but a heart cursed by the devil. Her addictions had beaten her down in every sense of the word. Jumping up off one of the blue-colored milk crates Nolan's always struggling family had been using as chairs, he was furious. Raising his foot, he kicked the crate over across the wooden floor. As it slid into the wall, Nolan now had his mother's full, paranoid schizophrenic attention. The troubled teenager was not only hurt by her words but also completely irate as well. How fucking dare she? After all he'd been doing in the way of making sure that at least his younger siblings didn't go hungry, here, this poor excuse for a mother was throwing him out. The nerve. The audacity. She wanted him to go live with his father, and she already knew what kind of sorry excuse for a man *he* was.

"I swear it's taking everything in my power not to nut all the way the fuck up! You straight tripping right now." He paced the floor, contemplating busting out the living room window after tearing down the dirty sheets that were nailed up for curtains. "A nigga ain't do shit to you. What the fuck!"

"Watch your mouth and the way you talk to me."

"Or what? You gonna throw me out of this hole-in-the-wall bullshit you got us living in? Is *that* what you gonna do?"

"Say *what?*" Although half out of her mind and off her meds, she tried to stand in hopes of going toe-to-toe with her son. She couldn't manage it and fell back down onto the couch.

"You heard me." Nolan had absolutely no respect whatsoever for the woman who had given birth to him as a teenager. "You must've forgotten that *I'm* the reason you even have money to halfway maintain like you do. I'm around here watching the twins so you can run the streets all day and night doing what the fuck ever. And you gonna do me like this? You know me and that baby daddy of yours don't get along."

"Nolan White . . ." Agitated that the bottle of wine was empty, the distorted-thinking mother of three threw it against the wall.

After it shattered, the oldest child at least had the mind-set to direct his younger twin brothers away from the glass. "Y'all go in the back room while I finish talking to Momma," Nolan strongly suggested, praying if he did leave, they'd somehow be safe from her wrath.

The combative mother and son then went back and forth for close to an hour. However, at the end of the boisterous argument, the result was the same as his mother had initially demanded. Nolan would gather his belongings and stay with his father. His mother knew the type of man she'd lain down and created him with. However, because her newest boyfriend of the week didn't like Nolan, the West Side and his father were his fate. In reality, Nolan had no idea whatsoever that his grandmother had threatened his mother. Calls would be made if she didn't let her oldest go and at least have a chance at a normal life.

The last words Nolan said to his mother still tormented him, even in his sleep. Nolan blurted out that he wished that they'd find her dead body in the gutter before Christmas. In truth, he knew that the way she was carrying on, partying, and living life so recklessly, his wish coming true was a strong possibility.

It couldn't have been any more than twenty minutes when Nolan was awakened from his dream. He'd heard the unruly roar of his father's voice from the top of the stairs. In full-body pain, Nolan wanted to get up and see what that madman wanted, but he couldn't bring his legs to function. Instead, he continued to lie there and pretend he was still asleep. He hoped his father would just go away, but that was far from the case. His footsteps got louder and closer. Nolan couldn't avoid what was coming next. He knew when his father saw his eye, he would flip out and threaten to send him packing back east for being a nuisance.

"Did you not hear me fucking calling your little black ass?" His blood boiled as he angrily towered over his son. He'd been down this road before with his disobedient offspring.

"Oh, dang. Naw, sorry. I was asleep," Nolan tried to lie as he turned his face toward the brown painted concrete wall wishing his dad would just leave him be. But that wish was not granted. He readied himself for another one of his father's infamous tantrums.

"Boy, ain't nobody sleeping that damn hard. Especially after hitting on peoples' kids with bats! Have you lost your fucking mind?"

Damn, okay, there it is. That was superquick. My father had to have gotten home right now, so how in the hell did he find out so soon? "Listen, Pops, let me explain." I stood to my feet so he could see my black eye. Then I took off my shirt so he could see what my back and shoulders looked like. As I stood there back turned, I was expecting some sort of unbridled anger for what someone had done to his son. I thought I would hear that those boys had that bat beating coming and more. But I didn't. In fact, I heard almost the complete opposite. Come to find out, my father, who was no more than a pussy hound, had been secretly messing around with the mother of one of the boys that I had beaten. That mother, along with her son, had just left from not only exposing my father's infidelities to his girlfriend but also throwing a brick through the picture window vowing further revenge if they ever caught me in the street.

"Explain? What the fuck is there to explain? Your dumb ass done came over here and ain't been shit but trouble since day one. I ain't want you here in the first place. This was all my mother's doing thinking you could change if you got out of that neighborhood and away from that deranged mother of yours. But, yeah, we see how that done

worked out. You done did some dumb shit that they outta
lock your ass up for. Matter of fact, I should call the cops
myself."

"Hey, you need to shut the fuck up down there talking
to that boy like that with your no-good-cheating ass.
What you need to do is be up here, gathering up your
belongings and getting the hell outta my house. And I'm
not playing around." My father's girlfriend never cursed.
That wasn't her style. But this was a special occasion.
Some random ho from a few blocks over had just broken
her window and vindictively proclaimed my father was
fucking her daily and helping her pay bills.

Slowly, I turned around to face him. It was as if he
were looking straight through me. There was no emotion.
There was no sympathy for my wounds. He acted as if
I were no more than a stranger to him. Standing there,
wanting to cry, I bossed up. I made up my mind that from
this point on, if he didn't give a fuck about me, then the
feeling would be mutual. Hearing the demands for him to
hurry up and get his belongings before they got thrown
out into the street, I knew what that meant for me. I had
already gotten in trouble for smoking weed in the garage,
taking the lawn mower away from the house to try to
make some money, constant days of detention, and many
other things. So, it was more than safe to assume that if
my father had to pack, so did I.

Ironically, as I stood on the porch, it started to rain
as it did the day I had arrived. At first, it was just some
drizzle, but then it turned to be a windy thunderstorm.
I stuck my hand out, allowing the huge drops to fill
my palm. I felt sad. It was strange. As much as I had
hated the notion of moving over here in the first place,
I had grown accustomed to not having a million people
running in and out all times of the night, like when I lived
with my mother. And also I was eating three times a day.

I didn't have many new clothes to call my own, but at least I had some peace of mind here. Now, as I watched my father load most of his things into his truck, I didn't know what my fate would be. I'd heard my mother had moved once again and didn't have a phone. But I guess my father would find her somehow and drop me off on her dysfunctional doorstep. I'd once again be her problem, which would make him happy. The only good thing that would come out of me leaving the neighborhood was the three fake goons that called themselves jumping me could not get revenge for that bat attack unless they were brave enough to come east to do so.

My father tried to plead his case with his girlfriend, but she was done. She said she was fed up with all of his lies and his low-down dirty ways. Throughout all of the screaming and loud threats of physical violence, some ugly truths were revealed to the entire neighborhood and whoever else was in ear range. Come to find out this had not been my father's first time getting exposed for his bullshit. Apparently, he was always on the prowl. However, this instance would be the last time he'd get away with being a dog on this street, in this house. His free ride was over at this address.

Pop's mug was ripped. He wasn't expecting this sudden eviction, but here it was. He had barely gotten the last box of his work tools out of the front closet and on the porch before his now ex-girlfriend and financial sponsor called him out of his name, slamming the door shut. My father was heated. Matter of fact, I don't think I'd ever seen him as mad as he was now. I don't know if it was because he'd just been thrown out or if he was pissed that the other lady had outted him. But whatever the case was, I knew that ultimately, he blamed me.

By this time, it was raining even harder. The sky was an eerie doom-and-gloom gray. Mumbling underneath his breath, my father headed toward his truck, and so did I. Before I could reach the passenger door, however, I was stopped dead in my tracks. He shot me an evil look. It was then that he dug into his pocket and pulled out a handful of loose change. Full of contempt, he opened his hand, throwing the change to the ground. As I stood there in the pouring rain with a swollen eye and my few belongings stuffed in a bag, I was told to get back to the East Side the same way I had come.

I knew he just had to be playing. I knew this was a bad joke. But unfortunately, it wasn't. Showing no signs of remorse, guilt, or shame, my father started the engine. Without making further eye contact, he quickly backed out the driveway. I was his son, his own flesh and blood. But to him, that didn't matter. I was invisible—a throwaway. Within seconds, his truck roared down the block, then out of sight.

There was nothing I could say. There was nothing I could do. I bent down to gather up the discarded coins on the pavement and scattered throughout the wet grass. I looked back up at the house, praying my father's girl-friend would have a change of heart and let me stay. Well, at least until the storm had stopped. I saw her standing by the broken picture window in tears. I still had a small bit of hope.

Then she walked away.

That day still haunted Nolan as it was the day that changed his life forever. After he'd made it back to the Far East Side during the violent storm, Nolan got off the third bus he was forced to take. Soaked to the bone, he limped around the block to his grandmother's home. With the showers still coming down, the mentally defeated teen stood on the corner in disbelief. Staring at her house and his father's truck that was parked out front, his soul was shattered. Once again, he had been shown that he meant nothing to the man whose blood ran through his veins. Not only had he made an injured Nolan spend a few hours in the middle of a bad rainstorm to get on the other side of town, but he had also left him to stand up on Eight Mile, not caring if he got jumped once more.

Seeing that vehicle parked there made the normally strong willed adolescent break down all the way. He wanted to go swing on his old man. He wanted to tell him that he wasn't shit. Deep down inside, Nolan knew his father wasn't shit. Truth be told, neither was his mother. Born in the struggle, he was cursed from both sides. With a lump in his throat, the man-child tried his best to be brave. He tried to fight it . . . but failed. The cruel, harsh reality of his life and what the future held set in. He was not even 16 years old yet and out in the world all alone.

Nolan's tears blended in with the rain as the traffic sped by. Not bothering even to go knock on his grandmother's door and give his no-good daddy the satisfaction of telling him that he was not welcome, Nolan kept it moving. He made up in his mind, right then and there, these would be the last tears he'd shed. Not only over his parents, but also anything else designed to bring him down.

Head held high, he slowly limped a few blocks over to find refuge from the weather and allow his injured body to rest. After a few hours of sitting on the porch of an abandoned house, the rain finally ended. By then, it was pitch black, and a confused Nolan still had not figured out what his next move would be. Returning to his grandmother's house was out of the question. And since he had no idea where his gypsy-ways mother was staying, that was also off the table and not an option. Using his soaked bags of clothes, he made a pillow. Exhausted, he curled up on the far corner of the porch, hoping he couldn't be seen. Before he knew it, the fatigued youth was asleep.

Chapter Fifteen

It was scarcely the crack of dawn in the low-income neighborhood. The sounds of the city garbage trucks pulling out of their home base yard one block over woke the homeless teenager. Nolan's swollen eye was all the way closed shut. The clothes he'd been forced to sleep in were still very much damp from the previous day. Not only was he hungry, but he was also visibly and mentally worn out. Doing some soul searching, he knew he wasn't the best kid he could have been growing up to this point, but he knew he didn't deserve what he was presently going through. The weight of the world was tragically on his shoulders.

Thirty minutes passed, and then the sun was all the way up. Contemplating his next move, Nolan buried his face in his hands. Still in deep thought, he lifted his head. It was then that he saw one of his homeboys from grade school, nicknamed O. P.

"Hey, what up, doe?"

"Damn, what up, doe, with you, nigga? What the fuck happened to your eye?"

"Oh yeah, this," Nolan proudly replied.

"Yeah, that, nigga. What the fuck? And, damn, what your ass doing back on this side of town anyhow?" O. P. was full of questions, starting with his friend's eye. He'd known Nolan since kindergarten and had never seen him in this bad of a shape. However, he would let him take the lead and reveal what Nolan felt he needed to in his own time.

"Man, these ho-ass faggots over near my pop's crib called they self getting down. But it is what it is." Nolan stood trying to fix his damp clothing and discreetly pushed his bags of belongings off to the side. He and his friend did indeed go way back, but that still didn't stop Nolan from feeling some sort of shame for now basically being homeless.

"I heard that. Well, damn." O. P. put one foot up on the stair of the porch, acting as if everything were normal. "I hope you showed they ass what was good."

"No doubt, my guy. I gave 'em some ninth-ending bull-shit, ya feel me?" Nolan managed to laugh while mocking as if he were swinging a bat.

"Dig that," O. P. cheered him on in the early-morning breeze.

"Yeah, my eye messed up some, but trust, they some-where mad they even tried that shit with me," Nolan smirked, giving O. P. a dap.

"That's what's up. Niggas gonna learn fucking around with Black Bottom boys will get ya all the way fucked up."

"True, true. But, what up, doe? What you about to get off into now?" Nolan changed the subject as he looked up one end of the block, then down to the other.

"Yo, I'm heading to the gas station to get a few loosies. You gonna make that hike with me or what? You ain't doing shit, so come on. Besides, I wanna holler at you about something."

Nolan was still pretty sore from the battle the previous day, but it was true, he had nothing else better to do. He couldn't risk his few bags of belongings coming up miss-ing, so he swallowed his pride. He bit the bullet, grabbing them. O. P. was from the streets like his friend. A known neighborhood troublemaker, he'd been kicked out of his house in the middle of the night and gone hungry more times than he chose to recall. He did not judge. He just asked Nolan if he had another bag he could help him carry, or was this it. Nolan handed him the small duffle bag, and just like that, they were on the move.

Reenacting blow by blow how he had gotten all three of his attackers together over on the other side of town, the two teens decided to smoke a joint. On the way walking back from the gas station, Nolan's boy explained to him his current situation. They were pretty much in the same predicament. O. P. revealed he was living a few blocks over in a house squatting. He said he was working on a bag he'd gotten from some older dude that ran the house. O. P. suggested he needed some help making something shake so that they could both eat. Nolan was all in. What other choice did he have? After all, he was homeless. Selling dope was the answer to his prayers. Nolan's life had gone from bad to worse within twenty-four hours. He'd lost a decent roof over his head. Now, he was willing to risk his freedom, as well.

Tall Rob ran the spot that his best friend was working out of. Nowhere in particular to be, O. P. lived there as well as a few other workers. Although Tall Rob didn't actually own the house on East Kirby, he'd commandeered it after one of his family members lost the property due to back taxes. He, like everyone else in the city of Detroit, knew that there were multitudes of vacant dwellings. So many, in fact, that no one department assigned to figuring out what was what could handle it. Tall Rob capitalized on their inability to do so. He had the lights on illegally. On the colder days, they used space heaters. There was no need for a stove or refrigerator. Most of the young guys he had staying as well as hustling there bought fast food on the regular. They were mostly from broken homes and used to living like savages.

At six foot five, Tall Rob had a few strict rules he'd made perfectly clear. All the drugs, be they weed, pills, or crack, would be provided solely by him. There were no outside drugs allowed in his "den of sin," as they nick-named it. Tall Rob gave his workers each a small sack. It was up to them to pay their ticket and also pay him rent if they chose to stay there. For the conniving middle-aged mastermind, it was the perfect setup because the majority of the teens were like Nolan . . . homeless and desperate.

Tall Rob did everything he could to fit in with the young group of men he was manipulating. He wore the latest Jordans that were released, turned his baseball cap to the back, and allowed his designer jeans to sag. He had the newest rap music blasting out of his vehicle's speak-ers when'd he'd pull up on the block. His plan was to appear youthful to blend in like he was one of them, not their superior. Tall Rob used that to keep the sometimes ambitious youth in line. He was wise enough to charge them for everything extra he could think of. The utili-ties were on illegally; yet, he still charged them for that. If he bought paper towels or toilet paper cheap off the streets, he charged top price for that too. As far as Tall Rob was concerned, not even advice was free. If he kept the struggling teenagers' pockets low, they'd never con-sider branching out on their own. They couldn't afford to. It was nothing more than modern-day sharecropping.

O. P. and Nolan each had a hundred-dollar sack. Join-ing forces, the pair was smart enough to have an angle to selling the marijuana as a team. Even though the weed was the same product, they would use a red sharpie to put a mark on half of the plastic bags. They then separated the bags, convincing customers that the "red bag special" was only for their VIP clients. Nolan and O. P. would act as if they were doing them a favor if they secretly served them the red bag against their boss's wishes. This ensured them a quick flip all the way around. Even though the other guys slanging various drugs out of the house made way more revenue than the two of them, the friends found a way to survive, if only barely.

Chapter Sixteen

It'd been almost a solid month since leaving from the West Side. And sadly, to Nolan's knowledge, not one family member showed interest in his whereabouts or well-being. Seeing as he was living a few blocks away from his grandmother's home, you would think he'd run into a relative or two. But he didn't. Nolan stayed in the house grinding, for the most part, sunup to sundown, trying to save the little ends he made. There were no trips to the mall with the other fellas jacking off their pay. No tricking with females. And no extra items he didn't need to maintain his hygiene. Nolan was on a mission. The teen was determined to get Tall Rob's foot off his neck.

Not naïve, Tall Rob saw that hunger and ambition in Nolan and tried to throw up every roadblock he could. Yet, it didn't work. The only thing he could do to slow down or stop the teen's hustle was to act as if he had no product or Nolan had broken a rule. Since all of the other guys living there knew their homeboy was not cut like that, Tall Rob had no other choice but to let him shine. He couldn't run the risk of fucking up team morale and appearing to be a hater.

O. P. had briefly made up with his mother. Having been down this road before, he knew it was only a matter of time before she flipped out again. And when that occurred, O. P. would once more be tossed out in the streets to fend for himself. However, in the meantime, he'd live in the celebration. He ate all the home cooked meals his mom prepared and took plenty of hot showers. He was able to not only wash his clothes but also leave them in his room, not worried about another guy stealing or wearing them. He offered to sneak Nolan in the basement daily while his mother was gone to work and each night when she would go to bed, but Nolan declined the offer. Not because he had pride, by any means, but because he was on his hustle and could not afford to miss any paying customers.

O. P.'s temporary change in residence had enabled Nolan to make double the amount a week now. Wanting to get some fresh air, finally, he stepped out on the front porch of the spot. Stretching his arms, he then made the short hike up to the nearby gas station. As he walked by his grandmother's street, his head didn't turn once. As far as Nolan was concerned, the entire generation could all kick rocks. He was living for self and only self. Of course, he hoped that his little twin brothers were doing okay, but the oldest son had to trust that God would cover them both because he knew his mother was still up to no good. He'd always love his siblings, but living how he had been the last few weeks, emotions could not come into play if one wanted to succeed in the dope game. Maybe one day, when he could support himself, he could support them as well, but for now, all Nolan could offer were silent prayers.

No more than three minutes inside of the gas station, he'd grabbed a honey bun, a few bags of Better Made hot chips, and a grape juice. Before the frugal teen could think of anything else he possibly needed to get by for a couple of days, he heard the bell ring on the door signaling that someone else had entered. Nolan was in the middle of walking down the aisle, items in hand. He wanted to stop. He wanted to just drop his stuff on the floor and exit. But he didn't. By the wayward teen's account and all he'd been through over the past few months, he was now a grown-ass man. That meant he feared no man, not even his mentally abusive father. *I swear to God if this old, played-out goofy nigga say some shit to me, I'ma nut all the way the fuck up. His best bet is just to leave me be before I test his jaw. I'm tight on all they asses over at Grandma's.*

"Well well well. Ain't this about some shit? And where in the hell your no-good ass been at?" the father barked at his son in his usual demanding tone, bringing attention to them both. That was what he liked to do. Get loud and act as if that made him right when it was apparent to all that he was wrong.

Nolan was seemingly unbothered. He stayed focused on what he was doing. He didn't say a word in response. Instead, he moved around his father, placing his snack items on the counter as if the boisterous man were no more than a stranger.

"Hey, little no-good bastard that probably ain't even mine, I know you hear me talking to your simpleminded ass. Now, I said, where in the hell you been at, boy? Your damn grandmother been asking about you." His scruffy voice grew louder, realizing he was purposely being ignored. The two other patrons inside of the gas station, as well as the attendant, all gave the animated man the stank eye for how he was carrying on. It was way too early for either of them to hear or see the next man clowning.

"Next," the Middle Eastern cashier waited for Nolan to place his items in the turntable portion of the bulletproof partition. He'd been working there for a few years and easily recognized both father and son. He'd always known Nolan to behave just as he was, quiet and with respect. And as for the elder of the two, Nolan's father was in true character as well, being loud, obnoxious, and a troublemaker.

"Hey, my main man, young Nolan. Good morning." Despite the obvious, the cashier still greeted his young customer with a smile, wishing he could eliminate what was going down on the other side of the bulletproof glass.

"Hey, Sam, how you doing?" Nolan nodded patiently, waiting for the price he owed for his early-morning snacks.

That pleasant exchange between the two pushed Nolan's egotistical father far over the edge. Not only was he embarrassed that his son had ignored his questions, but the surly in nature man was also pissed he'd done it in front of Sam. "Oh, so you can open that mouth of yours and speak, huh? I thought you had just lost your mind altogether. But, naw, you just being a stupid ass like that tramp mother of yours. I heard through the grape-vine she knocked up with another baby, crazy-minded, pill-popping bitch."

Taking a few deep breaths of the crisp morning air, it took everything in Nolan not to swing on his pops for the scandalizing remarks he was saying. But at this point, it was not only fuck him but also fuck his mother too, so, whatever. Nolan wisely fell back. He'd been around his father long enough to know that was just what his old dude wanted . . . attention. And there was no need to give him that satisfaction. He didn't deserve that much effort.

Being homeless had not only made the teen have to man up, but it also made him realize that his father was no more than a gloried bully that no one respected. The man was all bark and no bite. But now was not the time for Nolan to pull his old man's card. He'd let him do all the mouthing off. He wanted to ease his own guilt. Besides, the dedicated hustler had to get back on the block. Nolan knew there were always midmorning customers sliding by to grab a bag or two of trees before heading to work. And he needed every penny he could make to add to his come-up stash.

Paying Sam for his snacks, Nolan took the plastic bag and headed out of the door. Not ready to just let it go, his father followed behind, yelling obscenities. He loudly called his son every vile name he could think of, proudly announcing to his firstborn that he was disowned from the family. Nolan didn't bother to turn around. Why would he? His father had humiliated him for the last time when he was forced to take the bus home in the rain, so whatever he said mattered none.

Not slowing his pace, Nolan did slightly smirk, elated that he was disowned. Fuck 'em all had been his mind-set for months. Yet, the vile-tongued father was not done. When his harsh words didn't work, he would not be content until he got a reaction. Using both hands, he shoved Nolan in the center of his back, resulting in him dropping his bag. When the bag hit the pavement, it was quickly apparent that the glass bottle of juice inside shattered. The purple liquid filled the plastic. It was easy to see the grape-flavored juice had the chips and honey bun coverings soaked. It was then that Nolan's true tolerance level was tested. It took every inch of discipline he could muster. His jaw clenched, holding back his words. He knew if he turned around, the outcome would be nothing that his verbally out-of-control father expected or would see coming.

Aggravated, his father was heated that he'd not succeeded in provoking Nolan to react. He got louder and louder as traffic sped down Mt. Elliot heading toward the freeway. "You think 'cause you out here running these streets that you can be disrespectful to me? You think you can act like you too grown to answer questions about where in the hell you been? One day, you gonna regret this, you little motherfucker. One day, I'ma show you a thing or two about thinking you grown. You gonna need me one day. Then we'll see how big and tough you are, you li'l bastard!"

Naw naw naw. Don't turn around. Don't do it. 'Cause if you do, you gonna break this old fake-ass nigga's jaw or stump him the fuck out in the middle of this lot. Nolan didn't give in. It was as if his hands were tied. He remained strong and didn't even bother to pick up his bag and check if the other items were salvageable. Instead, the underage teen kept his head held high, never giving his father the face-to-face confrontation the immature man desired. Nolan picked up his pace, heading back to the house he now considered his temporary home.

Chapter Seventeen

A few days later, after the dreadful run-in with his father, Nolan was called down to the living room in the den of sin. Once there, he saw that Tall Rob had gathered the young hustlers around as he usually did weekly. Typically, it'd be on a Thursday midmorning to get ready for a heavy weekend. However, this day was in preparation for what was considered a three-day hood holiday. All of the sacks were doubled up because the first of the month would be the following day. That meant more than the usual amount of money floating through Detroit. Residents of the crime-ridden town would get their Social Security checks, disability checks, and the city workers would receive theirs as well.

Once Nolan had completed his business dealings with Tall Rob, he elected to go back upstairs to his room. There was no need for him to sit around and boast and brag about what he was going to spend his extra cash on. He was focused, not once forgetting why he was there and where he wanted to be. The rest of the guys were hustling backward, and Nolan had no problem whatsoever in letting them know when forced. It was the same routine each time they would settle up with Tall Rob. Before they would hit the streets to floss out with their pay, a dice game between some would jump off.

Having beaten everyone else out of their funds on the regular, Kev Cooper, the in-house bully, turned his sights on Nolan before he could hit the stairs. Boisterous and high, Kev tried everything in his power to persuade the house money miser to get in the game. Yet, Nolan didn't fold. Up until now, he never let any of the fellas living there get too familiar with him, and today would be no exception to that rule. He would serve his custos, then be ghost. For the time being, his homeboy O. P. was out of the crib, so Nolan would grind solo until further notice.

Not wanting to be bothered, he shook his head that he was not interested in throwing them dice. But a loud-mouthed Kev Cooper was persistent, not wanting to take no as an answer, even going so far as to pull Nolan back off the stairs in his direction by the shoulder. Nolan stumbled some but caught his balance, dropping his sack of weed on the step. That unwanted physical occurrence was all it took to awaken Nolan's sleeping inner beast. From that point on, he saw red.

"Nigga, have you lost all your damn mind? Don't ever put your fucking hands on me again," Nolan turned fire engine, making it clear he was not with the bullshit as rap music blasted out of a small floor speaker. He looked Kev square off in the eyes so there would be no misunderstanding. He wasn't with the fun and games.

A normal person would get the hint and fall back. But young fools that ran the streets thought otherwise. They were hardheaded and often had to be taught by a much-needed hands-on approach. Throwing both hands up, Kev broke out in laughter. He was not the least bit fazed by Nolan's outburst. In fact, it only fueled him to attempt to clown the usually reserved teen even more.

"Damn, so look, y'all," he pointed his finger in Nolan's face daring him to make a move while he tried downgrading Nolan's character. "The pretty boy done went and got some balls from some-damn-where. Maybe he got 'em outta his mother's mouth. Rumor has it her old pregnant ass be in the alley behind Auto Zone taking throat shots for a few dollars."

"What the fuck you just say?" Nolan bossed up as his fist clenched tighter. Even though what Kev was saying was probably right, especially after what his father had blurted out the other day, but so damn what? Who in the hell was Kev to try to clown on him like he couldn't get his ass handed to him? He may have been the top dog to all the rest of the crew living under that roof, but not him. Nolan was never going to be a sheep. No matter how poor he was. No matter how he dressed. And no matter how pretty and weak motherfuckers mistakenly thought he was. Nolan White was going to come out on top—or die trying. Blood flowing strong, the music lyrics blasting only motivated his rage more. What he had violently in mind for Kev would be nothing nice.

"Listen, y'all, hold up. Just chill out for a minute," Tall Rob interjected into the vicious word-brewing confrontation, turning his baseball cap backward. As he stood in between his two workers, one could only assume Tall Rob's maturity level would have kicked in. However, sadly, that was far from the case. It proved to be the complete opposite as he reached into his pocket, pulling out a few dollars. Chest stuck out, he tossed a hundred onto the floor.

"Y'all two doing all that jaw jacking. Let's see who really got heart. I got a c-note on Kev, and I'ma match anybody else that's betting on him too. And if Nolan fucks around and wins, which I doubt, then the pot is his. Now, who in?"

There were seven, maybe eight guys left standing around in the living room. The others had gotten their pay and were out. Tall Rob gloated as he dared each one of his young workers to step up and try to bet it up. Eager to increase their weekend funds, three of them put their money on Kev Cooper. The remaining guys had never seen Nolan go, let alone get loud and in his zone as he was now. They'd witnessed his boy O. P. act a fool, but never his sidekick. They opted not to risk the bet, but would definitely enjoy being spectators of the upcoming brawl. Extra cocky, Kev reached in his pocket and threw down not one, but two hundred-dollar bills onto the pile of cash. That made it an even G in play.

"I'm 'bout to beat the brakes off this asshole, then head up to Auto Zone so his mother can put in some work too," Kev taunted, promising that this would be quick. It would be a one-round knockout. "Yeah, y'all niggas better put them cell phones down from recording and get to calling the ambulance now. This bright-skinned soft pussy about to go night-night."

The vibe was intense. Nolan had a stone-faced gaze of emptiness. He'd had enough of Kev talking all of that rah-rah bullshit about this and that. Yeah, Nolan was quiet, that much was true. He'd been like that most of his life. But if a person started shit with him, Nolan had no problem ending it. This afternoon was no exception. If they wanted to see a reaction, he had time. And just like that, the sinister side of Nolan White's personality kicked into full gear. With a thirst for blood, he stepped to Kev Cooper, demanding he talk that garbage about his mother one more time.

Feeling as if this were going to be an easy win, his opponent hurriedly granted an underestimated Nolan his wish. Before he could manage to get the second disrespectful word out of his mouth, Nolan swung. As if it were a movie, his arm appeared to go in superslow motion.

A loud swishing sound rang out as his fist made direct contact with Kev Cooper's face. Immediately upon impact, Nolan could feel a throbbing pain shoot across three of his knuckles. Kev fell back into the mantle. Dazed, he tried to shake the hit off and stand strong, but he never got a chance to get right. Before he could, Nolan struck again, delivering another punch to the face, this time harder than the last. From the way his victim's mouth was now leaking, it was easy for Nolan and all gathered in the living room to see the damage. The resident bully had just gotten his shit blown out all the way.

Unfortunately for his challenger, Nolan wasn't done. Ignoring the aching feeling now spreading to his entire right hand, Nolan opened the left. After extending all of his fingers, he tightly wrapped them around Kev's neck. The guys who betted against Nolan repeatedly yelled for their boy to at least attempt to fight back. They soon saw that would not be happening. The quiet one had become unhinged. They had never before seen him in this state. His boy O. P., yes, but not Nolan. With a weird, dark, cold expression, he had started applying pressure to Kev's throat. The more Nolan closed his fingers inward, the more the boy's eyes bucked wide open, and he struggled to breathe. Nolan slow walked Kev up in a corner, never once letting up on applying pressure.

As much as Tall Rob hated to lose his money, he knew he had to break his two workers up before there was a murder in the middle of the living room. He was wise enough to know if that took place, it meant he'd lose not one but two long-term pay streams of income. So with the aid of a few of the guys, they successfully pried a deranged Nolan's hand from around Kev's neck, finger by finger. Once the grip was free, Kev had to be held up by his homeboys and led over to the couch. Not saying a word, Nolan went to the other side of the room pleased with himself for choking Kev out. The nigga with all the mouth wanted to scrap, so now he could deal with the embarrassing results.

Bending down, Nolan grabbed the money he'd earned up off the floor. He turned to look at the now silent crew along with Tall Rob. With a dead look in his eyes, Nolan firmly asked them flat-out, "So, we good on this, right?" No one spoke up against him taking the money, so he stuffed it in his pocket and took his sack of weed off the step. Before finally heading upstairs, he turned around once to ensure none of the occupants of the house, including Tall Rob, had a problem. Seeing as there was none, Nolan disappeared up to his room.

That young nigga gonna be a real headache in the future to anybody that crosses his demented ass. Tall Rob shook his head, still heated in disbelief he'd lost the bet but told Kev that getting a burner to get revenge for a fistfight was for suckers. Just accept the fact he got his ass kicked.

Like a warrior returning from battle victoriously, Nolan was still angry about the awful things Kev had said about his mother. He reasoned with himself that later on in the evening, he would go up to East Warren and see if he could locate her. It'd been awhile since he'd seen his siblings and prayed all was well with his younger twin brothers. After shutting the door, he slid the lock and placed the new bonus sack on the floor. Taking the thousand dollars out of his pocket, an elated Nolan lay back on the multiblanketed pallet he slept on nightly. Strangely, he calmed down as if what had taken place downstairs had not. Tall Rob had just been paid off and supplied all of his workers with more work, and now, Nolan had this extra cash. All was good. Ready to grind out another week, he glanced over to ensure he'd locked the door. He didn't want nor need any interruptions.

Reaching underneath the last wool blanket, he pulled out an over-the-calf white sweat sock. Removing a small

wad of cash, he brightly smiled. Nolan had just added
the thousand dollars to his ever-growing stash, bringing the total to $1,921. Everything was going just the way
he had mapped out. The loyal hustler had promised himself that when he got to an even two thousand, he would
strike out on his own. He would be done with Tall Rob's
opportunist tyranny. Since Nolan started working under his reign, he resented the man. Although over twice
his age, Tall Rob tried to dress young, speak young, and
most pitiful of all, the married man with children was infamous for sleeping with underage females. Rumor was
Tall Rob had several "outside" babies with teenage girls
scattered all across the East Side. His ungodly morals
where woman were concerned reminded Nolan a great
deal of his father . . . another reason he knew it was time
for him to move on and elevate his lifestyle.

Nolan had been looking toward the future. He had
been kicking it with a few older dudes in the hood he'd
grown up admiring. They had been slanging in the streets
as far back as he could recall. One of them saw Nolan
at the local store and informed him he had the plug on
some high-quality weed. He also knew an old woman
that rented out rooms by the week no matter what your
age was. So, a roof over his head would be secure as long
as he could pay. If Nolan made that move, it would be
bye-bye Tall Rob, hello independence. *Ain't shit gonna
hold me back from securing that gangsta bag and
getting the fuck outta here and this neighborhood! I'ma
'bout to come all the way up!* Thinking no more about
the over-the-top episode at the gas station or anything
else negative, Nolan focused on his future with his hard
earned stash laying spread out by his side.

Caught up in imagining what his life could be like if he
played his cards right, Nolan and everyone else inside
the den of sin were surprisingly interrupted. Initially,

there was a loud thunderous sound from the lower level of the dwelling, followed by multiple voices shouting out, "Detroit Police! Detroit Police! Put your hands up, Detroit Police!" Countless footsteps sounded as if an entire army had converged inside the house.

Instinctively, Nolan snatched his money up off the blanket. Stuffing his hard earned cash as deep in his pockets as possible, he rushed over toward his closed door. Without effort, he could hear the officers storming down the hallway, kicking in doors. In a panic zone, the distraught teen knew they were nearing his room. Like the other youthful drug peddlers located throughout the home, Nolan too scrambled, attempting to get away. Yet, there was no way to escape. The cops had not only all of the doors covered, but also as Nolan quickly found out, the windows as well. He took a deep breath. It wouldn't be long before he faced the inevitable.

Within a matter of seconds, the flimsy, wooden bedroom door with the Dollar Store lock on it was kicked in. As it dangled off the hinges then tore away from the frame landing on the floor, Nolan had no choice but to put his hands up or risk getting shot as the cop threatened if he'd not obey. Shoved to the floor and searched for weapons, the white officer ran his pockets as the black one stood over Nolan with a gun pointed at his head. *This Uncle Tom motherfucker and this cracker taking my damn money putting that shit inside they vest!* Nolan fumed as he was manhandled and handcuffed. Infuriated at what was taking place, he remained silent as they searched his room, discovering the bagged up weed Tall Rob had just given him.

Forcefully taken down the stairs, a handcuffed Nolan was shoved to his knees. Kicked in the lower spine, he was made to lie down on the living room floor with the others. The other cops turned a blind eye, behaving as if this abuse were the norm.

A female officer came in the house with a chip on her shoulder ten times worse than her male counterparts. With a notebook in hand, she took a pen out of her top pocket. One by one, the boys were asked their full names and ages. Several guys decided to play nice with the policewoman, hoping for some leniency, while others like Nolan bossed up. They chose not to say a word until provided with a lawyer. The few wanna-go-for-bad mouthy teens were roughed up on the female officer's command and promised more of the same if they didn't mind their manners.

There was only one person in handcuffs that wasn't sprawled out on the floor with the others suffering abuse, verbally and physically. And that was Tall Rob. A deer-caught-in-the-headlights-expression Tall Rob to be exact. But he was suffering in another manner, and that was shame, humiliation, and the contemplation of what his legal fate would be, and, of course, what his wife and family would think. There was no more of that wanna-be-a-young-thug spirit in his system now. The usually boisterous figure was as quiet as a church mouse. The officer appearing to be in charge of the impromptu raid had the middle-age man standing near the huge wooden table in the dining room. The table showcased all of the various narcotics, including weed, crack cocaine, heroin, and multitudes of street-craved pills. There were also some doctor prescriptions that had been stolen in home robberies and sold to Tall Rob, as well as a total of six weapons . . . four handguns, one rifle, and a semiauto-matic. All of the firearms were stolen, with the numbers scraped off. Then, of course, the cash, excluding Nolan's $1,921, which the two thieves wearing badges had stolen from him upstairs. He wanted to expose the rogue cops but knew that would only make matters worse for him while in police custody.

As select news reporters were let inside of the premises,
they received firsthand accounts of what was actually going down. A special spotlight focus was on Tall Rob and
what he'd been doing. The Detroit Police Department
Task Force allowed the reporters to snap a few pictures
of the illegal items on the dining room table and also
jot down the ages of the detained youth sprawled on the
floor, which they found especially outlandish. Tall Rob
lowered his head, refusing to answer questions without a
lawyer's presence. It was simple to see who the police felt
was ultimately to blame for what was taking place at the
address. And in the days to follow, when word got out,
the general public would feel the same.

O. P. had received a call from one of his girls that
some shit was going down at the spot. Bolting out his
side door, no doubt, he flew around the way to see
what exactly was taking place. Once on the block, it was
clear what was jumping off. It was a drug raid. Not just
a small-scale one, but it looked as if the entire law en-
forcement force had converged on the two-story home.
O. P. stood, mixing in with the other wide-eyed neighbors. Rubbing his face, he was relieved he wasn't posted
up inside with a sack. Looking up at the bedroom window he and his homeboy had posted up in, he hoped
Nolan wasn't home either. Yet, he knew his road dawg's
dedication to the grind, so nine outta ten times, his best
friend was indeed caught up in the sweep.

At least an hour passed before the teens were marched
one by one out the front door in handcuffs. Of course,
there was a growing crowd of neighbors gawking at what
was taking place. When it was Nolan's turn to be put on
display, he came out the door and down the stairs with
pride. Not once did he try to hide or lower his face. To
him, it was what it was. He was doing what he had to in
an attempt to survive in the streets. So, fuck everyone
that was there to judge.

Before he reached the dark-tinted window police van to join his cohorts, Nolan looked over into the crowd of onlookers. Two, in particular, stuck out. The first was his homeboy O. P., who clenched his fist over his heart, indicating that he had his back no matter what. Nolan nodded, letting him know that he was good and would stand tall.

Then the second face that stood out made Nolan want to throw up. The handcuffed teen grew increasingly sick to his stomach, locking eyes with his father. Nolan refused to give that man the satisfaction of seeing him in any type of emotional agony over what was taking place. He appeared nonchalant as if this little "bump in the road of his life of crime" was nothing. However, it was when his father mouthed the words, "Fuck you" that Nolan came to the realization. This was no coincidence. The cops had not just randomly picked this East Kirby address out of all the other drug houses in the city to run up in. His low-down father probably followed him back to the crib the other day and had vindictively called the law. He could only shrug his shoulders in disbelief at the level of hate in that old man's heart. Nolan's father and his toxic existence had found yet another way to ruin his son's life.

Chapter Eighteen

Kapri and Nolan

It was midsemester, and my immediate education status was up in the air. And that was thanks to that "brutal, uncalled for act of retaliation," as the Detroit Public School team of attorneys tried to argue to avoid a hefty settlement. As much as I complained the days leading up to registering, now here, it wasn't so bad. I didn't mind attending what was referred to around the city as being a "special education" school. Being looked upon as "special" meant special treatment, special rules, and, most importantly, special punishment when you broke those rules. I was good at it. It was right up my alley because I was a habitual rule breaker. Sure, the other kids that sometimes attended were more than a little rough around the edges, but I stayed clear of them as much as possible. They could do them, and I was going to do me.

Just like I had in Central, I stuck out from the others like a sore thumb. But this time, it was in a favorable way. This time, my differences were embraced and definitely celebrated by those in charge. I had scored so ridiculously high on the assessment tests that I was made an office assistant because they had no challenging classes to offer me. Also, when bored, I did tutoring after school for extra credit. Those "special things" enabled me to be up on everyone's business, secrets, and lies, both students and staff. With the supreme knowledge of all of that, I used it to my advantage. Sometimes for good, but most times for bad. I would plot, scheme, and get what I wanted one way or another, even if it meant blackmail.

"Hurry the hell up. Y'all act like I got all day to be messing around. This right here is not a joke, young men. Either get y'all truant asses registered in this school or ya getting locked back up—period. Your future is at stake, and you don't even see it." Aggravated, the group home counselor stood by the white passenger van with a clipboard in his hand. It was only nine in the morning, and the five remaining troubled teens had already worked his last nerve. If his wife were not pregnant and they needed the money, he'd have given the program administration his thirty-day notice.

"Dang, guy, give us a chance to get out of this mug," Nolan remarked, being the last to step out. "And chill out with all the school talk. We here, ain't we?"

"Boy, what's your problem with going to school? Don't you wanna read and whatnot? All of y'all need to stay out of the streets before you end up dead or locked up for real, not in that cozy environment group home you guys are at. The next stop is prison if you don't get an education."

"Look, man, as long as I can count money, what else matters? And for the record, naw, I ain't got no problem with going to school. School just always got a problem with me," Nolan spoke up as he and several other boys were being led into the office.

Since Kapri had been working in the office in between classes bimonthly, she'd see the salt-and-pepper-haired man. She found out that he was a juvenile group home counselor. He'd be with a handful of potential students to speak to the dean of students pertaining to attending the alternative school. Time and time again, it was the same outcome. Unfortunately, no sooner than the overwhelmed, underpaid man would come in and take the time to get the boys properly registered, the new students would never show up for class. Some ran away from the group home. Some committed more serious crimes and were charged as adults. While others just plain refused to attend. Up to this day, Kapri could care less what any of the delinquent guys did. She was living her life drama free from the bullshit that came along with that school.

It was Tuesday morning. This was the always grumpy counselor's day to come in and handle his regular routine with the wayward teens under the state's strict jurisdiction. From the outward appearance of this group, they seemed to be some of the most troublesome bunch as of yet. In particular, leading the pack was a fair-skinned man-child with mesmerizing hazel eyes. There was always one in every group that did the most, and it was him. He was the one with all the mouth and had a verbal opposition to every rule that was being explained by the dean of students. Extremely rude, it was evident to all he had a chip on his shoulder.

Kapri's first impression of him was that he should not be trying to come to this school but should be locked up like the wild animal he was behaving like. Asked by the administrator to bring in registration forms and a few extra pencils, Kapri turned her nose up at Nolan while shaking her head. Amused, he returned the favor by calling her a silly thot box underneath his breath so that only she could hear it. Kapri's first thought was to turn around and spit in his face. But since attending anger management classes, she'd learn to fight with her words, not physically as she was accustomed to. So instead, she decided to hit the boy where she thought it would hurt.

As usual, her hair was perfect, not a strand out of place. She'd just got her nails done a few days ago. And there was no question her outfit was on point. Gucci and Jordans never went out of style. So she was ready just in case his poor pimping ass had a comeback on standby.

"Damn, okay. Nice shoes, pretty boy. And what are those?" She pointed as she smirked. "Air Nots or something? Now, silly thot box on that, nigga," she said, planting her hands firmly on her hips. She cared not one bit about the adults in the room or what they thought. If they wanted to admonish her for what she'd said, Kapri would happily unleash her attitude on them as well.

Kapri had indeed hit below the belt, where teenage rules mattered. But it was all good. Nolan was used to being talked about because of the clothes he wore. That had been taking place since he was old enough to attend school, so that insult rolled right off his back. As the other boys in the office laughed at his expense, Nolan was stone-faced. He peered over at Kapri as if she were no more than filth for trying to embarrass him. The only thing he could think about at the time was if he'd still had that $1,921, maybe he could've had some halfway decent clothes. But the reality was, he didn't. After all he'd gone through at that house, he was flat broke and back to square one. And now, even though technically, he wasn't homeless any longer, he still had a juvenile record attached to his name, one that would follow him a lifetime.

Usually, Kapri could care less about going for the jugular. And if truth be told, Nolan had drawn first blood. So he had to take what he had coming, no matter how harsh in delivery. Kapri was in rare form but eased up. She could look into Nolan's eyes and tell deep down inside he was hurting. It wasn't just a plain bruised ego. The wounded pain she saw ran deeper than just her teasing him about his shoes. With compassionate intentions, she leaned over, whispering in his ear that she was sorry. Strangely, at that moment, the two somehow connected.

Off of her high horse, Kapri switched off her furious demeanor. She then volunteered to help Nolan quickly fill out his paperwork. That offered assistance was definitely okay with the frustrated keeper. The fed-up counselor was well aware Nolan couldn't keep quiet much longer. He'd witnessed the sometimes mentally deranged young men snap at the drop of a dime, and it wasn't a pretty sight. He wanted to get Nolan out of the building and back in the transport van before the dean of students changed his mind about accepting Nolan White and his rotten attitude.

When filling in the few blanks that he could, Kapri's heart started to break for the boy who had just called her a silly thot box. They were like night and day. That part was painfully apparent, just going over the top part of the paperwork. Growing up, Kapri's life was charmed. Her mother, even though a single parent, made sure of that. Even when she was pulling stunts and getting in trouble, her mother never once gave up on her. She stood by her daughter's side, showing not only love but also support. However, from what Kapri was writing on Nolan's student questionnaire, he didn't have any of that in his life.

At some point, Nolan excused himself to go to the bathroom. Kapri seized the opportunity to quickly scan over Nolan's student file records the group home counselor had left on the desk. She discovered not only was he a grade behind, but he was also basically homeless. Well, not really homeless. He was residing in a group home now, but that much she knew. The file explained that Nolan been residing in a vacant house that a group of boys was selling drugs out of. Apparently, after receiving an anonymous tip claiming a dead body was in the basement, and underage girls were being held against their will, the house was put on the fast track to be raided without investigation. When it was all said and done, there was no dead body or girls inside. But it wasn't a total loss and waste of police manpower. Shockingly to the public, it was uncovered that a grown man was the puppet master behind all of the illegal narcotics being peddled from the premise. He would be the sole one to be charged with the majority of the drugs in the highly publicized case.

Most of the teens were released to a responsible adult or guardian. Neither of Nolan White's parents' names was listed by him. Initially, he lied, claiming that they were both deceased. Although as much as the out-for-self youth may have wanted that fact to be true, it wasn't. The courts used records from the Welfare Office to track down his mother. After a few attempts were made, she opted not to go down to the police station and assume responsibility for her son. Therefore, Nolan was placed in the uncaring child abandonment system until he reached at least the age of eighteen.

This is a damn shame. Her unfit ass probably didn't want to answer questions about why she would have her underage child out in the streets like that. I swear my mother would never do any shit like this. Kapri's heart softened even more about his plight.

When Nolan returned to the area that they were working in, she wasted no time cutting straight to the chase. "So, dang, you live in a group home for some time now, huh?"

Nolan didn't hesitate or hold her up. There was no need to. He saw her clutching the beige-colored file in her hands with his name clearly written across it. It was easy to see that meant she already knew the answer to her question. But since she was cute, he played the game.

"Yeah, near the North End over off John R. You want me to say the address too?"

"Huh, what?" Kapri smiled while innocently sitting on the edge of her seat. She showed no signs of shame. She wanted Nolan to tell his business and speak his truth. She wanted to grill him more about his parents but would take what she could.

"What you mean 'what?' It don't say all that in there, with your good detective ass?" He pointed with a condescending smirk on his face. Nolan was used to girls trying to find out this or that about him. Yet, here this female was holding his life story in her hands and still asking questions like she was the police trying to verify an alibi or catch a guy up in a blatant lie.

"Boy, whatever. Damn, so all of y'all live there in the same house?" She motioned over toward the other side of the room, where the others were deep off in their own conversations.

"Me and the two fat ones do. The other dudes stay somewhere else. I don't know where, but not with us. Why? What's with all the questions you got for me?" He looked at her as if she were indeed the police on a quest.

"So what about your parents? I mean, what did you do wrong to get in the group home besides selling drugs at that house? And why didn't they come to get you?" Kapri rattled off question after question as she set the file down on the desk, anticipating his reply.

Once more, Nolan didn't hesitate in answering. He had nothing to hide. But by now, his tone became more serious as he was no longer smiling. "What about them? Shit, I was born. That's what I did wrong. Ya feel me?"

"Boy, are you serious right now or playing around?"

"Naw, straight up, I've always just been in the damn way. So, yeah, fuck my parents and fuck you if you keep grilling a nigga." Nolan didn't much like questions or those who asked them. He had every intention of trying to play nice, but this stranger was working his nerves overstepping herself.

"What? Damn. Okay, then." Kapri was confused at his outburst. She was far from being naïve, but this boy was like no other that she'd ever met. He seemed so sad, so broken. She had to fight back her potential tears.

"I mean, shit, girl, what's with all the questions?" He slid the registration paper over toward him. Picking the file up, he scanned over the top sheet, then the next. "Damn, brown eyes, I don't see all of that bullshit on here. Or is you just freestyle being nosy as a motherfucker?"

Blushing at the fact he'd noticed her eyes and spoke on it, Kapri still didn't deny that she was overly inquisitive. Nevertheless, the brazen teenager didn't stop there with her mini interrogation of his life. Finally, Nolan stopped her short. Cutting to the chase, he asked for her number and if she had a boyfriend. Kapri wasn't expecting that part, but wanting to hear more of this mysterious guy's story, she didn't think twice. She wrote it down, handing the small piece of paper to him. For the rest of the time he was there, the two of them stuck to the school-requested inquiries. When it was time to go, Nolan revealed he didn't have a cell phone of his own, but would find a way to call. Referring to her as brown eyes again, he promised to get at her later that evening after dinner. Kapri told him she'd be waiting, and she did just that.

Chapter Nineteen

Nolan had been using the community phone at the group home to stay in touch with Fiona. Since he'd left from the West Side, he'd been speaking to her on and off. She was far from his type of female, but he initially was using her to keep tabs on the three boys' he'd attacked with the bat. He'd heard that woman who had been banging his father was pressing charges against him for the assault on her son. That was until Fiona showed she was loyal to Nolan and had his back. She stepped up and let it be known to the investigating detectives that Nolan White had been jumped on first by all three of the guys, including the woman's ringleader son. She made it known he was only defending himself. Fiona made no mention that Nolan had been out of harm's way and returned with the bat seeking justice. Purposely, she omitted those facts. In the long run, the mother looking for justice felt it was best just to leave the entire matter alone before her son faced assault charges as well.

Nolan knew that part of his life was over. It was nothing but a bad memory of a summer gone wrong. He'd never go in that neighborhood again. That was, unless he was strapped and ready to take a human life. But Fiona, she was still all right with him for doing what she had done. She stood up and held him, despite being shunned by all of her friends. No matter how pesky she was, he knew she fucked with him the long way.

Over eleven guys living in the North East Side group home shared one phone line. There was always a long list, and that list was always full. Finally, it was Nolan's turn to use the phone. His first call was to Fiona. He'd gotten several messages from the office that she'd left, claiming she was his sister. She expressed she had some urgent family business to tell him. Nolan knew it was a lie just to get him to call her back. It wasn't that he was avoiding her. He just had to figure out how he was going to get up on some more cash. And sitting up on the phone kicking it with some random female wasn't going to help the cause. He'd make this call a quick one seeing as he was on a time limit.

"Yeah, Fiona, what up, doe, girl? What it do?" He addressed her as if she were one of the fellas, nothing more, nothing less. And to him, she was just that, no matter how hard she tried to be his girl.

"Dang, boy, where you been hiding at? I been calling and calling."

"Yeah, I know, I heard. But I been around here and there."

"Oh, for real?" Fiona replied with a bit of sass in her tone.

"Yeah, but so what's the big emergency with the family, since you said I was your brother and all that?" He cut it short. With Kapri on his mind, Nolan had no time for small talk with a girl he wasn't trying to get the pussy from.

Fiona giggled. "I know, right. Shiiid, I had to say something. The people who be answering the phone where you at be rude as fuck. So you know—"

"Look, Fiona, what's the deal? What's good?"

"Dang, Nolan, I mean, since you left from off East Kirby, you been MIA. What's going on with that group home? You tight over there or what? I started to catch a ride over that way, but I couldn't get in touch with you."

"You already know them ho-ass police took a nigga's cell phone too, so contact with anybody been limited. But, yeah, I'm good, just trying to put a few things together and whatnot. My homeboy in here, Trey, got some business on the floor outta town, so we working on that." Nolan looked up at the wall clock. The thirty-minute time he was allotted was ticking. He had to end this conversation quickly if he wanted to call Kapri as promised. He wanted to keep his word because that girl and her smart-assed mouth had been on his mind all day.

"Trey? I know a guy on the East Side named Trey. He like double dark and got dreads. He always stays strapped and got a missing front tooth." Fiona always wanted to put on like she knew everything and everybody, when, in fact, the only thing she knew on Nolan's side of town was raggedy-ass Eastland Mall.

"Naw, this ain't that guy. This dude lighter than me. They call him Bone Capone out in the streets. But anyhow, I'll get back. I gotta go handle some shit." Not giving Fiona a chance to respond, Nolan abruptly hung up the phone. Digging in his pocket, he pulled out the paper Kapri had written her info on. After dialing six numbers, on the seventh, he nervously took a deep breath. After a few rings, she finally answered.

"Hello, Kapri?"

"Speaking. Who is this, please?" She was using her "white voice," acting as if she didn't know it was Nolan, when, in fact, she'd been sitting on the edge of her bed waiting for his call.

Never at a loss for words, Nolan found himself tongue-tied. Even though Kapri had a smart mouth like one of the many hoodrats he'd kicked it with, it wasn't hard to tell she was much different. He knew whatever he was used to, this wasn't that. "Hey, girl, this is Nolan. Remember me, the one with the Air Nots?" He clowned his own self in an attempt to break the ice.

Awkwardly, Kapri laughed, a little embarrassed at what she'd said earlier. Despite being called out of her name, talking down on someone for being less fortunate was out of character. Once again, she humbled herself and apologized. "Look, my bad. But moving away from that, what took you so long to call? You just got finished eating dinner this late?"

"Umm, naw, but—"

"But what? It's not I'm thirsty or nothing like that. But if you say you gonna do something, then keep your word or keep it moving," Kapri advised, laying down the law as if they'd known each other for years, not a few hours.

"Whoa, hold up," Nolan tried to interject but was shut down.

"Naw, see, I was waiting this time, but if it happens again, I won't."

Nolan wasn't used to being told what to do. After leaving the West Side underneath his father's rules, he became his own man. Even Tall Rob knew not to push him too far. But here, this female was barking at him like she was running shit. Strangely, he wasn't the least bit offended. Nolan found that shit sexy as hell and knew this girl was the one for him. Unlike Fiona, Kapri wasn't trying to impress him. It seemed more like she had deeper plans for him . . . plans that only two people with a mental connection could share. Amused, he assured her that in the next few days, he would have a new cell phone, and they could kick it whenever. For the next twenty-five minutes, Kapri and Nolan chopped it up about their childhoods and how different they were.

"So, yeah, Nolan, my mother ain't so bad. Matter of fact, she holds me down when shit gets real. And where she works at, whenever I need to multitask on some school project, I can go with her and get on the computers and print stuff out. I mean, we have the internet at home, but at her job, the network is way faster. Plus, I used their free postage to mail out all of my college applications."

"Damn, girl, do you ever come up for air?" he playfully teased.

"Yeah, crazy. But you asked about me and my life and told me to make it quick, so, yeah, that's what a sista trying to do."

Fascinated with Kapri and her spunk, he conceded. "Okay, you right, my bad. Go ahead."

"Okay, so, damn, where was I?" She never missed a beat taking off right where she'd left off. "Oh yeah, and my father, he locked up. He killed somebody and been in prison since I was little."

"Damn, straight up?" Nolan was intrigued that as perfect as Kapri's life appeared, it was flawed just like his. Well, maybe not as bad, but there still were apparently a few hiccups.

"Yeah, I haven't seen him in years. My mother don't play that 'stand by your man' bullshit. And I can only visit my grandmother on his side every once in a while, on special occasions."

"Special occasions?"

"Yeah, special occasions. See, my granny a witch, and so am I." Kapri loved making that last statement to others for effect. That was her wow factor of any conversation. And, of course, Nolan's reaction was like anyone else's.

"What the fuck?" Nolan blurted out loud, causing the guys watching television in the dayroom to look in his direction. "You a *what?* Did your ass say you a damn witch? What the fuck is you talking about?"

"Yeah, my people from New Orleans. They into spells, chicken claws, voodoo, and shit. I'm an only child by my daddy, and I got the gift too."

"You bullshitting, right?" He hoped she was, but even though they'd just met, he knew she wasn't.

"Naw, Nolan, I'ma show you one day when we have more time. But forget about me right now. It's your turn to tell me all your business."

Nolan was dumbfounded. Since he'd first been kicking it with females at the age of ten, he'd never ever had one tell him no shit like Kapri just had. And even though they'd just met, he believed she meant every word she was saying. So, either she was, indeed, an ordained witch with some dirty down South powers, or it could be that she was just bat-shit crazy like his mother was. But however it went, Nolan decided that Kapri James was some kind of special, and he was feeling her vibe.

"Well, my story ain't as good as yours. I mean, you already saw my file at school. I have twin brothers by my mother and ain't no telling what my old dude got going on with his ho ass. My mother ain't shit. My father ain't shit. And right about now, I ain't got shit."

"Damn," was all Kapri could say.

"Naw, brown eyes, it's all good. Give a guy a few weeks. I'm about to come up and get back on my feet," Nolan proudly announced, hoping that Kapri would recognize his potential and stick it out.

"Nolan, listen to me and hear me good. It doesn't matter where you at now. It matters where you going later. Stay focused. Life gonna get better. Something good is going to happen to you, and it's right around the corner. All you gotta do is keep moving and keep looking for it. Trust me, Nolan, it's there. Besides, my witch senses telling me that," she joked, hoping that at least he'd smile . . . which, by the tone in his voice, she knew he had.

Nolan felt a weight lift off of his shoulders. He needed to hear that motivational outlook on what could be if he just persevered. Disclosing everything about himself, he then told his new confidante about his home-girl from the West Side, Fiona, and what she'd done to help him out with the detectives. Although amused, he wasn't expecting Kapri's raw response.

"Boy, bye. I already don't like your 'homegirl' or her name. She seems low-key shady. She just trying to be your girl. I might have to put a spell on that bitch one day." Once again, they both laughed, but Kapri was serious. Nolan was the first guy she really was feeling. She was prepared to plot, scheme, and do whatever it took *not* to hear Fiona's name again. Nolan didn't know it at the time, but Kapri was on several medications for not only anger issues but also obsessive behavior disorders.

When his time on the community phone was up, Nolan informed Kapri just to hold tight, and they would speak come Monday. "All right, then, we gonna kick it again on Monday."

"So, what your ass doing all weekend you can't talk? I mean, like that's twenty hours times two. Do the math," she firmly asked, knowing she needed to take her meds.

"Look, girl, slow your roll. Just know soon we gonna be able to kick it whenever. I already told you I'm about to come up again. And when I do, a nigga ain't never gonna fall anymore."

"All right, then. Okay, Nolan, do you. I'm done with all the questions. And I'll just see you Monday at school," she affirmed, easing up on her attitude.

"Girl, what you mean? Fuck a school. I got other business on the floor way more important than no school and classroom. I gottas come up and quick, real, real quick."

Kapri knew Nolan was one of those bad boys her mother had warned her about, but it didn't matter. She liked his confidence and was sprung by his swag. But even with her nose wide open, she still spoke her mind. "Okay, big boss baller. I feel you. But beyond that point, why in the hell you have me filling out all those papers earlier if you knew good and damn well you were not going to attend class?"

Nolan laughed before explaining that sometimes in life, a man gotta play "they" game until he could play his own. And the moves he was about to make would put him in position to finally be the master of his own destiny and a real boss baller, for sure. Lustfully, Nolan ended the conversation telling "brown eyes" to stay sweet and to look for his call Monday, or no later than Tuesday evening.

Chapter Twenty

For the first time in well over a year, Nolan finally felt a small bit of happiness. He'd been through the fire just trying to maintain. He'd been kicked out of his mother's run-down house, displaced from his father's girlfriend's spot, and robbed of all the money he had in the world. Basically, he was abandoned to fend for himself. Tragically, his spirit was damaged. And now, a random female he'd met on the humble had given him a tiny bit of hope. This female just said that she believed in him, even though he didn't feel that way about himself. Kapri James and her inspirational words had given him a fresh outlook on life. No longer skeptical, Nolan now felt confident what he and his boy were planning would work out. Sticking his head into the day room, he signaled for Bone Capone to meet him near the back hallway. Anytime the two of them would discuss their get-rich-quick schemes, they were careful to be aware of any of the others in the group home that were known for ear hustling. Those people then ran they bitch asses to the program's director snitching for an extra Honey Bun at lunch.

For the last few days, Bone had been telling Nolan that they should make a move with his older cousin. Originally from Ohio, Bone Capone had been in the streets getting money since birth. Unlike Nolan's parents, Bone's people taught him the dope game early on. He was in diapers holding the bag whenever their house would get raided. Often, the police would not cross the line and risk child abuse accusations by strip searching an infant. After relocating to Detroit, Bone and his moms continued to get money the long way. Everything with their hustle was going good . . . until a crooked cop out of the Eleventh Precinct got cocky. The slimeball wanted more than his usual monthly payoff. After a brief struggle, Bone Capone came out victorious, breaking the officer's jaw. Ultimately, that brawl landed the underage violent youth locked up in baby jail, which was another name for the strictly supervised group home.

"What up, doe, Nolan? What it do?"

"Okay, dawg, so you know that move you wanna make outta town?"

"Yeah, and, so what about it? What's good?" Bone eagerly inquired with his arms folded. Only seventeen, he'd been heavy in the game. Official in the streets, he already had major artwork on both of his forearms. "Jesus" on the right and "Only time will tell" on the left. Not one to play games, the fair-complexioned teen had long outgrown his present living situation. Ready to get back to the money, he was more than ready to get back to securing the bag.

"I'm thinking that everything you was telling me the other day after chow sound like a plan. I mean, shit, real talk, we ain't getting no money sitting around this bitch with these lames." Nolan motioned to all of the other occupants of the group home glued to the small television. Housing with them for over a month, he knew that he was cut from a different cloth. Most of them were content eating the garbage-ass food they were being served and gathering around to watch a whack-size television like some dysfunctional family. Even if Nolan hadn't received that pep talk from Kapri, eventually, the group home would have become too much to bear. Sooner than later, he'd be out. Bone Capone and his people out of state would just speed up the process.

Arms still folded, Bone looked around to see if there were any extra pair of ears or eyes lurking. Making sure the two wouldn't be overheard, he explained that he would get in touch with his cousin. Low-key, he and Nolan would pack their bags and be ready to be out the next night before daybreak. When one supervisor staff shift was about to end, and the next to begin, a lot of movement and confusion always occurred throughout the building. With no alarms on the various exits, that was the time it would be more than easy for Nolan and Bone Capone to slip out undetected. It'd be a good hour later after breakfast that a head count would take place, and their absence would be discovered. By that time, God willing, they'd be across state lines.

They'd been plotting on this getaway scheme for a few weeks, and up until now, Nolan had been hesitant. Bone was far from crazy. He could tell something was up with his homeboy by the way he'd been acting since they'd left that school. Not holding Nolan up, Bone cut off into him.

"Dawg, that was that crazy-mouthed girl from that school on the phone, wasn't it? Get it a hundred. She got your ass gone, and you ain't even smelled the pussy yet," he clowned him, knowing that shit was the truth.

Nolan didn't try to deny it. He announced to Bone that Kapri was some kinda different female. And he knew that he had to get his weight up if he wanted to be with an upper-class chick like her. Bone laughed, telling Nolan at this point he ain't give a shit if God came to him in a dream and motivated him to get this money. As long as his love-sick ass would be packed and ready to roll, all was good.

After they left the hallway from their, so to speak, "business plan of action meeting," the duo was met with stares of contempt and hatred from a guy from Southwest Detroit. Since the overgrown guy nicknamed Albino Abe arrived at the usually laid-back group home, he'd been dry hating on everyone he thought was more polished than he was. The fact that he claimed to belong to a gang meant nothing. If he wanted to run off at the mouth, then he'd get dealt with. Sadly for him, he'd picked the wrong time to step to Nolan or Bone. They had nothing to lose, knowing they were hours away from breaking out, so Albino Abe caught more than just their hands. He got stumped out, with Nolan finishing it off, slamming his shoe down on the boy's jaw, causing blood to leak. Dispersing before getting reprimanded, Bone and Nolan victoriously went to their rooms, daring any of the other guys to rat them out. Regretting that he'd let his mouth get his ass handed to him, Albino Abe soon got up from the fetal position he was left in, vowing revenge one day in the future . . . sooner or later.

Chapter Twenty-one

Welcome to Ohio . . .

"Damn, that was quick. This shit didn't take no time," Nolan remarked, looking out the window of the Ford Windstar driven by Bone's older cousin. The sun had just fought to come up, but couldn't shine. Clouds invaded the sky. It was easy to see the majority of the day would be dreary, but the weather didn't matter. Without a penny to his name, Nolan was determined to make this thing work out. It had to. After all, he had nothing to go back home to, so he was going to go all in full throttle. The hustle was going to be hard, and the grind would, without doubt, equal that. Nolan would be focused on making money, just as he did before the den of sin got raided. Knowing nothing but poverty since birth, the now runaway youth had never been out of Michigan. Embracing his future, he was hyped, enjoying the visual adventure of highway travel.

"Yeah, we done crossed over, but we still got a minute to go to get to Sandusky. At least another hour after we hit downtown Toledo." Bone Capone sat back in the passenger seat, drinking a hot chocolate from Coney Island. Although he'd not been back to his hometown for years, the born moneymaker was eager to see his old stomping grounds.

Both teens were elated to be free of the restrictions of the group home. Being that the State could only legally hold Nolan White until the age of eighteen, he would max out of the system in a few months on his birthday. Trey Walton's hold, aka Bone Capone, would be a little longer, but their circumstances were much different. Bone had a violent criminal case that required more incarceration, whereas Nolan was labeled a ward of the State due to abandonment. The authorities locating Bone would be much more significant than Nolan White, but with a short-staffed Youth Apprehension Team, neither of the two had to worry. They were now free to get money, no-holds-barred.

Passing through Perrysburg, Jayce turned the radio down. Half a mile later, he shook his head, pulling the van on the side of the freeway. Making sure the traffic flow was safe, the dreadlocked driver confidently got out of the vehicle. His cousin and Nolan followed him. The last few miles, Bone's cousin had felt that the older model Ford Windstar was driving rough. After turning down the ear-deafening music, Jayce knew he was correct. At the rear of the van, he got down on one knee. Kneeling, he looked underneath. He wasn't a mechanic, but it was easy to see that the muffler itself was partially loose, and there was a crack in the main connector pipe. Thinking quickly, Jayce told his passengers that he was going to attempt to make it to the next exit that had a gas station and nigga rig the muffler. Before they could get back in the van and be on their way, seemingly out of nowhere, an Ohio State Trooper appeared. He pulled over behind them with his lights flashing.

"Oh, hell naw," Bone mumbled underneath his breath, speculating if he should just break out and run. But since Nolan, his cousin, and he were in the middle of the highway, where was he going to go? Bone was forced to put on his police game face and wait for the lone officer to exit his vehicle.

"What these worrisome sons of bitches want?" Jayce chimed in speaking while barely moving his lips. He'd made the trip to Detroit and back at least twice a month and knew how the state boys operated.

Unlike the others, Nolan remained silent. Even in the worst-case scenario, the only thing that could happen to him was getting placed back in a highly supervised juvenile facility instead of the group home he'd just fled. Either way it went, Nolan was used to disappointment and would roll with the punches.

"What seems to be the problem with you guys?" the burly officer asked, cautiously approaching the trio. "Why you parked over on the side of the road? Y'all boys ain't out here urinating, are you? 'Cause if so, that kinda thing is a violation, even on the open highway."

Before Nolan or Bone got a chance to respond to the cop's wild assumption, Jayce spoke up. "Hello, Officer. No, sir, we are having some car trouble. I think my muffler is loose." He pointed toward the lower rear of the van. "I got on my hands and knees, and it looks like it." Jayce was quick to show the redneck his dirty hands. He knew how to play the game. He knew that the police, especially prejudiced white ones, loved the thought of a black man being down on their hands and knees needing help. So, Jayce played the role all the way. "I was gonna try to make it to the next exit and see if the service station had a hanger. That's the only thing I could think of, sir." Jayce gave the officer a dumbfounded look. Nolan and Bone still had yet to say a word.

With his hand on his gun, he walked a little closer to the van. The officer could easily see that the young man was telling the truth. "Yeah, I do see it hanging down some." While standing there, he glanced over at the other two boys. "And where all y'all coming from and headed?"

Jayce knew they hadn't broken any laws . . . well, at least not yet. And he knew that they didn't have to answer questions, but knew if he didn't continue to play along, things could go real bad, real quick. He didn't want or need any mishaps.

"Sir, I was just coming back from picking up my younger cousins. We were all hoping to have jobs at Cedar Point Amusement Park this summer. And a job fair on-site hiring orientation is taking place later on today," Jayce humbly replied, acting as if he were discouraged. "But now, I just hope we can make it. Would it be too much to ask if maybe you had a hanger or could help us in any way?"

The state trooper was used to young black guys traveling back and forth from Detroit to Ohio transporting drugs. So, automatically, his radar had been up, but now he'd lighten up on his suspicions. Over the years, he'd heard plenty of stories, but none as detailed as this job fair thing. And lastly, no thugs out doing wrong would practically beg for his assistance. Besides, by the way Nolan and Bone were dressed, he could easily tell they weren't drug dealers. Their clothes were far from expensive, and they both looked him in his eyes.

"Look, I tell you boys what. I'ma keep my lights on. Y'all stay close behind me, and I'll make sure y'all get up the road some to the service station."

"Thank you so much, sir. I really appreciate it. We all do, don't we?" Jayce nudged Nolan and Bone, who nodded in agreement.

"All right, y'all stay close behind me," he firmly ordered with a smile.

Seconds later, we were back in the van getting a personal escort. It was then that I looked down at my shoes and noticed small blood drops that must've come from me kicking Albino Abe. *Damn, I'm glad that state boy ain't noticed this shit and started asking questions.*

As they drove, Jayce busted out laughing at his cousin and his homeboy. "So, y'all ready to hit up this job fair? But I gotta drop this half pound of trees off before we do." He casually reached under his seat, pulling out a paper bag. He tossed it onto his cousin's lap to open. When Bone pulled out several bags of weed, we were both fucked up. I immediately looked out the front window at the cop signaling for us to go up the exit ramp where there was a service station. Jayce did just that, and the state trooper kept it moving down the highway, probably to attempt to catch some lawbreakers. It was right then and there that I knew that the time I was going to spend in Ohio was going to be epic.

Chapter Twenty-two

From April until late August of that year, things changed drastically for both Nolan and Kapri. The juvenile system runaway kept his word about getting a cell phone. As soon as he got his hands on some money and time, he called her. Kapri was done playing hard to get and was overjoyed to hear from the new "bad boy." Although not living in the same state, the odd couple still seemed to become close. In fact, the pair spoke almost every morning and twice at night. The new interstate best friends would trade stories about any and everything, even other people they may have been fond of. With the distance between them, it was a joint decision that until further notice, they would remain just cool.

Kapri

Kapri and her mother soon found out the verdict from the courts. Although she could not return to the Catholic schools in her area, after the battle royal the teen was involved in at Detroit Central, permanent expulsion was her fate with DPS as well . . . which was fine with both of the James women. Yet, one good thing did come out of Kapri's spitfire attitude and that lifelong scar on her angelic face. Another judge found the financially struggling school system liable in Kapri's attack. Mrs. James was awarded an enormous settlement that she accepted with a smile. Once again, she was the victor when wronged.

With cash never an issue, Mrs. James not only kept her job, but she was also promoted to supervisor over the entire office. And since her daughter had lost any chance of scholarship money and their windfall had placed them in a much higher tax bracket, some of the money was paid up front for Kapri's coming freshman year. Being homeschooled on a College Acceleration Program for the gifted, after a few series of tests passed with flying colors, her future was bright. An almost 17-year-old Kapri was enrolled in Michigan State. With nothing to keep her in the city, Kapri was happily shipped off to Lansing with her mother's blessings. Attending the summer semester would give her a chance to get familiar with the huge, prestigious campus before the crowds of the fall term students converged.

Nightly, Kapri would lie across her bed in the two-person dorm room talking to Nolan. Since enrollment was low at that time, the entire room was hers. With no friends to speak of except for her cousin Diane, life on campus was pretty much boring. In the midst of only homework to keep her company, Kapri's out-of-state bad boy was the only link to an exciting life. She lived vicariously through him and his illegal antics. Not really knowing what love or commitment was, the young girl was amused when he spoke of two females he had met that both worked at the same place.

"Are you for real? Naw, you must be joking. How can they both work in the same area of the park and not see your crazy ass creeping?" Kapri laughed at the thought of Nolan hiding behind bushes, checking to see if the coast was clear.

"Come on now, girl. How long we been talking? You should know by now I'm slick with mines all the way around." He stuck his chest out with pride.

"All right, slick black man. Don't mess around and get caught up." She still had that bossy demeanor and a short fuse that Nolan had come to love.

"Never that, so get outta ya feelings. Besides, you know I'm just wasting time with these birds until you ready to give it up to a real one."

Kapri shook her head, shrugging her shoulders. She was still a virgin and had no intention of giving up the pussy to just anybody, Nolan included. "Okay, well, then, you best keep giving them dumb hoes the dick."

"Oh yeah? It's like that? So, I guess a brother gotsta keep dreaming about getting in them panties." Nolan continued to tease, low-key wishing he could get out of the friend zone.

"Yeah, silly. It's just like that. But on another note, I've been forgetting to ask you if you have spoken to anyone in your family yet?"

A few brief moments of eerie silence came on the line before Nolan angrily replied. The response was the same as it had been since the two of them first met. "Naw, girl. You know none of my so-called people give a fuck about me. And even the ones that used to pretend they cared is fake as fuck."

Kapri regretted asking, fully knowing it was a sore point of conversation with her friend. Luckily, an interruption occurred to their now awkward conversation. "Dang, boy, don't bite my head off. But, look, I'ma call you back later. Someone's at my door. Probably my study group leader that's been getting on my damn nerves. He be too extra."

"*He?*" Nolan quickly questioned with a slight bit of jealousy.

"Yeah, he. But don't worry, he old as hell and all about them books," Kapri whispered, not wanting the person on the other side of the door to hear what she was saying. Especially if it was the guy she was referring to.

"Yeah, all right, brown eyes, cool. No problem. You know I'm always around for you. Hit me back later when you free."

Although Kapri thought both females he was dealing with to be plain stupid or blind not to see through Nolan and his bullshit, she felt special that he trusted her enough to let her into his otherwise shielded life. She listened to everything he had to say, except when it came to Fiona. For some strange reason, Nolan was still in touch with that hoodrat. Kapri didn't understand it, but in the back of her mind, one day, she'd put an end to that, once and for all. Down the line, whenever she would decide to get serious with Nolan, any contact with random hoes would come to a halt—even if she had to do some family-inherited black-magic spells to get her way. But for the time being, getting good grades was her main goal. Kapri was going to stay in the books and leave the streets to Nolan.

Nolan

Elated with his current circumstances, Nolan stayed upbeat and positive. Blessed with a pocket filled with money and wearing new 'fits every day, what more could a young thug ask for? The days of wearing run-over shoes and hand-me-downs were no more. Even though he had to keep a gun tucked in his waistband for protection, the past few months since arriving in Ohio had been nothing short of spectacular. Having come from absolutely nothing but poverty, Nolan was now making more money out in the streets of Sandusky than he ever did back in the D. With no one looking over his shoulder or dry checking half his money as Tall Rob did, the teen was living the American Dream. Just as Bone Capone had promised, they had a secure roof over their heads and a bag waiting on them. This was all Nolan needed . . . a chance to come up.

It took no time for the infamous pair to get down to business. Moving as smoothly as they did, it was like taking candy from a baby. Posted up, eager to get paid, the drug addicts in the neighborhood were soon singing their praises. However, Nolan and Bone Capone had an equal amount of hate coming in their general direction. Not only from the police but also from a rival crew of imported hometown locals as well. Nolan couldn't say that he blamed them for being heated. After all, if any guys from the West Side of Detroit came over to the East trying to set up shop on his block, there'd be hell to pay. Any other dudes may have been intimidated. But not Bone Capone and certainly not Nolan. They were on a mission to get money, and as far as they were concerned, only God could come down on the block and stop their hustle. Fuck the police! Fuck the local pussy-ass niggas! And fuck anyone else that had intentions other than theirs.

Unlike the emotional bond Nolan shared with Kapri, those sentiments were far from the case where Fiona was concerned. Still thankful that she'd had his back against her childhood people, that game had played itself out. The West Side female predator had shot her load and ran that guilt trip into the ground.

Not really caring if she lived or died, the scheming teen still found a use for her. Since Fiona was hell-bent on being his friend and showing her loyalty, Nolan put her on a mission. Even though he was content living out of town and making money, his mind was still on his mother and two brothers. As much as he attempted to get that dysfunctional portion of his life in the back of his thought processes, it kept creeping up to the surface.

It was easy for him to blame his mother for her ratchet, seemingly coldhearted actions, but the twins were fault-less in it all. And now that he had made a little cash, his conscience wouldn't allow him just to let them twist in the wind. Nolan knew he had no intention of going back home to Detroit anytime soon, so instead of texting Fiona as he usually did, he opted to call her. In no more than one ring, the clingy female answered.

"Yeah, hello, hey now, Nolan," her tone was always annoying. And more than that, Nolan despised how she said his name, so long and drawn out. Just hearing Fiona's voice made him want to hang up and forget his plan. Taking a deep breath, he thought about his brothers' certain poverty circumstances, thanks to their mother, and sucked it up.

"Hey, what up, doe, girl? I need you to shoot a move for me." He cut straight to the chase, not giving her an opportunity to start whining or lying about this, that, or the third. "I need you to call my boy O. P. and link with him."

Fiona was more than eager to do whatever her long-distance crush asked of her. After hearing about Nolan's homeboy for some time in passing, now she would be able to put a face to the name. Quickly, she responded before Nolan changed his mind. "Of course, I will. No problem. What you need to do or go?" She started search-ing her closet for something to wear in hopes that O. P. would go back and tell his friend how good she was looking. Fiona's delusional thoughts even imagined that O. P. would try to push up on her, resulting in Nolan getting jealous. Then finally, he'd come clean and confess his love for her. Nolan's deep voice snapped her back to reality.

"Look, in a few days, O. P. gonna hit you up. I'ma need you to go over on the East Side wherever he tell you to be."

"Okay, and?" Fiona replied, somewhat sad the designated meeting was not about to immediately take place.

"And you and him gonna handle some business with my old girl," Nolan surprisingly revealed.

"Old girl, as in your mother, mother?" And just like that, Fiona was back on cloud nine. *Damn, hell, fuck, yeah! He wants me to meet his mother. I knew he been low-key feeling a bitch.*

Nolan was getting annoyed with Fiona's voice and wanted to end their conversation much sooner than later. "Yeah, my mother. Damn, is you slow? Look, O. P. gonna call you in a few days, so just be ready to roll out. He'll tell you what's good when y'all link." Before she could get out another whinny word, he hung up.

Chapter Twenty-three

It was just another typical day on the block in the inner city of Sandusky. The sun was beaming down, and it was extremely humid. Even the breeze that would occasionally blow in by way of Lake Erie was on pause. That sweltering summer heat didn't stop or slow down the hustle, though. If you smoked crack, shot dope, took pills, or chose to drink a fifth of cheap rock gut gin every single day . . . Whatever your addictive poison of choice was, the weather was never a factor. Just like the mailman, come rain, snow, sleet, or hell, getting high was a mission that could not be stopped. Even more committed than the postal carriers of the world, the crackheads, dope fiends, pill poppers, and drunks never took days off. Not Sunday, holidays, or nights. Truth be told, those days, folks even went harder.

Doing what they do, Nolan was holding down a spot on Vine Street, shaking the bag. Bone Capone was posted up over on West Osborne, doing the same. They were making money hand over fist. Although they were not located far from each other, there was no competition. As far as they were concerned, there was more than enough money and drug addicts to go around. Unfortunately for one set of neighborhood dealers, they failed to share their sentiments. Jayce had warned them about the infamous crew that had long since migrated from Toledo, but those words were just that to Nolan and Bones . . . words.

They were there to make money, not friends. And any distraction to that would be eliminated.

"Yeah, guy, what up, doe?"

"What up, doe, with you, my nigga?" Nolan placed his cell on speaker as he emptied the contents of a sandwich bag filled with weed. He was glad Bone Capone had called so they could touch base on the ticket. Having banged all day, Nolan knew he was about at point zero and would need to re-up soon. They had sometimes been going six days straight, at least fourteen hours a day since arriving. The struggle was real, but the come-up was official.

"It's been kinda slow my way, but you already know me. I'ma make this shit do what the fuck it do." Bone Capone's past credibility to get money in even the worst situations was never in question. The only one that could stop his shine or grind was God.

"So, listen, Bone. Why don't we call it for today and hit up the park or something? I like money just as much as the next man—shit, probably more. But real talk, we been going hard like a motherfucker since we touched down." Nolan finished rolling up and lit the blunt. After hitting it strong a few times, he went on. "Day after day, I been watching all these people flood this city headed over the way. A nigga like me wanna see that shit firsthand again. That shit be off the chain."

Bone Capone couldn't contain his laughter. "Dawg, again? You act like you ain't never been to Cedar Point coming up. That shit be too hot during the day. And besides, you can see them dusty-ass bitches any day."

"Man, are you serious? Up until I was like twelve, I ain't even leave off the block unless I was over my granny's crib. My old girl or pops, whenever he showed his face, wasn't on no tip like trips and shit. Matter of fact, when my mother was on, we was lucky even to eat that week. And as for them females, hoes ain't never a factor in my moves."

It was nearing three in the afternoon. The intense morning rush was well over, and it was the end of the month. And after all that Nolan had revealed, it didn't take much convincing for Bone Capone to agree to call it for the day. They called Jayce informing him of their plans so he would know both spots would be temporarily dark until the next day. Bone Capone's older cousin knew the fellas had been putting in long hours and deserved a break and some downtime. Truth be told, he'd expected them to fall off way before now and head back to Detroit. But his family and Nolan had proven to be solid soldiers in the game.

After changing into some of the new 'fits they'd gotten from the mall, Nolan hit up his boy telling him that he was ready to roll out and hopefully get with some hoes. Meeting halfway, the two Motor City natives hopped in a cab, destination Cedar Point Amusement Park. Unfortunately for Nolan, that spur-of-the-moment excursion away from the grind gave him a flashback to the first time he and Bone Capone hung out there. That afternoon would soon become the gateway to two occasional lifelong headaches. In between the fun and excitement of the bright lights, roller coasters, and food, it was there that he linked up with not one, but two females that worked at the park. One chick he and his homeboy nicknamed Popcorn, since that was what she sold at one of the various concession stands. She was born and raised in Sandusky and had another job as well. The other girl they jokingly referred to as Snoopy because she worked in the Snoopy and Peanuts area of the park. This was a summer job for her. She stayed with her aunt, who also worked at the park. Cedar Point was so gigantic the girls had not met each other and were none the wiser of Nolan's playboy antics.

Never one to be cheap, he hung out with Popcorn some days and Snoopy on others. When he ate good, they each ate good. When he would go splurge at the mall, he'd make sure he would look out for them too. Used to having nothing, he found it was hard to see the next person struggle, especially a female he was dealing with, regardless of whether he truly loved them. Of course, his heart was with Kapri, but she was the next state over in school, still playing hard to get. So for fun, he knocked Popcorn and Snoopy off to pass the time.

A few miles away from the long bridge gateway to the amusement park, Bone Capone instructed the driver to pull over. Doing as he was told, the middle-aged bearded man turned into the crowded lot of a liquor store. Once he parked, Bone Capone gave him a few dollars to stay put until they returned. He and Nolan then got out of the rear seat heading inside of the store. The game plan was to purchase a few shot bottles of Paul Masson and Henny to take on their adventure. The already-weed high pair didn't want to get drunk, but to just have a nice little buzz while getting on the rides, having fun, and talking shit to whoever they were near. The store was packed with customers probably with the same idea knowing the prices for booze inside of Cedar Point was sky-high. And also, in Nolan and Bone's case, they were underage and knew they'd get carded at the various concession stands. But at the local stores, the owners lived by the motto of "money talked, and bullshit walked." So, since they had cash on hand, and plenty of it, they were good to go.

With a few bags of chips and cookies and a bottle of cold water to satisfy their current munchy status, Nolan paid the clerk for those items along with the shots. In a good mood, ready to turn up, Nolan and his homeboy strolled to the exit talking about the females the self-proclaimed player had on his line, hoping he didn't run into either one later. Not paying attention, Nolan accidentally shoulder bumped a guy in passing. He and Bone were exiting the store while the flamboyantly dressed guy and his two friends were coming in.

"Shit, damn, my bad, dude. I ain't see you," Nolan swiftly remarked, not even bothering to make eye contact.

"Yo, pretty boy, watch where the fuck you going!"

"Nigga, say what?" Nolan paused. His normally mild-mannered expression changed. The teen was not immediately looking for any trouble, but definitely was not willing to avoid it either.

"You fucking heard me. Y'all fools come from Detroit think y'all running shit around this bitch. But, naw, that ain't the case."

It was then that Bone Capone, like Nolan, was ready to put in work. From the East Side of their hometown, they were both trained to go. "Whoa, pussy-ass nigga, who the fuck you think you talking to? You must wanna end your day somewhere at Urgent Care."

Nolan irately double downed on his manz statements of impending violence toward not only the dude he'd bumped but also his two sidekicks as well. "Yeah, and if you keep running off at the mouth talking that Detroit bullshit, you gonna catch more than these hands, you and these funny-style fuck boys you rolling with."

"You hold the fuck up." Conrad was prepared to show he was just as hard as the two young hustlers he'd easily recognized as the dudes that had come to town and set up shop in what was once their sole territory. The fact that the Old English D baseball cap-wearing Nolan and the arm-tatted warrior Bone Capone were standing tall at this moment meant nothing to the Toledo native. As far as Conrad was concerned, his little cousin, his homeboy, and he were in Sandusky from jump selling product in that area. So, even if theirs was weak, so damn what? They had set down stakes first. "You young niggas think this shit a game. We play for keeps out this way. It's do or die."

Nolan smirked. He found Conrad's statements of who did what and when humorous, as did his boy. "Oh shit, now I get it. You that bitch-made sissy all the custos been talking about. They said you be out here crying like a baby that y'all ain't making no money. Yo, Bone, these them Toledo faggots. Yeah, boy, the streets been talking."

"Oh, shit," Bone Capone joined in on the joke as the other people in the store looked on, wondering what was going to happen next. "So, this that whack-ass, old, dried-up lame running off at the mouth like I won't smack the dog shit outta him."

"What you say about my family?" one of Conrad's homeboys finally found the courage to speak up.

"Word is you was somebody's bitch behind them bars. Yeah, that's you. You piss sitting the fuck down," Nolan interjected, ignoring the shorter of the three men who was trying to get loud.

Threatening to call the police, the store owner urged the five irate black men to leave his business and move off of his premises. Not wanting to spend the night in the Erie County Jail, each group did as was asked, but not before vowing certain bloodshed the next time their paths would cross. Nolan and Conrad stood toe-to-toe, ready to do battle despite the promise of seeing the cops.

"Yeah, nigga. The next time I see your ass, you better be ready." Conrad flexed with his crew behind him, acting as if they were ready to do something.

"What up, doe?" Nolan tossed the bag with the chips and small bottles of liquor into the open rear window of their still-awaiting cab. With murder on his mind, he turned his baseball cap to the back. Not caring if the guy was strapped or not, he was on the verge of socking Conrad dead in the mouth to ensure things popped off. "Why wait, gay boy? I'm ready now. So, what's good?"

"Yeah, what's good with all you lames? Me and my manz will air this parking lot out right damn now." Bone Capone didn't have his pistol nor did Nolan. Yet, he was good at reading people and could easily tell ole boy with all the mouth and his crew weren't holding either. But just the same, he knew he could back them down with words. With absolute certainty, he saw pure *coward* written across all three of their supposedly tough asses, especially the one with an eye patch. He appeared to be the biggest pussy of them all.

"Stop fronting like y'all about that life and shit," Conrad continued to try his luck, even though he was shaken.

Before the apparent leader of the pack could get any more words out, Nolan's fist clenched and connected with his jaw. The force of the blow knocked Conrad to the pavement. Had it been the other way around, Bone would have been right in the mix—guns, knives, throwing hands, whatever. But that was far from the case with Conrad's people. It was as if they were frozen as Nolan ran up their homeboy's dental bill even more.

And with that brutal exchange of bloody blows leaving Conrad leaking from the mouth, the store owned stepped out into the parking lot. Phone in hand, he once again demanded peace . . . or else. Thankfully, without further incident, the man got his wish as the two opposing crews parted ways. Conrad and his boys headed back to the hood to not only tend to his wounded mouth and bruised ego but also to concoct a concrete plan to regain their territory, while Nolan and Bone Capone calmly went on their way to the amusement park to have a good time as planned. Nolan used the bottle of water he'd purchased to rinse Conrad's blood off his knuckles once they arrived at the ticket entrance. He then made sure to tip the cabdriver an extra twenty for holding them down back at the liquor store when he could have just as easily pulled off, wanting to avoid being caught in between possible gunfire.

Chapter Twenty-four

With determination to live like young kingpins, Nolan White and Bone Capone were making things shake in a major way in the small Sandusky town. With cocky attitudes and bigger-than-life personalities to back it up, the revenue was pouring in. Doing what they do, they had caused several drug houses in the vicinity to shut down entirely because they couldn't keep up. There was no competition. The product Jayce was supplying them with was way more potent than anything around the way that the guys living in Toledo were pushing. It soon became a seemingly well thought out domino effect in the general area. Although the nine-five hardworking neighbors were elated to see some of the dangerous drug houses close their doors, the dealers weren't as happy.

After seeing several of their comrades fall to the wayside, Carlos and Conrad, who were cousins, and One-Eyed Tre decided they were not going to be forced into an early drug dealer retirement as well. Especially after the high-energy exchange of violent threats made against each other a few weeks back, and Conrad getting his jaw rocked. Vicious-minded intentions, they knew they had to make a serious power move to stay relevant. There was no way they were going to allow no young cats from Detroit to run them back home to Toledo. That part of the game was out of the question.

Daily, the desperate trio schemed and plotted their survival in the game. After a few evenings of watching their prey like a hawk, Conrad, who was a known bend-over-bottom sissy behind bars, came up with what he believed to be the perfect plan. One of the girls Nolan was spending time with lived down the block from one of the migrated Toledo guys' few remaining spots. Their first plan was to cut off into the chick to see if she'd be willing to set her boyfriend up. But in reality, Conrad knew she wouldn't be down for that course of action. That uppity female not only wasn't cut like that, but also she always gave Conrad the side eye. He'd tried to kick it with her repeatedly, and constantly, she shot him down, expressing that she knew he was on the down-low. And to further make his chances zero to none, it was also rumored that Conrad was HIV-positive. He constantly disputed those facts, just as he did when Nolan cut off into him back at the liquor store confrontation. But the truth always came out in the wash whenever a real true gangsta was anywhere around and could see through Conrad's fake demeanor.

The next option that little cousin Carlos threw into the ring was to ambush Nolan and just let the bullets fly as they may. His reasoning was to have an old-fashioned shoot-out. "We should just run up on they asses and start busting. I mean, after all, we just can't let them punk us out again."

"Again? What you mean *again?*" Conrad raised his eyebrow at his cousin's recount of what had jumped off with their first face-to-face with the Detroit boys.

Carlos could tell he'd struck a nerve saying what he'd said. One-Eyed Tre could now feel the sudden tension in the room as well. Not wanting to beef out with his old peoples, Carlos tried to clean up his statement. "Naw, cuz, I was just saying let's go hard at them bitch-made niggas, guns blazing. They won't even see the shit coming. Then, *bam!* We all Gucci. Back to business as usual. We making money, and they ass dead as a motherfucker."

As much as he would like for it to be that easy, Conrad knew that wasn't a realistic possibility. He was quick to point out that even if they did that and came out victorious, the spots Nolan and his partner-in-crime Bone Capone held down would still be pumping hard at some point in time. It was common knowledge that Jayce was the real man behind their gangland Detroit invasion movement. And without a blink of an eye, he would just import some more Motown thugs to come grind. Naw, the real boss move was they had to not only take Nolan White and Bone Capone out of the game, but they also had to make those blocks and cribs hot. Carlos had always been slow since he was a small boy. So most of the ideas he continued to come up with only got worse as he kept speaking.

Conrad and Carlos at least tried to come up with a plan that wouldn't leave them looking like straight pussies in the aftermath. However, One-Eyed Tre had an entirely different mind-set. He had no reservations with being a rat and labeled a snitch. They could opt to call the Erie County Illegal Narcotics Hotline or the state police and let them do the dirty work. The cousins looked at their homeboy with disgust, knowing that's how One-Eyed Tre had lost his left eye in the first place and was wearing a patch . . . snitching. The only reason the coward was still around in the crew was he was good at cooking up. While the cousins decided to have some bit of honor, One-Eyed Tre was prepared to make a call at any moment in time.

"Yo, let's just hold tight." Conrad ordered his cousin and the one-eyed snitch to stand down for the time be-ing. "He'll be coming back over that stuck-up bitch's crib one night soon, and when he do, I got something in store for that nigga. He gonna go back to Detroit in a body bag for fucking up our bread. And his boy gonna be on that same one-way ride across state lines."

Chapter Twenty-five

It was well past eleven when Nolan finally called it. Today had been one of the best days out of the week. About his paper, the young, determined hustler stayed until every customer had been served. It was like back at the spot on Ferry. He'd be the first one up and the last one to close his eyes. Nolan had spent the few previous nights with Snoopy, treating her like a queen, something she wasn't used to. But it was Popcorn's birthday weekend, so now the tables would turn. Now, she would have the pleasure of Nolan's company and receive the royal treatment for the next few days. He was slightly exhausted but pushed through. He promised Popcorn he would be over at her house when he closed shop. So it was what it was. He wished like hell he could just be with Kapri and cut all this bullshit out with random females, but he was a man, a young one with needs and eager to fuck.

As Nolan White would try to be a man of his word, the hardworking hustler took a hot shower to try to shake off his weariness and wake up. While he allowed the hot water to flow out of the showerhead covering his body with wetness, he thought about the last few weeks and what Fiona had done for him. As much as Nolan hated to admit it, she had come through once more when needed. Although she could never truly be his main girl or even a side chick, Fiona played her position well when given guidance. O. P. had given Nolan a blow-by-blow account so vividly that it was as if he were there on the block.

O. P. got in touch with Fiona. He joked with Nolan that she answered on half of a ring. Without having to ask twice, she was with the shit. Without hesitation, she got a ride over to the East Side of Detroit. Once there, she met her crush's homeboy at Coney Island off I-94 on Mt. Elliot. Fiona thought he looked all right, but he was no way as fine as Nolan was, at least in her eyes. After small chitchat about who she claimed she knew and whatever else, they headed to his car. Smoking him over once more, Fiona mumbled under her breath that O. P. had nothing on her man Nolan, especially the way he was dragging his left leg like some creature in a low-budget horror film.

After pulling off from the restaurant parking lot, the awkward pair then set out to do the huge favor asked of them both. And that was first to locate his mother and report back not only where she was living, but also how she was living as well. After that, Nolan wanted to know if his little brothers looked like the woman who had given birth to all of them, was doing right by them. He knew how his moms practically allowed him to raise himself in the unsafe streets and get off into all sorts of mischief but prayed the twins, young as they were, wouldn't suffer that same fate.

Thankfully, it didn't take too long for the word on the street to get back to O. P. on the woman's whereabouts. Sure, Nolan could have just as easily had his manz ride down on his old girl, but she would take one look at O. P.'s face and bolt. Fiona was a female and could approach her in a more casual, nonthreatening manner. When O. P. pointed the woman out standing in front of a Chase Bank begging for spare change, Fiona got out of the car. While vainly hoping O. P. was looking at her ass as she walked, she casually went toward Nolan's mother. The closer she got, it was hard to fathom that this weather-beaten-faced lady had spit out a nigga as fine as Fiona believed Nolan to be.

"Hello, miss, how are you today?" Fiona questioned with a calm persona and a smile smugly plastered on her face.

"I'm okay. Do you have some spare change? Or maybe a dollar or two?" Nolan's mother upped her standard begging ante seeing that her prospective sponsor was dressed to impress and could probably afford it.

Fiona paused. She was thrown off her square. For weeks on end, she'd imagined coming face-to-face with the woman she wanted to be her mother-in-law. Yet, this part of her fantasy never played out like this . . . some deranged lady up on Gratiot panhandling folks for pennies, nickels, and dimes when they went in or came out of the bank, or in her case, dollar bills. But for Nolan, Fiona would do just about anything short of committing murder. And maybe that as well if he asked her in the right way. Swallowing the lump in her throat, Fiona finally answered the question that had now been repeated several times. "Umm, sorry, I don't. But I'm Nolan's girlfriend." She lied, but at this point, neither Nolan nor O. P. was in ear's range to verify or deny her claims. "Nolan is your son, right?"

Nolan's mother took a few steps back, and a strange expression came across her face. It was as if her eyes drifted off into a place of darkness. Fiona waited a few seconds, then asked again, "Is Nolan White your son or not? I'm his girlfriend, Fiona. He sent me to check on you."

It took some time, but the woman came out of her impromptu trance. She then had a few questions of her own that Fiona did her best to answer. Outside of telling Nolan's mother that her oldest son was in some part of Ohio, she thankfully got her to put her guard down. The two then walked to a nearby Dollar Store and purchased some items she felt the woman needed. O. P. was still out of sight but close by, watching what transpired. Soon after, Fiona returned to the car, telling O. P. to pull off. With an address memorized in her head and a sketchy description, she told O. P. to hurry up and get over to the house where the twins were supposedly living at before Nolan's mother showed up and found out her oldest son was plotting. Parking on the corner of the block, in less than ten minutes, she showed up. O. P. and Fiona reclined their seats and waited to see if there were any signs of the twins.

In the meantime, Fiona called Nolan telling him her version of what had transpired. She had done just what he asked: gave his mother a Green Dot Card with seventy dollars loaded on it, and told her that Nolan promised to put seventy dollars every week on the card for her to buy his brothers some groceries or fast food. As long as they ate, that was all that mattered to him. Nolan had gone to bed hungry on more than a few occasions under his mother's care.

Within an hour or so, Nolan's mother emerged from the house with the two boys in tow. Although they didn't look too bad, they didn't appear to be picture-day ready either. Making sure they were out of sight, O. P. got out of his car. It was then that Fiona paid attention to the noticeable limp he had. She sat on the edge of her seat as he ran up to the small bungalow. Once on the porch, he looked through the front window, not surprised that the inside of the dwelling appeared pretty much empty. Making his way around to the side of the house as well as the rear, O. P. repeated the process of being Inspector Gadget. From what he could tell, there was nothing but a few mattresses on the floor and two wooden chairs and a table. Shaking his head, O. P. headed back to his vehicle. Fiona's and his job were complete. Nolan would get what he was looking for and have the satisfaction of blessing his twin brothers, hopefully, with food.

Hitting the freeway heading west, O. P. soon dropped off Fiona. Anxious to get some privacy, she barely shut the door of his vehicle before running up her walkway. Thirsty, she couldn't wait to get into the house and talk Nolan's ear off. "Hey, baby. So, yeah, like you already know, I met up with your mother. And—"

"Yeah, and she was looking crazy, I know, but what about my brothers? They was good, right?" Nolan quizzed, getting right down to what he wanted to know.

"Yeah, the kids, they looked okay to me from where I was sitting in the car. But like I was saying, when I first met up with your mother, she seemed to like me right off the bat. I told her how tight you and me was, and you was like my man and shit." Fiona steered the narrative of the conversation back to focus on her. "And she was all happy and whatnot and even told me that I looked cute. And you know I was. Let me tell you what I had on."

Already, he was over hearing the tone of Fiona's annoying voice, coupled along with the fact that she'd skipped right over the main reason he'd sent the bitch on a mission off rip—the twins' well-being. Enraged at her nerve, it took everything in Nolan's power to keep his composure down to a decent level. "Look, girl, you got me all the way fucked up. First, don't nobody give a shit if my mother liked your punk ass or what in the fuck you had on. That shit don't matter to me," he barked out while shaking his head in disgust. "And why you lied to her saying I was your man is another issue altogether!"

"But wait!" Fiona tried to interject and was quickly shut down.

"But wait, my black ass. You need to stop being a bug and play your position where you and me is concerned. I already told you I kinda got a main girl. But on another note, did my ole girl look pregnant or have a new baby with her?"

"Naw, she ain't look pregnant or ain't had no baby. But back to what you said first, who you mean, your main girl?"

"Come on now, Fiona, stop playing yourself." Nolan laughed at the fact this nothing-ass bitch he occasionally dealt with when need be had the nerve to try to stunt on him.

"You talking about that fake bitch named Kapri you be bragging about so damn much? Like she some helluva type of smart female? She from the hood just like you and me," Fiona smartly replied, sucking her teeth.

"Look, I be trying to be cool with you just on the strength you looked out for a nigga, but don't jeopardize your half-assed friendship with me. Matter of fact, I got shit to do. So, yeah, go do whatever it is you do. I'm out."

Unfortunately for Fiona, the best she could get the remainder of the evening was a few text messages of gratitude from Nolan. And then her fantasy boyfriend stopped responding. Hell-bent on one day being his one and only, she still wasn't deterred by that disrespect. Fiona would get some rest and just start back calling. Nolan White would need her again one day. And when he did, she'd be Johnny-on-the-spot.

Nolan was in the shower so long, the hot water was turning lukewarm at best. He snapped back from thinking about his mother and her awful parenting skills that had his mental still messed up and the lengths he was going through to help his siblings. Nolan knew that he'd come a long way from growing up in the gutter and vowed never to return to living as he once had. He had grinded out all summer long and had multiple stacks of money saved. The once young boy with no more than one change of clothes had clothes in the closet and lying around with tags still on them. If all continued to go as planned, he would be able to get the new truck he'd been eyeballing every week. And maybe one day, he'd buy a crib of his very own, right out. But for now, Nolan had a date with Popcorn.

Exhausted, he had to make tracks before he got sleepy again. Getting dressed, Nolan tucked his pistol in the rear of his waistband, threw on a baseball cap, and was out the door. Once on the porch, he took a deep breath of the crisp night air. Moments later, his cab pulled up, flashing the spotlight upon the house, searching for the address. Nolan waved at him to kill that light. He jumped in the rear of the cab and tossed twenty to the driver in advance of him even asking for a deposit payment.

"What up, doe? Yeah, run me up the way to the store on the corner, then I'll tell you where to next." Nolan's game plan was to stop by the store, grab something to drink, and then some grub. He'd be on Popcorn's doorstep shortly after midnight by his calculations.

Chapter Twenty-six

Kapri

School at State was everything Kapri imagined it would be. For the first time in her life, she was on her own. She and she alone determined when she would go to sleep and wake up. And when and what she would eat. No longer was her mother there to be her overseer. Never one to be considered a wild child who was known to run the streets, Kapri loved reading books and teaching herself about things the average female in the hood would never consider learning. Her ability to pick up on this and that assisted her in reading different, impromptu situations whenever they would occur.

Ray Bradford was a graduate student. He was a few years Kapri's senior. Fresh out of high school, Kapri had been assigned to be a part of the school's Academic Study Achievement Program. The program was geared to assist incoming students with following proper study habits. Naïve to Ray's lustful glances, Kapri was focused on maintaining a decent grade point average. Nothing more, nothing less. At what would seem odd to most, Ray would find reasons to call or text Kapri late at night or in the wee hours of the morning. Cloaked in the reasoning of needing some reference notes or if he may have left a folder or two while they were at study group together, Ray was conniving. It was as if he were obsessed with the barely of age female. The older man wanted to make sure she was going to bed alone and waking up that way. Other people in their group would notice the extra attention their so-called leader would bestow upon Kapri but tried to ignore it. The other girls were just glad the mustache-shaven-off, gold-wired-frames-wearing creep was not focused on them.

It was midweek, and Kapri had completed most of her assignments with ease. She had not been attending the study groups lately. Not only was she growing bored with all of the strict rules Ray was putting in place, but she was also starting to notice him singling her out. Far from crazy, the clever teen started testing him and his intentions. Kapri would show him a paper that her professor had already signed off on as being above average. Ray was none the wiser and would break down all the ways that the assignment was inferior. He urged Kapri to meet with him for extra study sessions even when she insisted she had other plans. As of late, she'd been complaining to Nolan about the older dude and how she felt she was being pressed. Nolan promised her one day he would have so much money saved up she could get her own private, handpicked tutor. That promise made Kapri happy and look toward the future.

Just coming back from having lunch, Kapri stopped in the common area of the dorm to speak to a few friends. No more than five minutes had gone by when Ray seemingly appeared from nowhere. It wasn't like Kapri was dodging the man, she just simply didn't want to be bothered. "Oh, hello, Ray. How you been?"

"Wow, so Kapri James in the flesh. Dang, girl, you just done gave up on getting good grades, huh?" Ray spoke as if he were her father attempting to scold her.

"What you mean?" Kapri snapped back quickly, immediately getting an attitude. She was at her wit's end with Ray, who was always popping up out of nowhere. And lately, he had amped up his weirdness by hovering as if he were her keeper. Kapri sat there thinking if she wanted to be mothered, she would have stayed home with her own mom.

"I mean, I haven't seen you in the group, so—"

"So, and? You acting like that study group is a job or something," she huffed. "I thought it was for if you need extra help. I swear I don't get it. You be doing the most."

"It is but . . ." Ray replied, pushing his glasses back up on the arc of his nose.

The people Kapri were speaking to were starting to feel uncomfortable and left Kapri and Ray alone to hash out their apparent differences in thinking. Their leaving only made Kapri madder. Something inside of her snapped. She was trying to keep her cool, but she was done. The Detroit hood girl from around the way was ready to make her appearance. Ray had pushed every wrong button wired to Kapri's emotions. Before Ray or anyone else in ear range could prepare themselves, Kapri got to going. By the time she was done, Ray was standing in the middle of the room, looking like a fool as Kapri stormed up the stairs. But strangely enough, Ray was not discouraged. Delusional in his thought process, he reasoned with himself that the young girl truly did want him deep down inside. She was just confused and high strung. He'd give Kapri some time to calm down and would approach her again once he returned from his trip up North to visit his aging and sick grandmother.

Once up in her dorm room, it took Kapri damn near twenty minutes to calm down from her very much warranted public rant. Pacing from side to side in the small room, she had to breathe in and out slowly to regain her composure. She wanted to call her mother and tell her about the creep, but she knew her mother. She'd drop everything she was doing and be on her way, probably with another hammer in her purse or even her gun ready to use on Ray. Phone in hand, Kapri considered calling for all of five minutes, but she didn't want her mother to think she was weak. She didn't want her to think she couldn't handle life as an adult living on her own. And telling Nolan was out of the question just because he would nut up as well. So, instead, Kapri reached out to her cousin, Marie.

After telling what had just jumped off, Marie got Kapri off a hundred. Finally, back in her right mind, Kapri got caught up with family business on her father's side. Needless to say, that conversation was full of revelations that would come in handy later down the line.

Chapter Twenty-seven

Carlos was sitting on the front porch of the spot, smoking a blunt. It was a little after midnight, and the block was quiet for the most part, as it had been most of the day. When he was just about as high as he wanted to get, a pair of headlights turned the corner. Although he hoped it was a customer, Carlos knew those days of making late-night money had trickled down since the two-man Detroit drug invasion. Paranoid, he leaned back in the shadow, making sure his pistol was close by. Within seconds, he realized it was just a cab. Yet, with the aid of the bright streetlight, he easily peeped out who he thought was Nolan in the rear seat. Wasting no time, Carlos stood, then raced into the house. Quickly alerting Conrad that this was the perfect time to make a move on the dude that had blown his shit out at the store, his cousin readily agreed. After weeks of scheming, their great master plan was to catch Nolan and his homeboy slipping and kidnap them. Of course, there would be no ransom notes of money involved, just pure torture, ultimately resulting in the D-boys' demise. But the longer they waited for Nolan and Bone Capone to slip up was the longer they were not making money. So plan or not, it was time. Both strapped, the eager, bloodthirsty pair bolted out the front door. Jumping off the wooden stairs, their adrenalin was pumping.

As they hit the side of the house, One-Eyed Tre came on the porch. Having just come out of the bathroom taking a dump, he didn't know where Conrad or Carlos were headed, but he could tell it must've been some kind of serious since their guns were drawn. Since it was dark, it was hard for him to see which way they were headed once his friends had reached the backyard. Cutting through the alleyways was part of the game when running from the law or, in this case, trying low key to creep up on a situation. Not knowing what to do next, One-Eyed Tre ducked back inside of the house and retrieved his gun off of the coffee table. Coming back on the porch, he looked down the block seeing the taillights of some sort of vehicle. The make and model he couldn't quite make out. It was times like these that made him hate the eye patch he was cursed to wear. Taking a few steps down off the porch, he still couldn't see clearly up the block.

"Hell yeah, that's the punk-ass nigga. Told you so." Out of breath, the two men crouched down on the side of the house as the light inside of the cab came on. "I knew he was gonna be back over here, hitting that uppity hood pussy. Now, we gonna get rid of at least one of our problems."

Conrad was seething with rage. He felt his internal hate for Nolan increase. Holding his gun in one hand, he used the other to rub his still-sore jaw. Just thinking about how the young boy had handled him at that store caused his blood to boil, and his taste for revenge to increase. He'd put one up top while he was running down the alley, so he was ready to go. In a matter of minutes, when Nolan would exit the cab, he and his cousin would get the drop on their soon-to-be victim. Sure, they would not be able to torture him, but at this point, as long as the end result was death, it would be a win.

"Yeah, guy, I'm on my way over to ole girl Popcorn's crib. It's her birthday weekend, so I'ma chill over there tonight."

"Dig that. Is you gonna get your ass outta that pussy in the morning and open up shop on time or what?" Bone Capone clowned his homeboy. "You know Jayce got a new package in and word from his testers is that shit stronger than the last. So you know we gotta be all over that bag."

"Come on, now, fam. I ain't missing no money over no damn bitch. I'ma be there bright and fucking early." Nolan hand-signaled the cab to make a right at the next stop sign he got to. "So, yeah, bet, I'm 'bout to pull up at her crib and eat this damn food, sip off this bottle, smoke a li'l something something, then rock that cat to sleep. I'll holler at you in the a.m."

"All right, then, do you. Peace," Bone Capone ended the conversation.

"Yeah, pull over right behind that silver car on your right." No sooner than the cab did as instructed, the driver hit the interior light. Nolan looked over at all the stuff he had. Shaking his head in disbelief at how much money he'd just spent, he called Popcorn. It went straight to voicemail. He tried again and got the same result. *Bitch probably in the shower,* he reasoned, trying not to get angry.

Nolan then dug into his pocket. Pulling out a ten-dollar bill to go with the twenty he'd already had on deposit, he tossed it to the driver, telling him to keep the change. After looking up toward Popcorn's house, he gathered up the bags and exited the cab. Before the big tipper could get out good, the driver sped off in hopes of catching another fare before calling it a night.

"Damn, why I ain't call that bitch back to come help a guy with all this bullshit she wanted?" Nolan mumbled underneath his breath with both hands full, now standing in the middle of the street.

Fumbling with the bags, he backed up some and set them down on the hood of Popcorn's car. Before he could take out his cell and call her once more, something told him to look toward his left-hand side. It was then that he took notice of a guy standing on the porch of a house a few doors down. Nolan was from the streets and could tell the lone guy now down on the stairs seemed to be focused on him and his actions. Automatically, he remembered that Popcorn had told him some guys from Toledo had set up shop there and were slanging. When the guy turned his face, the streetlight caught it. It was then that Nolan saw buddy was wearing an eye patch just like one of them dudes that was in the store talking shit. Leaving the bags on the hood, Nolan eased on the far side of the vehicle. Taking his pistol out, he turned his baseball cap to the back. He knew the chances of there being more than one Negro in the hood with an eye patch suspiciously lurking in the middle of the night were slim to none.

Nolan White wasn't a killer by far, but he was ready for whatever. He'd gone too far in the game to now give it all up to the devil on the humble. All the days of target practice shooting in the basement of vacant houses were about to come in handy. Letting them guns sing out on New Year's Eve back home in Detroit had also readied him to be prepared for anything. So if man-child minding his own business had to put fire to a Negro's ass, then so be it. It was go time. Tightening his fingers on the rubber-gripped handle of his gun, bravely and without reservations, Nolan White wanted all the smoke.

Conrad grinned with satisfaction as his intended target got out of the cab. With what appeared to be a bunch of bags, he watched him like a hawk as Nolan paused, then placed his packages on the hood of a car. His trigger finger itched to go to work. *Hell yeah, motherfucker. Put all that bullshit down so a nigga can get a clean shot off on that ass!* This was it. This was the time he'd been waiting for since initially hearing about the two Detroit hustlers. The two of them, under the guidance of Jayce, had successfully edged Conrad and his crew damn near out of business. He and his boys were struggling to eat regularly. And although this was going to make the block hot, he didn't care. The spot down the street was dried up anyhow. Conrad didn't give a fuck if they indicted the entire block. Carlos, One-Eyed Tre, and he would just set up shop elsewhere. As long as they didn't have to be worried about Nolan or Bone Capone showing up and upstaging them with product, all would be gravy.

"Yo, hold up. What the fuck he looking at down the way," Carlos whispered, nudging his older cousin on the shoulder. "What this lame doing? Why he going back behind the car like that?"

Conrad eased up slightly, trying to see through the bushes. Looking in the same direction that Nolan was, it became obvious exactly what their target was looking at. *Son of a bitch! That ho-ass nigga Tre is about to fuck shit up all the way! And, damn, now, why the hell is he bringing his blind ass off that porch?*

There was thick tension circulating in the night air. Both parties felt it. The promise of death was poised to make an appearance and alter lives forever. As Nolan was posted on one side of the block behind a car, gun clutched, Conrad and Carlos held down the other side, waiting for the perfect opportunity to open fire. The atmosphere and its surroundings were like one of those action movies you'd watch on television. The stage was now set for a perfect storm. It was a little past midnight. Just the right time for an all-out gun battle to occur in the middle of a mostly quiet, yet densely populated neighborhood street.

It was a shift change at not only the police department but also the hospital staff as well. Nolan, Carlos, Conrad, and any others that may be cursed enough to be caught in the middle of pistol play and struck by a stray bullet would appreciate those facts. That would mean help would be on the way in a timely manner by alert personal trained to save the lives of not only the innocent victims but also the corrupt lives of the criminals as well. With the presence of One-Eyed Tre bringing attention to himself, adding fuel to the already-burning hot fire, Conrad couldn't risk losing his window of opportunity. He could quickly tell that Nolan had peeped game and knew something was up. The time to act was now.

Chapter Twenty-eight

Popcorn and Snoopy

"Bitch, how did you get my number?" Popcorn angrily yelled into the phone.

"Don't worry about all of that. Just answer the damn question. How long you been fucking my man, Mac? *That's* what this call is about," Snoopy hissed, wanting to get all of the truth out in the open.

"*Your* man? Ho, if half of what you saying is true, then that's *our* man. So it's whatever at this point."

Popcorn was the most sensible out of the two females Nolan had been dealing with. Snoopy was the trouble-maker. Yet, no matter which one felt they had the upper hand in what was an apparent situation of a dude getting caught playing both girls, the crazy part was neither of them knew Nolan for real. Not even his government name as he had them both calling him Mac. He had come up with that name on the spur of the moment because number one, he liked eating Big Macs. And number two, he felt it was best not to let any of the people in Sandusky know, including the chicks he was lying down with, his true identity. That way, if anything gangster ever jumped off and he had to get out of Dodge, no one would have anything but a false name to call out.

"Well, like I said, he on his way over here right damn now."

"What?" Snoopy raged, ready to explode.

"Matter of fact, that's him calling me right now, back-to-back, but I'm sending his grimy ass to voicemail. I'ma deal with him face-to-face."

"Ain't that some foul shit. Mac ain't shit!"

The girls went back and forth, exposing their stories and cross-referencing his. After a short time, they discovered that he'd met both of them the same day at the amusement park, probably minutes apart. Snoopy told her sisterwife that Mac had been with her the previous nights. Popcorn informed her that her birthday was the next day and repeated that Mac was supposed to be on his way over to hang. It was then that they both revealed that they each were late with their period.

After exchanging more information, the scorned pair of potentially pregnant females thought about having Mac meet up with both of them at the same time. Then let him explain what was really good. However, just when they were close to coming up with the perfect plan, Popcorn quickly rolled off the bed and hit the floor. Having dropped her cell, she started crawling on her hands and knees to seek refuge in her closet. It seemed like the world was coming to an end as the thunderous sounds of a barrage of gunfire rocked the walls of her house. Snoopy was left on the line repeatedly saying hello, as she could easily hear the multicaliber fireworks display going off as well.

Chapter Twenty-nine

There was no time like the present. Conrad sprang up from the cover of his hiding spot. Rushing from behind the bushes, he spoke no words. Instead, he aimed his gun and fired off round after round. Although second-guessing if they had made the right decision jumping the gun, so to speak, a nervous Carlos followed suit. As he emerged from the darkness on the side of the house, his gun was now extended as he tried to find his mark. Confused and scared, he ran to the far side of the street, ducking behind an old-school Chevy. Before he could get any more than two shots off, he saw Conrad get hit, then take off toward the alley. It was then that he sadly realized he was left alone on the block to face Nolan. One-Eyed Tre had since run for cover, praying not to get hit.

Nolan didn't have to get ready. He stayed that way. Quickly, he turned his attention from the guy with the eye patch and caught a glimpse of a figure jump out of the bushes. The next thing he knew, he was under fire. With the heart of a lion and the will of a champion, the Black Bottom-raised teen did what the streets of Detroit had trained him to do: react. Although he was used to carrying a gun, Nolan hoped he would never have to use it. But in all honesty, he knew being in the game, chances were he'd have to at some point.

Without hesitation, he put in work. Knowing he was outnumbered, he carefully pulled the trigger, making sure each bullet counted. The first guy was letting 'em go, one after another. Thankfully for Nolan, the man was hitting everything *but* his mark. Popcorn would have to replace the windows on her vehicle as first the driver's one shattered, followed by the rear one. Nolan gave as good as he was getting. Creeping toward the trunk, he let off a shot, striking Conrad in the upper thigh.

What the fuck! Hell yeah, that bitch nigga hit for sure! Seeing the bullets hit the man and his body jerk some brought a strange feeling of joy to Nolan. This was the first time he'd ever shot someone—and it felt good. It felt as if he wanted to shoot the man repeatedly. The tables had turned. The attacker was getting attacked. Firing once more, striking the shoulder area of his now-victim, Nolan imagined the man was his own snake-backstabbing father, and he was settling up some old business they had. *I could do this bullshit all day! Niggas gonna learn fucking with me!*

Nolan was breathing hard, never having been in this dire situation before. He'd often let a nigga catch them hands, but this was an entirely whole different animal. Momentarily, he took more electrifying pleasure in watching the guy he'd now recognized from the liquor store beat down retreat somewhere behind a house. However, the longtime mentally troubled youth's celebration and break from being under siege was not yet over.

On the other side of the street was the second of the two gunmen behind the old-school Chevy. Nolan was now in a kill-or-be-killed zone. As he watched and waited, it didn't take long before the second guy emerged, trying to make a run for it while shooting. Once more, Nolan aimed and fired. And once more, he knew he'd struck gold. Carlos was hit. He stumbled, then fell to the pavement, dropping his pistol on the way down. Crazed and half out his mind, Nolan wasted no time running up on the now-injured man. As he stood victoriously towering over the wounded man, Carlos begged for mercy. Thinking of his father once more, Nolan showed none as he let off two rounds, one directly into each of Carlos's kneecaps.

"I guess you ain't gonna run up on another nigga. I should kill your bitch ass!" Nolan threatened while making sure he didn't see the first guy return from the back area of the side of the houses. Unfortunately, while Nolan's attention was on that task, he failed to notice that One-Eyed Tre had come out of hiding and had somehow crept up on him.

"Yo, get the fuck away from my people. Drop that fucking gun, nigga," One-Eyed Tre ordered, seeing and hearing his homeboy Carlos moan in utter agony.

Nolan was no coward by any means. In fact, he had no fear of much since being a small child. The only thing he had was a strong will to survive. And there was no way in hell he was ready to die in the streets of Sandusky as a John Doe. There was no question that his family could care less about his well-being as a whole, but at least if he were in Detroit, they might claim his body. Of course, Nolan knew the odds weren't good because the dude had his gun pointed directly at him, but he wasn't going out like no pussy—period.

"Look, ho-ass nigga, what you trying to do? You wanna do something, then do it, bitch! Make that shit sing or shut the fuck up and take what *I* got for *you!*"

It was apparent to One-Eyed Tre that Nolan was about that life and was not backing down. Just as Carlos second-guessed them running up on Nolan, it was now One Eye's turn to do the same. Standing there ready to shoot, he regretted the fact that he just didn't call the police on Nolan and his boy, Bone Capone, from jump. So, what if everyone around the way knew he snitched again? That was his known MO. "Nigga, just drop that gun. I'm not playing."

"Dawg, just shoot his ass! Shoot him and get me some damn help. I can't move my fucking legs," Carlos pleaded repeatedly.

"Yeah, dawg, just shoot me now . . . or else," Nolan taunted as if he were invincible.

Forced to make a move before one was made on him, One-Eyed Tre fired off one single round out of fear. The flash from the gun lit the side of the house for all of a millisecond. Then came the immediate aftermath of his actions. One-Eyed Tre stood there, trembling. Carlos was in sheer disbelief. He started to cry like a baby, fearing he was going to bleed out. Nolan, in turn, sinisterly smirked that the half-blind fool had put a slug in the side of Popcorn's side door. He then wasted no time returning fire.

Unlike his attacker, Nolan was deliberate. He aimed for the stomach. No sooner than One-Eyed Tre doubled over falling to the ground in pain, Nolan callously used the side of the gun to most certainly brutally blind One-Eyed Tre in the other eye. With each time he raised his firearm, bringing it slamming down on One-Eyed Tre's face, his adrenalin had him hyped. Nolan's drive and definite willingness to commit murder increased. This incident was his first taste of blood, and the way it felt . . . it would not be his last.

Realizing that with the ear-deafening barrage of gunfire that had taken place, the onset of police was sure to follow. Getting locked up for attempted murder or any other possible charges was not an option. It was time to get out of Dodge. Wisely, Nolan fled the scene as quickly as possible. He knew neighbors would feel it was now safe to peek out of their doors and windows, so he definitely didn't want to be around for that. Sure, he'd done nothing wrong but defended himself, but the law wouldn't take that part in consideration when locking him up for having a gun in the first place.

Fast jogging at least six blocks over, down one alley, then another, and finally crossing a major street, Nolan sat behind a garage to catch his breath. He was no fool and knew what had to happen next. Popcorn was blowing up his cell, but he didn't answer. He'd hit her back when he handled his business. Calling Bone, he told him briefly some of what had just jumped off. Still trying to process what he'd just done, he told him to get with Jayce and meet him at his spot as soon as possible.

Back on the move, Nolan saw a bike in the rear of one of the houses he was passing as he cut down the alleys to stay out of sight. He quietly opened the back gate and slowly rolled the bike out of the backyard. Once on it, he was at his spot within eleven minutes.

Just as he was putting his key in the door, Bone Capone was turning the corner. Jayce was right behind. Once all three were in the house, Nolan gave them a more thorough reenactment of the ambush than he had a chance to do on the phone. Hearing him out, the three knew that the streets were about to be hot. And neither Nolan, Bone, nor Jayce wanted to feel the heat.

Nolan and Bone needed to leave town and possibly set up shop somewhere else. Jayce would stay behind and tie up any loose ends that needed to be dealt with. Besides, he had other spots throughout town still pumping, making money. Knowing that this was Nolan's first time handling something like this, Jayce asked him for the gun he used so he could get rid of it. But Nolan wasn't as green as he thought. He'd watched enough episodes of *The First 48* to know not to trust his fate in the hands of the next man. Without blinking an eye, he claimed he tossed it into one of the many murky sewer lines that ran along the nearby lake by the city. Jayce, of course, didn't doubt him or his word.

Bone Capone was heated that those three lames tried to make a move on his homeboy. Loyal to point and principle, he wanted to go over on Popcorn's block and shoot the three niggas his damn self just for trying that dumb shit, but his cousin was right. Things were gonna be on edge around their way. He had people in another part of Ohio, so he opted to head there and let things settle down. He wasn't as hot as Nolan was possibly going to be, but they had to be precautious just the same. Saying their goodbyes and vowing to meet up down the line and run shit, he left to pack and get his affairs in order too.

Nolan, on the other hand, had nowhere to go . . . no family . . . nothing. As Popcorn and now Snoopy both continued to call and text him back-to-back-to-back-to-damn-back, he could only think of one person that cared about him. And that was Kapri. Quickly gathering all of his belongings in four huge Home Depot bags, Nolan went to his secret stash and stuffed all his money in his pockets, front and back. The streets were already buzzing about what had gone down. So time was ticking for Nolan not only to get out of Sandusky but also Ohio as well. Jayce had one of his trusted drivers on the payroll come by and pick up Nolan. He also sent a package of some strong dope he'd just gotten in just on the strength. He knew Nolan had been nothing but straight up and a real soldier for the movement. Nolan was told to flip it wherever he landed and hit him up if he ever wanted to do business again. Jayce hoped one day in the future, that would be the case.

Chapter Thirty

Once on the highway, Tone, the middle-aged driver, made sure to do the speed limit. No way did he want to risk getting pulled over by the state boys. As Nolan settled back in the passenger seat, he finally felt he could breathe. It was like he'd been holding his breath since the first gunshot rang out. He was no longer a virgin to bullet mayhem. One guy, he hit in the leg. With an oh-well-fuck-him attitude, Nolan didn't know where he went or how he was. Yet, the shooter knew for a fact that the dude on the ground crying for his mommy would never walk straight again . . . if he even walked at all. And old boy that took one in the stomach would need a shit bag for some time to come. And nine outta ten, somebody to help him put it on since he was now blind in *both* eyes. Nolan felt no remorse, laughing to himself. The only thing he hated was that he'd wasted all that money on food and liquor and had left it sitting on Popcorn's car.

Taking his cell off of vibrate, Nolan saw a slew of text messages and missed calls. Now a safe distance away, he'd return Popcorn's calls and see what the status was with what popped off outside of her house. Snoopy would have to wait. But first, he wanted to call his girl Kapri and let her know he was headed her way. It was almost three in the morning, but he knew she wouldn't mind. They'd stayed up talking all times of the night throughout the summer. Plus, this was an emergency.

"Hey, Nolan, what's going on? What time is it?" Kapri's voice was groggy. She had been asleep for hours. Having an early-morning class, she wanted to make sure she was well rested.

"Hey, brown eyes, so, guess what?" Nolan said in a hopeful tone. After all, he had nowhere else to go, so at this point, all he had was hope. "I'm heading your way. I'm coming to see you."

Kapri thought she was hearing things. She must've heard wrong. After all this time of talking on the phone and promises of visits, Nolan claimed he was truly on his way. She sat straight up in bed. "You coming here, up to school? When?"

"I'ma be there in a few hours, cool?" On edge, he waited for her response.

"Yeah, crazy boy, of course, it's cool. I got a class in the morning, but I guess I can miss it. I can't wait to see you." Kapri was stunned but elated. She and Nolan had not laid eyes on each other since that day they first met, but it was like she'd known him forever. All of the long hours they spent on the phone, she was in love. And even if it would not last moving forward into the future, right now was good enough for her.

"All right, bet. I'll make it up to you missing your class, I swear to God. I'm just geeeked I'ma be able to kick it with me girl."

"Nolan, you ain't gotta swear. I'm just glad to see you again. And yeah, I can't wait."

"Me too." His voice softened to almost a whisper as he was feeling wanted and loved by someone unconditionally for the first time. "So, I'ma jus' hit you when I get on your campus, and you can give me directions from there. Until then, go back to sleep."

That was settled, and Nolan was ecstatic. Once he reached Kapri, he knew she could give him some insight on what moves he should make next. Even though D-Boy hustler was making money hand over fist, he was glad to be leaving Sandusky and all the turmoil that came along with living there. But before he wrote that town off forever, he needed to call Popcorn. Then maybe Snoopy's off-the-chain ass to say goodbye. After all, spending time with them wasn't all that bad or torture. Besides, Popcorn could give him a read on what went down after he got ghost.

"Mac! Mac! Is that you? Oh my God, why you ain't been picking up? I thought you was dead or something. Where the fuck is you? I been calling you like a motherfucker!" She was going ham, not giving him a chance to answer even one of her multiple questions.

"Damn, girl, why would you think I was dead? Where that come from?" Nolan played it off as if she were bugging. "I was asleep."

"Nigga, asleep, my black ass. I know you was outside my house earlier with that shooting bullshit. So stop playing stupid with me. What the fuck, I know it was you." Popcorn argued with an attitude that he was acting dumb. "You know the police was knocking on my damn door."

"Okay, so what they want? What they say?" He finally started coming clean to a certain degree, knowing she knew the deal or at least some of it.

"How do I fucking know? I ain't even open the damn door. I don't wanna be caught up in all that shit. Niggas shot in between the houses and shit. Flashing lights and ambulances. Nigga, that's the shit they drag bitches down to the station for hours grilling them about. I went outside to look at my fucked-up car real quick before the cops pulled up, and that's how I know it was your fake ass over here!" Popcorn's voice got louder as she got off into her supposed boyfriend's ass.

"Why you think that so hard?" Nolan wanted to see her reasoning.

"Uuum, let me think. Probably because them bags you left on my damn hood."

"Oh yeah, damn, okay, then. So, yeah, I was there. And them ho-ass niggas from down the street tried to go in on me. They tried to catch me slipping."

"Yeah, well, Mac, from the looks of things, you the one that came out on top. But I guess you always come out on top, huh? You slick like that."

"What's that supposed to mean?" Nolan puzzled. He knew she was pissed since he had to lay two niggas down right outside her door, but that wasn't his call. They acted, and so he reacted.

"Why don't you ask that bitch that work at the park with me that bullshit? The one you was with the other night. Yeah, Mac, the one you been fucking while you been fucking me! Ask *her!* Yeah, we talked. We talked for a good while, you snake-ass nigga."

Nolan didn't know what to say. After months of doing this and that, he was busted. The only thing he could do was shake his head. This just wasn't his night. Although Popcorn and Snoopy were both cool females to hang with to pass the time, they weren't Kapri. They weren't wifey material. They were both something to just fuck on. "Okay, so, now what? It is what it is. What you want me to say?"

"Oh, for real? It's like that? You trying to be all cold-blooded and boss with it? Well, guess what? I'm pregnant, and so is ole girl," Popcorn announced as if she felt she'd had some knock-down-and-dragged-out information.

"Okay, and? What you telling me for?"

"Boy, what you mean?"

"Look, both you stupid hoes can give them babies back to God. Or raise 'em ya damn self! A nigga like me ain't trying to hear none of that," Nolan casually replied as if he were speaking on nothing of great importance.

"Oh, it's like *that?*" Animosity was in her tone, as well as it should have been.

"Yeah, it's just like that," he sneered with certainty.

"All right, then, Mac, I'ma tell the police it was you. I'ma bring 'em over to your damn house too. So, let's see *you* boss up about that," Popcorn loudly threatened with fury and hurt at the same time.

"Oh yeah? Well, good luck with that, bitch. Knock yourself out. Do what you gotta do. And your new best phone friend, you can tell her that too. I'm out." Exhausted, Nolan hung up and then blocked her number. He followed suit with Snoopy as well. There was no need to read any of the multiple texts or listen to the sure-to-be hot-talk voicemails. Whenever he got to Kapri, he'd toss the cell he'd been using and buy a new one, new number and all. He would cut all ties. And Popcorn could go to the cops all she wanted. Only thing she could say is she was fucking some nigga from Detroit named Mac. Closing his eyes, Nolan anticipated and speculated what the next part of his life would hold after touching base with Kapri.

Chapter Thirty-one

It was a little shy of six thirty in the morning. There was a small bit of moisture circulating in the air. As Kapri stood on the front stairs of her dorm in a Michigan State sweatshirt, she took notice of just how quiet it was on campus at this time of the day. Since this was the summer session, she could only imagine what it would be like come fall. She was excited for all of that to take place. But for now, she was minutes away from a new adventure. With her cell phone ringing once again, she knew it was Nolan. He must've followed her directions and was now at the point where she told him to call her back. Answering, she stayed on the line with him, talking to him the final mile since it had a lot of twists and turns.

In no time, she saw a car turn into the far end of the student parking lot. As the vehicle got closer, Kapri felt a lump in her throat. She was nervous yet anxious at the same time. Moments later, Nolan stepped out of the passenger side. It was then that she felt her legs get weak. She thought she was going to pass out.

"Hey, girl! Hey, brown eyes." He ran up to her, sweeping her off of her feet in a strong embrace. "You miss me or what? Damn, it's good to see you."

Kapri was smiling so hard it seemed like her teeth were ready to jump clean out of her mouth. "Dang, yeah, I'm happy. It looks like your ass got taller. And look, you got a beard growing." She rubbed the side of his face.

Nolan patted her on the head, laughing. "Well, damn, it looks like you got shorter. But your eyes got even prettier."

While the two of them were having a mini reunion on the stairs of the dorm, the weary driver interrupted, asking Nolan where he wanted him to put his bags. He already had the trunk open waiting for a response. Nolan left Kapri's side and helped the man take the three huge bags out of the trunk. He then took the last one out of the backseat of the car. Before Nolan allowed the man to pull off, he got one last, smaller bag out of the corner of the trunk and gave the guy some money. Kapri was confused about all of the gigantic bags her just-arrived impromptu guest had brought but didn't say a word. First, they would get all his things up to her dorm room and figure the rest out later.

"Okay, Nolan, please tell me what's going on," Kapri asked while helping him drag the last bag through her door. Luckily, it was early, and none of the other residents were up or around with prying eyes. With the amount of bags Nolan had with him when he pulled up, someone would assume he was trying to move in.

"I will, but first, gimme a hug, girl. Damn, I've been dreaming about you for so long. Now we here. Now we together."

After months of having a long-distance relationship, Nolan and Kapri shared their first kiss. It was long and drawn out like in the movies, not awkward in any way. Kapri had butterflies and felt dizzy when Nolan loosened his strong embrace. She was still standing on her tiptoes because of Nolan's height. But that part didn't matter to her. She knew when they first met, there was just something about this bad boy. Now, after all of the time they spent on the phone getting to know each other, coupled with this kiss, Kapri knew this was real. She could feel it. The lovesick teen believed she and Nolan could go the distance. To her as well as him, it didn't matter that they were young. They both were determined, and that was half of the battle.

When the pair broke apart, Kapri sat on one bed, while Nolan posted up on the other. He thought about just putting the moves on her for the pussy right then and there but chilled. He could tell by the way she was looking at him that time would soon come. Nolan begged her not to judge him for what he was about to say. And without question, she agreed.

"Come on, now, Nolan. Seriously, when have I ever judged you?" She leaned back across the pillow.

"You mean besides the day we met, and you clowned my shoes?" he smartly replied.

Still embarrassed, Kapri apologized yet again. Only this time, it was in person, and she had a huge smile plastered on her face. "Oh my God, I told you my bad a million times. But whatever. It looks like your ass done came all the way up. So, yeah, you good. Now, tell me what's up with you. Why you really here?"

The two of them spoke constantly, and Nolan never held anything back from his best friend. So besides what happened the night before, Kapri was caught up to speed. Rubbing his hands nervously together, he once again asked not to be judged. Then he went on expressing himself and revealing his truths. When his confession of street crimes and gunplay and whatnot was all said and done, Kapri stuck out her hand while shaking her head.

"Nolan, gimme that damn gun, crazy nigga. We gotta get rid of that hot-ass motherfucker! I can't believe you risk riding across state lines like that."

"Huh, what?" Nolan didn't expect that simple response. After all, he'd just told Kapri he shot some dude twice, then another in his kneecaps deliberately, then probably double blinded a blind man after he put a bullet in his stomach at close range. Gimme that gun was it? "Did you hear all of what I just said?"

"Yeah, baby, you just said you had one long night putting in work, handling your business, and doing what had to be done," she reaffirmed. "Now, like I asked, gimme that gun."

Digging in one of the garbage bags of his belongings, he took out the dark blue T-shirt he had the pistol wrapped in. Giving it to Kapri just as it was, what she did next they would come to laugh about for years to come. Kapri took the T-shirt over to her desk. After instructing Nolan to make sure the double bolt lock was on, she turned on the television and the radio. Sitting down at her desk, she unwrapped the shirt and took the gun out. Looking at it as if she were a scientist, the girl from around the way that was used to getting straight As in school showed her other skills.

First, she took the clip out and told Nolan to take any remaining bullets out. Then she checked to make sure there was not one up top. Then, to his surprise, Kapri broke the weapon down, disassembling it piece by piece. Nolan was practically speechless. He didn't know what to say or think.

"What the fuck? How did you learn how to do that shit?" His eyes bucked.

"My mother carries a gun and sometimes a damn hammer in her purse. But it's my father's side that's really about that life. One of my father's brothers taught all my cousins and me one day when I was over there. That's part of the reason my mother despises them so damn much." Kapri shrugged her shoulders, smiling. "Plus, of course, them special powers I told you I inherited."

Nolan knew his girl was dead ass about that black-magic bullshit she was always claiming, but it didn't matter. Because it was right at that very moment that he knew Kapri James was the female he was destined to marry someday. She was the woman of every hood hustler's dreams . . . book smart and street smart, plus, fine as hell. When she was done telling him that they would dump parts of the gun in various dumpsters throughout the outskirts of the city as well as some directly in the basement's incinerator, he could only smugly grin. The next thing he did was take the dope he had handing it to her. He then took all of his money out of his pockets and tossed the knots and stacks onto one of the beds. Nolan told his girl he had no real idea how much it was, but she could count it and let him know how much "they" was working with. Glad that she had a bathroom attached to her room, Nolan just wanted to take a hot shower. When he did that, Kapri started counting while thinking the same thing as he had, that one day the two of them would be married.

Later on that night, the couple made love for the very first time, over and over again. And like everything else when it came to Nolan and Kapri . . . It was spectacular.

Chapter Thirty-Two

Kapri canceled all of her upcoming classes. Luckily, it was not like high school where you went all day, five days a week. College schedules were much different and flexible, which worked out perfectly in her case. The two of them were having the time of their young lives. After the first day of going here and there, they made a joint decision to go to a used car lot. Once there, Kapri picked out a late-model Chevy Blazer, her favorite color, red. Since she was the only one with a valid driver's license, the vehicle was put in her name and paid for in cash. With a temporary paper tag in the rear window, she and Nolan were on their way.

Nolan had been camping out in Kapri's dorm room secretly for almost a week and counting. Each knew that they'd have to make other living arrangements for him soon. And Kapri knew she would have to make up those skipped classes. But for one last day before apartment hunting for him, they decided to live it up as bosses. Nolan was going to the local café to grab them breakfast. Then they were going to the mall to buy matching tracksuits for an end-of-the-summer concert. Kapri only had a T-shirt on and no panties when Nolan opened the door to leave. To both of their surprise, there stood a stone-faced Ray pretending he was about to knock . . . when all along, he'd had his ear pressed up to the door for some time.

"Damn, what up, doe?" Not expecting to see anyone, Nolan took a few steps back.

"Hello." Ray's tone was dry at best as he gave who he'd believed to be his competition a cold, dark stare.

Kapri heard Ray's annoying voice and came from behind the door, peeking over Nolan's shoulder. "Oh, hey, Ray. What's happening?"

"You have not been in class or even to study group all week. I came to see what issues you may have had." Ray's voice continued to be cut and dry as his eyes quickly surveyed the room as much as possible. Seeing that only one of the two twin beds appeared to have been slept in, he seethed with jealousy. His inner soul felt as if it were growing rock hard. It took everything in his power not to lash out right then and there.

As Ray stood there questioning Kapri, Nolan quickly realized precisely who this buster was. This was the creep that had been pestering his girl over the previous weeks. Whereas part of him wanted to just swing on him, Nolan could tell by his looks, Ray-whatever-his-last-name-was, was a total goofball. "She just been extra, extra busy, dawg. You know how it is when old friends link up, don't you? Shit gets real wild, and a nigga forgets all about time." Nolan put even more salt in the game by stepping back and wrapping his arms around Kapri, who giggled, telling him to stop playing.

This entire scene had become way too much for him to deal with, although Ray wasn't the least bit surprised. Low key, he'd been stalking Kapri since the day Nolan arrived. He'd even dry snitched, making an anonymous call to the resident dorm manager, which obviously did no good at all. The virus was still there. However, this particular day, Nolan's unwanted presence was getting to him. Ray had fallen asleep enraged and woke up in that same mood. He had to come knock on her door. He had to see Nolan face-to-face. And, of course, he had to see Kapri, the object of his twisted affections. "Excuse me, I sure I don't know how 'niggas' forget about anything," he sneered with a facial expression of contempt.

"Look, Ray, I'm busy right now," Kapri cut him off knowing if he went any further with his smart, condescending tone and words, it might set Nolan off. "I'ma be back at class and study group next week for sure. So I'll see you then." Rudely, she then shut the door in his face.

Ray was livid. As he momentarily stood there, he could easily overhear Kapri and her visitor laughing at his expense. That only added fuel to the fire. Out of sorts, he marched down the hall to the far end staircase. Once inside of the small platform area, Ray then started to bang his head on the wall, attempting to calm himself down. He'd wanted Kapri since the day he'd seen her. Now, this no-class thug was getting the pussy that belonged to him. He was on the verge of exploding. As he stood there pacing in the small area contemplating his next move, he saw Nolan leave and headed down the other set of stairs closer to Kapri's dorm room. Waiting a minute or two to make sure he was gone, Ray rushed back down the hall to at least finally express his affection to Kapri and ask her to leave that punk alone and be solely with him.

Dang, why is Nolan's butt back so soon? He must've forgotten something. Without bothering to double-check if it were him, Kapri swung open the door. Straightaway, her enthusiastic smile changed to a disapproving frown of resentment. Totally justified, Kapri caught an instant attitude. Fed up with his antics, she went right in.

"Oh, it's you. I thought you was my boyfriend. What you forget to say? I already told you I'd be back next week. So, umm, what part of that don't you freaking get?" she then attempted to close the door some since she was only T-shirt clad.

Ray was not in the mood to be shut down or have his feelings dismissed. He came back to win his girl, and in his distorted mind, that was what he was going to do. Raising one hand, he stopped his beloved from closing the door any further. Just looking at her angelic face and beautiful legs, his manhood stiffened. Taking a quick glance over at the bed drove him wild. That sight was all a delusional Ray needed to push him over the edge. In a flash, he imagined being on top of Kapri in that bed, legs spread wide open. That fantasy caused him to snap. Before she could protest, he shoved her back away from the door. Before she could resist, he quickly shut the door behind him. Kapri's first instinct was to scream out for help, but Ray had other plans. Without warning, he rushed up to her before she could utter a word. Using his hand, he covered her mouth, forcefully pressing against her lips.

As Kapri's eyes widened in fear, Ray seemed to be getting off even more. By him only having one free hand, he had a tough time trying to control Kapri. Not only was she born and raised in the hood, but she was also good with her hands, and that fact Ray would soon discover. Struggling to stay on her feet and keep his free hand from violating her, Kapri reached up, socking him in the face and trying to scratch his eyes out. However, Ray was like a wild animal that couldn't be tamed. But Kapri was a beast in her own right. With him attempting to keep her mouth covered so that she could not yell out, Kapri managed to bite the inside of his hand. Just as she'd gotten a good piece of meat biting down, thankfully, Nolan busted through the door, hearing the commotion out in the hall.

"Yo, dawg, what in the fuck is you doing?"

"Nolan, Nolan . . ." Hysterical and in tears, Kapri was glad to be free of Ray's violent attack and attempted rape. "Oh my God, this motherfucker was trying to—"

After snatching him off of Kapri, infuriated, Nolan wasted no time going to work. Ray was a grown man and indeed had a few pounds on Nolan. Yet, that part didn't matter. The teen street warrior saw nothing but red for what this man was trying to do to his girl. Every strong-arm sock in the jaw, he made sure Ray would remember him and this day. Each tight-fisted punch in the eye, Nolan warned Ray what would happen to him if he *ever* dared put his hands on his girl again. The multiple blows to the mouth were followed with promises of Nolan killing Ray's entire family. They all came in play seemingly at the same time. And it was with certainty that Nolan meant each threat. Ray tried to fight back but didn't have the same luck in overpowering Nolan as he almost had with an innocent-minded Kapri. Nolan saw the fear in Ray's swollen eyes but didn't let up, not once, finally body slamming him to the floor. When he got him on the ground, he wrapped his hands around his throat and started to choke him damn near to death. The only thing that made Nolan stop was Kapri pulling on his arms.

"Baby, baby, wait. Wait! You can't kill this nigga here. If you do, the cops gonna come up here. Baby, please." Frantic, she pleaded, making Nolan let go.

Ray's damn near lifeless body was sprawled out on the dorm room floor. He was visibly bruised, battered, bloody, with a swollen eye, lip, and all. With him out of commission, Kapri took the opportunity to kick Ray dead in the nuts, inflicting even more excruciating pain. Then she spit in his face after kicking him in the mouth as well. Nolan tightly hugged Kapri, asking if she were okay. With tears streaming down both cheeks, she reassured him that she was. Being more than a little shaken up, she was glad he'd come back when he did for whatever reason. But deep down inside, Kapri, a virgin until recently, felt not only violated but also would forever be traumatized.

In semishock and denial, she'd seen these types of things take place in movies and heard about the reports of rapists on the loose in Detroit, but never in a million years could she conceive of that crime happening to her.

As luck would have it, most of the residents on that half-empty floor had gone to class. That gave the young couple a moment to figure out what to do next. Even though Kapri undoubtedly wanted Ray dead for what he tried to do, she knew they couldn't kill the man in her room. If they did, she and Nolan both would be going to jail for murder, not to mention the drugs they had stashed there. They had to think quickly.

Kapri put on some track pants and went to look in the mirror at her face. Ready to put a bullet in Ray's head, Nolan wished they hadn't got rid of his gun. With his foot pressed down on his chest, Nolan stood over Ray, wanting him to try to make a move. If he did, the creep foul Negro would regret trying to rape Kapri even more than he probably was now.

Chapter Thirty-three

It was painfully clear that Nolan's time hanging out with Kapri at school had come to an abrupt and unexpected end. Although the couple intended in finding him somewhere else more permanent to stay, Nolan decided that he needed to get back to what he knew and had grown to love . . . hustling. He was eighteen now, and the State of Michigan no longer would have him under the jurisdiction of care as a minor. The once runaway youth was free and clear. With money in his pocket, not to mention a bag of drugs, there was no reason he couldn't return home to Detroit to set up shop.

As Ray lay on the floor bleeding from both his mouth and nose, Nolan got pissed all over again and stumped Kapri's attacker in the stomach. Watching Ray react in agony, once more, Nolan wished he had his gun . . . or anyone else's for that matter. With authority, he instructed a now fully dressed Kapri to pack all of his belongings scattered about back into the Home Depot bags. After doing so, he told her to pack herself a bag and make sure she had enough clothes for at least a week or so. Stepping over a dazed Ray, who was blacking in and out every few seconds, she got the job done. Nolan then dug in his pocket, tossing Kapri the keys to the truck.

"So, okay, brown eyes, pull the truck around the back where you said the elevator y'all use to move in and out is at."

"Okay." Kapri didn't know what Nolan's game plan was, but she was down for the ride, no questions asked. She owed him that much, especially after what awful fate he saved her from.

"And bring up one of them dolly carts we saw when we was in the basement handling our business." Automatically, she knew he meant a part of the dismantled gun they tossed directly into the incinerator.

"All right, bae. Are you gonna be cool when I leave?" she quizzed, hoping Nolan would be able to control himself and not end Ray's no-good life—even though his demented ass definitely deserved death by any means available.

Kapri was gone no more than ten minutes when she returned with the cart. Thankfully, it was big enough to fit all of Nolan's bags, the bags of new items they'd happily purchased over the previous week on shopping sprees, and Kapri's things to boot. With Ray now halfway coherent, part of her wanted to spit in his face again, but she controlled her emotions.

"Okay, now grab the rest of the stuff off your desk and get all our stuff outta the bathroom. Then come check this out," Nolan had broken a broom in two pieces and was pushing one part under Ray's throat, probably praying for him to move so he could shove it straight through his neck.

Unplugging her laptop, Kapri placed it in her book bag along with a few of her school books and her cell charger. Rushing into the bathroom, she cleared the items off the sink with her arm, filling a plastic bag. Returning into the room, she went over to Nolan's side. He handed her his phone, telling her to push *play* on the screen. When she did, she saw a video Nolan had just made with Ray confessing to trying to rape her as well as stalking her. The video also had pictures of Ray's cell, which had candid photos of Kapri taken without her knowledge or consent, further proving the older man's ill intentions. She smiled, content in knowing that if this ever got out, Ray's life, career at the school, and also his freedom would be snatched away. Nolan had Ray's driver's license too, as well as he made him check in his watch. With all of those things, including Ray's cell phone, the young couple was almost ready to head out.

"Look, baby, I need for you to take our stuff down to the truck. I would help you load it, brown eyes, but me and this pussy-ass nigga right here got just one more bit of unfinished business to take care of." Nolan pushed the broken broomstick harder into Ray's throat, who was now crying for mercy. Nolan wished he would attempt to move and give him a reason to finish it.

Kapri had only been around Nolan for a short time. And after what he'd confessed to her he'd done before fleeing Ohio, part of her was scared to leave, not knowing what he was truly capable of. It was evident that if she had not just stopped him, he would have choked Ray all the way to sleep—for good.

Heading toward the door, Kapri opened it wide, rolling the completely packed cart out into the hallway. "Listen, Nolan, are you sure you don't want me to wait for you?" she asked, praying he would say yes. Unfortunately, that was not what she heard.

Nolan winked, then grinned. "Naw, girl, I'm good. Now, are you sure you got everything you need for a few weeks or so?"

Kapri scanned the dorm room she'd considered home all summer. Satisfied that she had all of her needed personal belongings on the cart, she glanced over at her man. Nolan had a cold, black-hearted look in his eyes that made her scared of him, yet strangely, even more attracted to him at the same time. "Yes, bae, I have everything."

"Okay, then go ahead and take our stuff down. And when you get it all packed, just call me, and I'll come down. Cool?"

Kapri had to trust Nolan. What else could she do? She couldn't snitch on Ray without getting Nolan in trouble as well. So, she did as she was told, pushing the cart to the freight elevator. Once down on the bottom floor, she quickly went out the doors and loaded the truck. Placing her book bag and purse on the passenger seat, she called Nolan, who immediately answered and informed him she was done. He told her to sit tight. He was on his way down.

As she sat there, her heart racing, she started to think about what she was going to tell her mother about her abrupt absence from school if she ever found out. With the weight of that on her mind as well, she tried to calm down and tell herself that everything was going to work out for good. Minutes later, Nolan exited the building. Opening the door, he moved her stuff to the rear seat and got inside. Kapri wanted to ask him where Ray was and what 'unfinished business' the two of them had. But by his dark expression, she opted not to. Instead, she drove off the campus and followed the signs to get on the highway, I-96 East.

Chapter Thirty-four

They traveled on the bumpy interstate road for at least twenty minutes. The trip was silent for the most part, with neither speaking. The only thing that interrupted that awkward silence was Nolan calling his boy O. P., telling him that he was headed back to the city and had a package with him that he needed help to flip. Nolan then informed his friend that when he and his girl touched down, he'd also fill him in about the wild shit that had jumped off back in Ohio. After ending that conversation, once more, the silent ride continued. Both the driver and passenger had a lot on their minds. This day had started picture-perfect, no worries. Now, as they drove in deep thought, that was not the case. The day had gone from sugar to shit just like that. Now, here, the in-love couple were heading home, not knowing what the future held. Nolan and Kapri's lives were about to change forever within ninety minutes when they would arrive in Detroit.

Damn, a nigga wasn't planning on going back so quickly. I wanted to get my mind right and figure shit out. This shit is all the way fucked up. First, I had to get outta the way in Sandusky and don't know if them three motherfuckers I shot is dead or alive. And now I'm moving the same way from back at that school, just all random and outta the blue with it. Shit is mad crazy for real, for real. But at least I got this bag Jayce blessed me with. So, I can definitely build on that. Plus, I'm holding this cash, so I'ma be good. We gonna be okay. I'ma marry this girl one day. Kapri definitely wifey material. She done proved she got a nigga's back when the chips is down.

Reaching over, he placed his hand on Kapri's lap as she drove. Lying back in the passenger seat to get more comfortable, Nolan fought off the not-so-fond memories of emotional turmoil he'd suffered, not only growing up but also now as well. Closing his eyes, the troubled youth continued to plot out his next plan of action that would leave him and his woman set. Now, he would have to operate differently than being solo because Kapri was in his life to stay. And even though she didn't realize it yet, Nolan knew nine outta ten times, his girl would never return to Michigan State. He'd pretty much made sure of that before leaving that dorm room.

Kapri kept her eyes focused on the road, but was also contemplating her future. *Damn, what am I gonna tell my mother? What am I gonna say if she ever finds out I've been skipping classes? And now, I'm coming back to Detroit. Especially with a dude she doesn't know, and even if she did, would not approve of. Damn, this is so, so messed up. She gonna be so pissed and so disappointed. I'm not even gonna tell her I'm not a virgin no more. 'Cause if I do that, she might pull that hammer out of her purse and hit me in the head with that son of a bitch. Oh, hell naw. Hopefully, I can get back to school without her even finding out.*

Feeling some sort of way, Kapri found a small bit of comfort as Nolan placed his steady hand on her leg. She glanced over at him and smiled at her bad boy, who was now her hero. Those thoughts of Nolan being her knight in shining armor quickly turned her mind back to the horrendous act of the attempted rape. *Oh my God, I swear my head is starting to pound. Never would I think that what happened back at school would've*

*jumped off. What in the fuck was wrong with Ray?
Why would he even pull some ho shit like that? I mean,
what was he thinking? I ain't never ever led that asshole to think I'd be with him in no way. I'm just glad
Nolan came in when he did and stopped him. And I'm
glad he beat the blood outta his crazy ass. I just wonder what happened when he had me go and load the
truck. I know whatever it was, Ray had that shit coming. I just hope my baby didn't go too far with it. But if
he did, fuck it. I'ma ride with Nolan forever and a day.
Period!*

With the lovesick and confused teens wondering
what the near future would be like now that they were a
couple, each felt that together, they were invincible. The
mutual feeling was that their love and strong bond would
conquer all, and nothing or no one could ever tear them
apart, ever. Unfortunately, soon, their loyalty to each
other would be put to the test. Passing a sign that read
Detroit, forty-seven miles, Kapri yelled out Nolan's name,
causing him to open his eyes and sit straight up quickly.

"Damn, baby, what is it? What's wrong?" he puzzled,
looking out the front window.

"Nolan, don't turn around, but the damn state boys
are coming behind us. They just pulled out from that
rest area. What should I do?" Kapri was in a frenzy, first
thinking about the drugs they had in the truck, then
second, her mind flashed back to Ray and what may have
jumped off back in her dorm room. Maybe he'd called
the police on them . . . or worse than that. *Damn, I hope
Nolan ain't kill that motherfucker back there! Oh my
God!*

Nolan reached over, placing his hand once more on
her knee. "Listen, bae. Just be cool and drive the speed
limit. We ain't did shit wrong. And besides, you trust
me, right?"

"Yes." She fought back the tears.

"You know I got you, right?"

"Yes." Her heart raced.

"Okay, then. As long as you know both them things, then we always gonna be Gucci."

"Baby, I hope so." She tried to pray for the best, even when the state boys' flashing lights came on. "Because they on us for real, for real. I gotta pull over."

"Just go ahead and do it. And remember, I got us now and forever." Nolan was prepared for whatever would come next . . . even if Kapri was not. Since birth, his life had been fucked up and full of chaos. Yet as long as he knew his girl was riding with him, nothing else mattered. Whatever the outcome, they were a team and would remain that way until the end of time.

When the blond, blue-eyed trooper got out of his car, he placed his hand firmly on his pistol. Making sure the traffic was clear, he cautiously approached the driver's side of the truck. With a stern expression etched on his face, he instructed Kapri to kill the engine and step out of the vehicle. Nervously, she looked over at Nolan for reassurance, then complied and did as she was told.

Even though it seemed like this was possibly the end for them . . . This was just the beginning and not the last time their backs would be up against the wall.

Stay tuned . . . It definitely gets greater later!